Sky-in-the-Eye

Tony Letts

March 2024

'... The Outlaw Josey Wales meets Dances With Wolves...'

'... bold, unflinching style...'

'... highly readable...'

'... the narrative is imbued with a sense of high stakes...'

'... captured my interest from the start and held it to the last...'

'... very well structured...'

'... builds progressively...'

'... fast paced...'

'... keeps the reader hungry to continue...'

'... a book for everyone...'

'... always interesting and exciting...'

'... I couldn't put it down...'

'... made me cry...'

'... loved getting to know the characters...'

'... sorry when it finished...'

'... visceral and powerful...'

Sky-in-the-Eye

adventure, love and tragedy
on the American frontier

Tony Eaton

Sky-in-the-Eye
Published by The Conrad Press Ltd. in the United Kingdom
2024

Tel: +44(0)1227 472 874

www.theconradpress.com
info@theconradpress.com

ISBN 978-1-916966-30-7

Typesetting and cover design by Michelle Emerson
michelleemerson.co.uk

Artwork by Sue Eaton

The Conrad Press logo was designed by Maria Priestley

Printed and bound in Great Britain by Clays Ltd, Elcograf
S.p.A.

Contents

Author's note

Although *Sky-in-the-Eye* aims to be a rip-roaring yarn encompassing the heartwarming and the heart-breaking, it contains an underlying warning that is more pertinent today than at any time.

To help emphasise the worldwide implications, the inevitable preconceptions associated with real events that may make it appear parochial have been avoided by making this story is a work of fiction in which all characters, peoples, locations and incidents are imaginary.

Tony Eaton
February 2024

Foreword

I lived my life on the American frontier at its most rugged, where violence and depravity were more commonplace than kindness and morality. This narrative pulls no punches, but contains nothing gratuitous, as each incident is important to the story.

From the uplifting to the distressing, I will tell my story in a bold and unflinching manner. I challenge you to set aside your inhibitions and accept that each event is integral to a life that encompasses everything from the most inspiring to the most disturbing. If you don't read each page with the same intensity, you will never understand my battle to retain a sense of honour and to find love and peace of mind.

Some parts of my story are difficult to relate. I normally avoid thinking about them because each time I do they come back in vivid detail. We all have incidents in our lives we would prefer not to remember, but, together with the good, they make us what we are and recounting them in detail is the only way to ensure you will know exactly who I am and precisely the sort of people who have influenced my life. To sanitise or avoid even the smallest particular would be a betrayal of the truth. I did not invent atrocities and I am not alone in having them inflicted on me. Survivors' memories may vary, but the one thing we have in common is we are unable to avoid the explicit detail.

You may prefer to see the worst events through the soft filter of retelling or to avoid the worst by skipping a few pages, but we who have suffered first hand did not have these luxuries. Failing to describe the upsetting in the same detail as the uplifting would be unfaithful to the truth and give you a false impression.

To understand who I am, the pictures in your mind must be as close as possible to those in mine. If you prefer to pretend that bad things don't happen and don't have the courage to face them, stop now. If you value the truth and are prepared to confront it in all its guises, I invite you to join me in this unexpurgated story of my life. We may not have shared at first hand all my ups and downs, but I will do everything in my power to make your experience as close as possible to mine.

So, let us be brave together, me in the telling and you in the reading. Only then will you fully understand the experiences that made me who I am and what I will become.

Jimmy Kidd

Book 1 - Jimmy Kidd

1

Schmidts

I couldn't speak. I could hear what people were saying and I understood. I could formulate responses in my mind, but I couldn't articulate them.

Mrs and Mr Schmidt were the kindest of people. I arrived on Mr Schmidt's horse sitting in front of his saddle and leaning back over the saddle horn to bury my face in his chest. He had one arm around me to keep me safely seated and to hold me close. The front of his shirt was soaked with my tears and dribble as I cried silently into his shirt, but I had no memory of what had occurred prior to that moment.

As far as I knew, my life had started the instant I saw Mrs Schmidt running from her house and gasping, 'What .....?', but her husband cut her short as I felt more than saw him shake his head. Although I had no idea what he meant, she understood without explanation. Her husband passed me down to her and she held me close as she carried me into their house.

I heard others ride away with muted goodbyes as she carried me to a rocking chair next to their fire. For the remainder of the day she sat there with me on her lap, holding me close and soothing me in softly spoken German. I didn't understand anything she said, but I was comforted by her soothing voice, her homely smell, her matronly appearance and the softness of her touch. I stopped crying and just sat as she rocked slightly back and forth. Mr Schmidt brought me some bread and water, which I nibbled and sipped, but I didn't want to move preferring to stay cocooned in her arms.

I eventually looked up to see the most kindly, slightly chubby face topped by silver hair that was held in a loose bun. Although small, Mrs Schmidt's body seemed well padded and very comfortable.

It was dark outside and Mrs Schmidt said, 'Com mine little *schatz*, I vill tak you to bed.' I was big enough to walk, but small enough to be carried and so she lifted me gently, carried me to a small room and laid me on a little bed. I didn't want to be left there and sat up, but she pushed me back gently so my head rested on a soft pillow. She covered me with a blanket and sat next to me on the bed stroking my head and singing:

'Geh' ins Bett, kleiner Depp,
Mach schon, komm, sei nett,
Denn es ist schon so spaet!
Mach's Licht aus, komm, sei brav
Und geniesse den Schlaf,
Den das Sandmaennchen saet!

Schlaf mit ein'm Aug' offen,
Und halt' dei' Kissen fest!'
Go to bed little fool
Go ahead, come on, be good,
Because it is already so late!
Turn off the lights, come on, be good
And enjoy sleep
That the Sandman sows!
Sleep with one eye open,
And cuddle your pillows.'

It was a lilting lullaby and, being exhausted, I fell asleep without realising.

I woke with a start.

I knew where I was and knew I would be safe, but there was an inner fear that made it impossible for me to stay in the house. It was in a house similar to one I had lived in before and I knew it wasn't safe because the roof held menace.

I had to get somewhere safe and so I rose without making a sound. Looking out the bedroom window, I could see it was still dark. I opened it as quietly as I could, slipped out and crouched beneath it looking around for danger.

I could see the outline of a barn about fifty feet to my right and made a quick dash to it. Easing the door open just enough, I squeezed in and looked around. There were bales of hay and straw piled high to my right and a slightly messy pile to my left. The sweet smell of hay was pleasant and reassuring.

I heard movement to my left and, as I turned, felt something wet and cold on my neck. I started back, but, in spite of my fright, could still not utter a sound. Standing next to me with its face not more than a few inches from mine was the most enormous dog I had ever seen.

I should have been scared witless, but I wasn't. It may have been that my capacity for fear was used up, but I suspect it was because, in spite of its size, the dog looked funny. Its head was too big for its body and its coat comprised tufty hair sticking out at all angles. It wagged its tail and so I held my hand out. It sniffed it, licked it and then moved away to lie on its side on a bed of hay. I followed, lay down next to it and curled up as close as I could get with my back pressed against the warmth of its chest. Although it looked wiry, the dog's coat was soft and it was nice and warm. As I fell asleep, I felt a protective paw being laid across my arm.

We were woken by my name being called repeatedly, 'Yimmy, Yimmy vere are you?'

The barn door burst open and Mr Schmidt was standing in the doorway silhouetted by the brightness of the day. He stood there looking alert and capable even though I thought he looked ancient with his facial lines and thinning hair. It took a few moments for his eyes to become accustomed to the dark interior of the barn and then his attention was drawn to us as the enormous dog got to its feet and trotted over to him. He spotted me and called, 'I've found him, Granny, he's in here with our Meg.'

He held out his hand. I walked to him and took it. It seemed too big and horny for someone so lithe, but I liked the way it felt. As we walked out of the barn, Mrs Schmidt came up to us and said, 'What were you doing in there, Yimmy? You have a much more comfortable bed in the house.'

I just looked at her as Mr Schmidt said, 'We can't guess what he is thinking, Granny, but he has been through a lot and if he wants to sleep in the barn with Meg, then we should let him.'

Mrs Schmidt walked back to the house. Mr Schmidt and I followed still holding hands.

The house was made of logs and looked familiar. The barn was big, as was the corral that held some horses that looked strange to me. I was used to seeing big, heavily built horsed suitable for pulling a plough or wagon as much as riding, but these were much finer and seemed frail by comparison. I wondered what use such fragile-looking horses could be.

That evening after we had eaten, the Schmidts and I sat around their fireplace. Mr Schmidts said, 'Ve haf a big house here, Yimmy, because we had two sons. When they grew up, they married goot girls from our homeland, Deutschland. They lived near us for a vhile and had kinder of their own. Our enkelkinder called us 'Granny' and 'Gramps' and we were all very happy until our boys vent to var and vere both kilt.'

He put his head in his hand and sobbed. Mrs Schmidt got up from her chair and put her hand on his shoulders. This helped him regain his composure and he was able to continue, 'Our daughters-in-law did not want to stay here in a land they thought was foreign and so they vent back to the homeland. They took our enkelkinder with them and we haven't seen them since.'

He was overcome again and Mrs Schmidt took over, 'That was years ago and ever since then there has been a giant hole in our lives. Ve know that ve cannot replace your mum and dad and they will always be vith you because you have your mum's light blue eyes and your dad's dark complexion, Yimmy, but ve vould be pleased if you vould like to make your home vith us.'

Her speech meant nothing to me. I knew I must have had parents, but I had no recollection of the people she mentioned. When she had finished, she went back to her chair and sat down. For several minutes, we sat lost in our own thoughts, crying to ourselves, them because of their lost sons and grandchildren, me because of my confusion and lost memories. Eventually, I rose, went over and kneeled between their chairs and took Mrs Schmidt's hand in my left hand and Mr Schmidt's in my right. They raised their heads and, looking at them in turn, I nodded. They both rose from their seats, kneeled next to me, each put an arm around my shoulders and laid their heads on mine. Through her tears, Mrs Schmidt said, 'From now on ve vill be your Granny and Gramps, Yimmy.'

*

I had no alternative and so that was what happened. Over the next few months, we settled into a pattern. I was still

6

unable to speak, but the Schmidts and their workers spoke to me. To begin with, they explained the work on their farm. They bred and sold horses. To help them, they had two field hands: Asuka, who was a wiry man of average height with black hair and smiling eyes and came from a country called Japan. Tor, a giant of a man with unruly, sandy hair from a place called Denmark. I watched each day as they worked with the horses and learnt that the animals I first thought looked too delicate to be any use, were based on a breed called Arabs and were not only sturdy and reliable, they were more intelligent, faster and more agile than any other breed of horse.

Tor's main job was to arrange for the mares to be covered by one of their stallions and then to look after the mares and their foals until the foals were ready to back. They were then passed to Asuka who backed them and trained them before they were sold. Mr Schmidt managed the whole undertaking and organised the sale of the trained horses to people who wanted the very best riding horses. Granny looked after the house and tended the garden, mostly growing vegetables.

Each day I would watch Tor and Asuka at work. I would then have my evening meal and, to begin with, Mr Schmidt would walk me to the barn where he would bed me down with Meg because if I slept anywhere other than with Meg in the barn, I had terrible, vivid nightmares. One evening, Meg was waiting at the back door of the house and from that day on she would come for me each night and we would walk to the barn together.

Life settled into a routine. I would sleep in the barn with Meg, get up and have my breakfast in the house. The rest of the day I would spend watching Tor and Asuka working with the horses, doing simple chores for them and helping Granny tend the vegetable patch.

Six months into this routine, there was a dramatic change.

One morning, Meg and I were walking from the barn to the house for breakfast. We were part way across the yard when I noticed a strange dog barring our way. He was about half as tall as Meg, but twice as wide. He stood there four-square with his front legs spread looking like a bull about to charge. Meg stood looking at him quizzically for a moment before deciding she should make friends. She trotted up to the strange dog with her tail wagging, introduced herself by putting her nose to his, when he attacked. He jumped up and grabbed her by the throat. Being so much heavier, he knocked her on her back and stood over her pinning her to the ground.

Meg squealed and I bellowed in outrage. Grabbing a fist-sized rock from the ground, I launched myself on the dog's back locking my left arm around his throat and beating him repeatedly in the head with the rock in my right hand. I was small and didn't have the strength to inflict any real damage on his thick skull, but I hit as hard as I could while screaming like a banshee. He let go of Meg, reared up, shook me off his back and turned to face me. I jumped up.

I didn't think I had hurt him and I was sure he could

tear me to pieces, but my anger was up and I shrieked my defiance in his ugly face. He could have torn us both to pieces, but it was probably the noise of me screaming and Meg barking at him that unnerved him, powerful as he was. As he turned tail and fled, I hurled the rock at him, hitting his hind quarters as he beat his retreat.

For minutes after he had gone I howled, screeched, shrieked, roared and shouted. All the frustrations of six months of silence since my unrecalled ordeal came out in a prolonged outpouring of previously unexpressed emotion. Everyone came running. Granny, Gramps, Tor, Asuka and Meg just stood dumbfounded as I poured everything into vocalising my pent-up feelings.

Eventually, my vocal eruption subsided to a whimper. Granny came over to me, knelt down next to me and took me in her arms. I buried my head in her shoulder, my tears soaking her dress. I mumbled, 'I love you, Granny.'

My body stiffened and I shuddered. Shocked, Granny held me at arm's length. With my eyes wide, I looked into hers and said, 'I remember ...'

2

Commencharos

My parents and I had lived in our little log house on the prairie for several years. We were poor, but they eked a living from the land and our two-room home was well built. By dint of hard work and careful planning, we were able to keep warm when it was cold and had enough to eat throughout the year.

Mum and Dad knew the Commancheros' reputation for fast, ruthless attacks and so they were on constant alert. Even so, when they hit us we were taken by surprise. Around twenty of them broke clear of the trees about half a mile from our home and galloped straight for us. Dad grabbed me and ran for the house. I could hear the drumming of their horses' hooves getting closer and closer and was sure they would run us down. The crack of their guns increased our fear as the bullets flew around us with a 'whoosh' and ricocheted off the ground with a 'zing'.

Fear seemed to add wings to Mum's and Dad's feet. We reached the house before they hit us and slammed the door.

'Bar the door, Jimmy,' shouted Dad as he and Mum

pulled their rifles from the rack on the wall and rushed to the windows.

I dropped the thick piece of oak into the brackets to bar the door while their rifles cracked as they returned fire. Rushing to a window and peering over the sill, I was thrilled to see they had unseated two riders who fell like rag dolls from their horses and landed with a bump in our yard. My joy was short lived as they fanned out each side of the house and disappeared from view in a thunder of hooves and clouds of dust. In less than a minute, we heard them breaking through the roof.

Dad grabbed me and shouted in my ear, 'Out the back and into the hide'.

The hide was a small tunnel dug into the hard packed earth of the corral. It was just below the surface and the entrance was a small hole facing away from the house making it virtually invisible from anywhere but up close. It was just big enough to hold me. Dad had told me that, if we were ever attacked, I was to slip into the hide and stay there until the danger had passed.

We couldn't see any Commancheros from the back window. I slipped through and crouched below it while I looked around. I still couldn't see anyone and so I made a dash for the corral. Moving around to the back of the hide to get to the entrance, I looked back at our house for the first time and saw that I'd made it unseen because all the Commancheros were on the house concentrating on breaking through the roof. I dived into the hide, crawled as far forward as I could and kicked the dirt from the floor behind me to close the entrance.

It was pitch black and quiet. I hated the dark. I felt ahead of me to see how far I was from the front. As I did so, I found a short, stout stick. Picking it up, I pushed it into the earth in front of and a little above me. After a few moments pushing and twisting, the stick broke through the surface. Light was coming through the hole, but it was only a pencil thin shaft and so I pushed the stick in again and wiggled it around to increase the size of the opening.

I could now see out and, as I did so, I heard a cheer from the house followed by two shots and two cries of pain and then banging noises and shouting.

After a few seconds of silence, the front door burst open. A Commanchero staggered out, bleeding from a wound in his chest. He collapsed a few steps from the door and was immediately followed by two men dragging my mum and then more men supporting my dad as he staggered out. He was bleeding from cut in his head. I guessed Mum and Dad had shot at least one when they broke in, but had then been overwhelmed. It looked as though a vicious blow to dad's head had brought the uneven struggle to a quick end.

The others poured out shouting with excitement. Most of them gathered around my mum laughing as they squeezed her boobs and lifted her skirt. She screamed and spat and struggled so much they couldn't hold her and so one slapped her in the side of the head. As she was struggling so frantically, she was moving away as the blow landed and so she didn't feel its full force. However, it seemed to knock a lot of the fight out of her and so she just stood panting and staring her hate at the filthy men laughing as they stood around her.

A large, swarthy, ugly brute stepped forward. He had a scar from just below his left eye, across his lips to below his mouth, which twisted his features into a horrific parody of a grin. He seemed to be the leader. Standing in front of mum, he moved his left hand behind her head to grab a fistful of her shoulder-length blond hair and yanked her head back. She spat in his face. He just laughed and grabbed her left boob in his right hand squeezing it so hard it made her gasp.

'Don't knock her about. Keep her looking good and we'll enjoy her more. She'll soon be obliging.' His men laughed in lustful anticipation.

Letting go of Mum, he walked over to my dad, wiping the spittle from his face as he did so.

Dad's arms had been tied to the rails of a fence so they were stretched out wide as though he was being crucified. This made him squat slightly as the top fence rail was below his natural shoulder height.

When the Commanchero leader was close enough, Dad kicked out at him, but his crouched position made this difficult and so his kick was awkward and the leader avoided it easily.

'Tie his legs to the lower rail' the leader ordered.

Two men pulled his legs from under him and tied them to the lower rail so that dad was hanging from the fence by his arms and legs. As he moved in close to dad, the leader took a long, wicked looking knife from a sheath at his side. He pulled Dad's shirt from his trousers and tore it open. Dad's eyes were open wide with horror and my mum let out a shriek. The leader turned towards her and grinned. But mum's shriek was nothing compared to the blood curdling scream of pure pain and terror that came from Dad's throat as the leader sliced open his belly in the same way mum did when gutting a rabbit. Dad's guts spilled to the ground. Mercifully, he lost consciousness and slumped forward.

I didn't understand how someone could be so wicked and cruel and wanted to look away, but I couldn't tear my eyes from the scene. Turning his back to dad, the leader returned to Mum. She was frozen in terror with her eyes and mouth wide open, but unable to utter a sound. The whole group of sadists shouted in triumph and turned towards her.

The leader pushed his way to the front of the crowd shouting, 'Stand back, you'll each get a turn.'

They stepped back a few paces leaving mum in the centre of the group. She was obviously completely traumatised because she neither moved nor uttered a sound. The leader went behind her, squatted down, lifted her dress from her heels and used his razor sharp knife to slice it from hem to neck. Her dress fell forward and he sliced down each of the sleeves, allowing it to drop to the ground.

He then cut off her underclothes, leaving her standing naked in a circle of slavering animals. Still standing behind her, the leader dropped his knife and slid both hands under mum's arms to grab her boobs. The appreciative crowd roared their approval as he pulled and squeezed them. He then dropped one hand down, grabbed her pubic hair and pulled it, forcing mum to thrust her hips forward, which delighted his audience who shouted their approval and suggested other things he might do for their entertainment.

Pointing to a couple of his men, the leader commanded, 'Lay her out.'

They grabbed her arms and legs and pulled her to the ground where they spread her in the shape of a cross. Such was her state of shock that mum lay as she was placed without moving or uttering a sound.

For a few moments the crowd stood looking at her, lost in a reverie of lustful anticipation. Their trance was broken as the leader moved without a word to kneel between mum's splayed legs. He had his back to me and so all I could see was him dropping his trousers and pants and leaning forward over mum. After a while, he moved his bottom up and down vigorously for a few moments before he kneeled up and looked around his men with a satisfied grin.

They knew what he meant when he said, 'Take her one at a time. That way she will last longer and you can have her as many times as you want.'

They all stood around and watched as they took turns to repeat what their leader had done by kneeling between mum's legs, dropping their trousers and pants and pumping their bottoms up and down before getting up to make room for the next one.

It seemed to go on for hours. At one stage, Dad regained consciousness and, despite his horrific wounds, realised what was happening and mustered enough strength to repeatedly shout, 'God no! God no! God no! God no!....' before succumbing once more to his own pain and passing out.

Eventually, their enthusiasm waned. Some retained their interest for longer than others and, as they continued with Mum. The remainder ransacked our little house and barn, taking anything that may have been of use to them and then setting fire to the buildings.

When they were ready to go, the leader went over to the last man who was still bumping mum. He pulled him off and threw him to one side saying, 'Mount up, we're going.'

He then knelt between Mum's legs again. He had his back to me and was obscuring mum's body, so I couldn't see what he was doing. All I could see was him doing something with his knife as he squatted between mum's thighs. When he stood up, there was blood flowing and mum was writhing and shrieking.

Leaving their fallen comrades, the Commancheros rode away to the sound of crackling flames and my mum and dad howling over and over while I screwed my eyes shut and covered my ears trying to muffle the screams as I cried repeatedly for it to stop.

*

Without realising, I had fallen asleep. I woke with my face resting on the floor of my hide made muddy by my tears. It took a few moments for me to remember where I was, but, when I did, I started shaking and had to steel myself to look through the peep hole. I saw the smouldering ruins of our barn and house. My mum was lying where the Commancheros had left her. She was no longer screaming and was perfectly still in a dark circle where her blood had stained the ground. My dad was hanging lifeless from the fence with the ground below him muddied by his blood.

Between me and them was a man leaning against the corral fence being sick. It was the sound of his retching that had woken me. He stood, wiped his mouth on the back of his hand and then down his trouser leg as he moved away. Behind him was another man on his knees, also being sick. There were others standing around looking at my mum's and dad's bodies with their heads in their hands or shaking their heads in disbelief.

I recognised them as neighbours who lived in the local town and farmsteads. They must have seen the smoke from our burning house and barn and had come to see if they could help. It looked as though they were totally unprepared for what they found.

Two of them went into the burnt remains of my house. They picked up a charred body and brought it out. 'We know it's not Mrs or Mr Kidd and it's too big to be young Jimmy, so it must be one of the Commancheros,' guessed one of the men.

'It looks as though the Kidds got off a few shots killing three of them out here and one inside before they were overpowered,' said another, 'But where's young Jimmy?'

'Perhaps they took him with them,' said the first.

'I doubt it,' continued the second, 'It's not their style. Unless his body is hidden around here somewhere, it's my guess that young Jimmy got away and ran off.' He put his hands to his mouth to form a trumpet and called, 'Jimmy, Jimmy, you can come out now, it's safe.'

Another called, 'Come on, Yimmy, it's me, Helmut Schmidt. You know me, I von't let anyone hurt you.'

I wasn't frightened of him or the others, but I didn't want to see my mum and dad up close and so I stayed hidden.

Another man joined them and spoke nervously, 'Let's get these two buried as quickly as possible. We can then hunt around a bit for Jimmy before we head home.'

The others agreed and several more men came over to lift mum and cut dad down from the fence. They carried them away and for an hour or so I heard the sound of shovels in the hard earth as they were digging graves. I heard some muttering, which I assumed were prayers, before a large group of men came into view leading their horses. There was some sort of discussion that I couldn't hear, but guessed they were deciding on what to do next. I heard something to the effect they would, 'Leave the bastards as carrion,' by which I assumed they meant the dead Commancheros.

'What about Yimmy?' asked Mr Schmidt.

'We've been here hours. If he was around, he'd have shown himself by now,' said the nervous one.

'I'm not happy,' continued Mr Schmidt, 'I'd like to look around more carefully.'

The others had mounted. I was now more frightened

of being left alone and panicked. Kicking out behind me to clear the entrance, I wriggled backwards until I was clear of the hide and stood up. Startled, the twenty men turned as one while reaching for their guns before they recognised me covered in dirt with my face caked with mud and streaked with tears.

Realising I was traumatised, Mr Schmidt walked slowly towards me. As he did so, he spoke quietly, 'It's okay, Yimmy, nothing will hurt you now. I know you're frightened, Yimmy, but I vill take care of you.'

I found his German accent soothing and his words reassuring. Tears were coursing down my cheeks as he knelt in front of me, took me in his arms and held me close. I sobbed silently into his shoulder. He picked me up, carried me to his horse, lifted me in front of the saddle and mounted so he could hold me close as we rode slowly away from the ruins of what had been my home for the first five years of my life.

3

Education

I had been standing looking into Granny's eyes, but seeing nothing as I recalled the greatest drama in my young life. I knew I was five and that I had lost my family in the most tragic circumstances.

Breaking away, I rushed over to Meg. Inspecting her body, I found her wounds were superficial and so I held her close and said, 'I love you too, Meg.'

So my period of silence came to an end. I can only guess that the shock of seeing Meg being attacked broke through the barrier created by the trauma I suffered when mum and dad were killed. I would never become talkative, but I could now speak.

I continued to sleep with Meg, but from that day on we slept in my room in the house. I was happy with Granny, Gramps, Tor and Asuka and helped as best I could.

Over the next few years I learnt about horses. I was taught to ride bareback on a little old pony called Asher, who was the companion for injured horses when they had to be kept away from the main herd. Although I was too young to realise it at the time, throwing myself into this work and wholly accepting my new life helped me come to terms with my loss.

*

Several months after my sixth birthday, all five of us were sitting having our evening meal, as normal. I was next to Granny and, as she got up, her elbow knocked her best milk jug off the table. Without thinking, I caught it before it hit the ground. 'Well done, Yimmy,' said Granny, 'That's my best milk jug and I vould be very upset to lose it.' She kissed my forehead as further thanks. As she did so, I saw Asuka looking at me in a quizzical way.

Later that evening, I was playing with Meg in the yard. Asuka came up to me carrying a smooth stone about the size of an orange. As he threw it from one hand to the other, he asked me, 'Can you catch?'

I replied, 'I think so.'

Without another word, he lobbed it to me in a gentle arc. It was coming down directly in front of me and I caught it with both hands. He asked me to throw it back, which I did. He took three steps back and gently lobbed the stone to my right. I caught it in my right hand.

Getting the idea, I threw it to him and this time he lobbed to my left. I duly caught it in my left hand. He increased the distance between us by another couple of steps before he threw the stone harder so that it travelled in a much straighter line to my right. I caught it in my right hand and returned it. He repeated the process to my left with the same result. He then hurled the stone in a straight line to my right. I caught it again, this time moving my hand back as I caught it to cushion the impact. Once again, he tested my left side and I responded in the same way.

I was enjoying the game. He changed it, pointing to a fence post about twenty feet away, saying, 'Throw the stone as hard as you can to hit that post.'

I pulled back my right arm, pivoted on my left leg and hurled the stone at the post, hitting it dead centre about three feet above the ground. Asuka walked over to the post and scribed a cross at the point I had hit it. Tossing the stone back to me, he ordered, 'This time, hit the cross.'

I hurled the stone with all my might, hitting the centre of the cross. He made me repeat it six times with exactly the same result. 'Okay, Jimmy, come here.'

I walked over to him. He knelt in front of me so we were about the same height, held up his hands each side of his head with the palms facing me and said, 'Punch my hands as hard as you can.'

I stood square on to him throwing hooks so I punched his left hand with my left fist and his right with my right. I pivoted my upper body with each punch, which seemed the natural thing to do. I was pleased that I knocked his hands back with each punch and edged forward trying to drive him back, but when I got close he caught my forearms to stop me. Holding my arms he asked, 'Would you like to learn karate?'

'I don't know,' I replied, 'What is it?'

'It's a very special way to fight. If you start now and

work hard over many years, you will not only learn to win a fight against almost any man, you will learn when to fight and when not to fight, how to judge a man and how to be calm when everyone else is panicking.'

As a six-year-old boy, I didn't understand most of what he said, but I thought it would be good to be able to win a fight against any man and so I agreed, 'I would like to learn karate.'

When we told Granny and Gramps, Granny's reaction was to shake her head and say, 'I don't want him to fight.'

Gramps nodded in agreement.

My response was, 'I don't want to fight, Granny, but if I have to, I want to win. If mum and dad had been better prepared when the Commancheros attacked, they may be alive today.'

Seeing her resolve wavering, Asuka reinforced the point, 'If I teach him, he will fight less often because I will teach him how to avoid fighting, but when he has no choice, he will have the best chance of winning.'

This obviously resonated with both Granny and Gramps. They looked at one another. Granny nodded and Gramps said, 'Okay, if it vill help to make him safer, we agree.'

Asuka continued, 'In my country, we call it a martial art, which means it is not simply fighting. It will give him a variety of skills that will include how to deal with many problems that life will throw at him. I would not choose to teach just anyone, but I have seen something special in Jimmy. He is kind, able to work out problems quickly, has very fast reactions, is well coordinated and from his fight with the strange dog, he proved he is brave. He is not very big, but size need not matter. As we say, '*it's not the man in the fight, it's the fight in the man*' and Jimmy has a lot of fight in him.'

Asuka suggested that, as I was so young, my training should be little and often and they agreed he would work with me first thing each morning and after work each evening. We would start with half an hour sessions rising to one hour when Asuka thought I was strong enough.

We started the following morning. I was expecting to start punching and kicking and so I was disappointed when Asuka made me practise stretching exercises and slow movements that seemed to me to be more like dancing than fighting.

'The moves in karate need you to be flexible and so you must stretch before you learn them,' Asuka explained. 'You must also be able to control your movements. Dancing and fighting are similar because in each one you must have complete control of your body. In my country, the best fighters are beautiful dancers.'

In my young mind, this turned dancing from something sissy that was for girls into something far more masculine. I'm sure that was exactly what Asuka intended.

So I threw myself into training with great enthusiasm. I was early for each session and wanted to continue beyond the time Asuka judged it would be best for me to stop.

My enthusiasm was rewarded.

One morning after we had been training for a few months, I went to our training area to find Asuka waiting for me. He had with him a plank of wood that was about nine inches wide, one inch thick and eight feet long. Around the top eighteen inches were wound many layers of a thick material that formed a padding. We dug a hole about three feet deep, placed the unpadded end in the hole and packed the earth tight around it so that the top five feet stood straight up from the ground.

'This is your *Makiwara*,' Asuka explained. 'It is the striking-post on which you will both toughen your body and learn many of the karate blows.'

I added hitting the Makiwara to my training regimen. I learnt to hold my hand out straight with my fingers extended and to hit with the outside edge of my hand in a chopping action. I learnt to clench my fist with the thumb wrapped around my fingers and to hit with the bottom knuckles nearest the hand like a boxer. Asuka called this the hammer. I learnt to keep the lower knuckles straight and to bend my fingers at the middle knuckles and to hit with the middle knuckles. This was to strike places like the throat, which were normally protected by the chin making it difficult to hit with the club fist. Asuka called this the spear.

During the first few months, I had to toughen my hands and feet. To do this, I had to hit or kick the post in exactly the way Asuka told me. He was very strict and gave me punishments like running around the corral or doing lots of press-ups if I tried to hit too hard or in the wrong way.

He would admonish me time and time again with, 'If you hit wrong or too hard to begin with, Jimmy, you will damage yourself and get into bad habits. If you do either of those things, you will never be a good fighter.'

My training progressed over the ensuing months and years, during which time Asuka introduced exercises to build strength and stamina in addition to flexibility. My hands and feet hardened to the point I could hit the *Makiwara* as hard as possible. As the years passed, my strength grew and the hardness of my hands and feet grew correspondingly. When I was twelve, I hit the post so hard it disintegrated. I though Asuka might be angry, but he just smiled and made a new *Makiwara*.

When I was ten, Asuka decided I was big enough to learn holds and throws and so we added sparring to our schedule. It was then I learnt Asuka was not only a good trainer, he was also a good exponent of karate. For many years after, the only time I threw him was when he let me. It was not until I was sixteen that I felt we genuinely competed and was able to throw him a few times on merit, but even then I was not certain he was not letting me. After one particular bruising bout in which he had thrown me time after time, I became despondent. 'I'm useless,' I complained. 'I've been training for ten years and I still can't even beat you, a middle-aged horse trainer.'

He smiled, went to his room and, after a few minutes, came out holding a rolled up scroll. He passed it to me. I unrolled it, but was no wiser. It was very ornate and impressive, but there was no proper writing on it. Instead, it was covered with all sorts of strange symbols that seemed to have been painted on. It looked more like a work of art than a document. 'What is this?' I asked.

'Those marks that look like symbols to you are writing in my language. They say that this certificate has been awarded to the karate champion of Japan.'

'How did you get it,' I asked.

I was embarrassed as he laughed and said, 'You are being uncharacteristically stupid, Jimmy. I won this just before I left Japan. You see, I may be middle aged to you, but I am not just a horse trainer. I was selected at the age of five to go to a special school. I studied there until I was eighteen and when I left I was their star pupil, a karate black belt 5th dan, which is one of the highest qualifications possible.'

I was speechless. After a few moments, he carried on, 'When I saw you catch the milk jug when you were only six, I suspected you were special. The stone throwing was a test, which confirmed my suspicions. For the last ten years I have worked with you and, far from being useless, you are the best pupil I have ever known. You are good at everything needed for karate, but, in particular, your reflexes are the fastest I have ever seen. You are much faster than me and, if my experience didn't allow me to anticipate most of your moves, you would beat me every time. That won't last much longer, Jimmy, because you are gaining experience and one day soon you will have the beating of me.'

This was the first time anyone had spoken to me in this way. In spite of my best efforts, Asuka had been able to beat me every time, but now I realised I was competing with a champion and being beaten by him was an honour rather than disgrace and he was telling me I had the potential to be better than him. This could have made me conceited, but much of my training to that point emphasised the importance of being humble.

I was deeply touched and went up to Asuka and held him close. As he overcame his Asian reserve and put his arms around me, I mumbled through the lump in my throat, 'Being trained by you is a great honour, Asuka, but you have placed a heavy burden of responsibility on me. To be worthy of you, from now on I must work even harder to fulfil trust you have in me.'

*

Our local town was Smalltown, about twenty minutes steady ride from our home. The school there was run by Miss Sharp, who could not have been more inappropriately named as she was small and round and had a kind, patient personality. She taught pupils between the ages of seven and fourteen in one class on Monday through to Thursday each week from 8 am to 2 pm. The class size was dependent on the number of kids in the area within that age group whose parents wanted them to attend. There were fifteen covering the whole age range when I started at the age of seven.

Granny and Gramps took me on the first day in the buggy, as they wanted to make sure I settled in. Miss Sharp's reaction to me was the same as all women, 'His eyes are so blue and he has such long lashes,' she cooed.

I was still at the age that this embarrassed me and so I was a little taciturn to begin with, but Miss Sharp's motherly nature soon won me round.

After the first day, I rode to school on Asher with Gramps, Asuka and Tor taking turns to escort me there and back. Although the older boys asserted their authority, this was accepted by the younger kids and so the atmosphere was generally friendly with little bullying.

I settled in easily and, although I was never going to be a top grade student, I enjoyed the lessons and things like basic arithmetic and English came with just a little effort. I enjoyed working with numbers and I was intrigued by words and was surprised to discover the richness of my language, which provided so many ways to express oneself. This fascination led to an increase in my vocabulary.

Although I enjoyed most subjects, the one that most caught my attention and sparked my imagination was history, especially military history. The Romans were my favourites and I was most impressed by their army. I could see how their success was built on rigorous training, discipline, the best equipment and, most of all, fastidious organisation. Although I thought many of their punishments were too harsh, I could see the benefits of organising troops into small units of eighty men in a century, which combined to make cohorts, legions and armies. I especially admired their insistence on choosing battle sites that most suited them and their versatility and speed of manoeuvre on the battlefield.

I noted that their three major losses at Cannae, Teutenberg Forest and Carrhae and their eventual downfall were all as a result of a departure from these principles. I also had great respect for the Parthians, who were highly organised, too, and whose archers on horseback were a match for the Romans.

*

On my eleventh birthday, I went in for breakfast, as usual. The other four members of my family were standing around the table with great big, silly grins on their faces. I had no idea what this was all about until I saw that, laid out on my place at the table, were a hunting knife, a leather sheath and a whetstone. As I looked up, they said, 'Happy birthday,' in unison.

The knife was a present, the best birthday present I had ever had.

I picked it up. It was obviously old, as the rosewood handle was smooth from many years of wear and stained by countless sweaty hands. Below the handle was a metal guard and then a blade, about eight inches long and about one and a half inches across at its widest point. It was blackened with age, but I could see it was of the highest quality, would hold an edge and last forever.

Gramps took the knife from me and said, 'Yimmy, this is not a toy. It is a tool and ve believe you are old enough to use it responsibly.'

My chest swelled with pride and I resolved never to betray their trust.

It was a Friday, which meant I didn't have to go to

school and so, after my morning training and breakfast, Gramps sat down with me and spent an hour showing me how to use the whetstone to maintain the blade and achieve the sharpest of edges.

The sheath was as old as the knife. I could see the new stitches where Granny had spent hours repairing it and so it was as serviceable as a new one. I threaded the sheath onto my belt, placed the knife in it and strutted around for the rest of the day feeling very grown up and important. I wasn't allowed to take it to school, but put it on my belt as soon as I returned home each day.

*

Working with the horses, karate training and going to school made my life routine, which is probably what made a pretty innocuous incident that occurred shortly after my twelfth birthday stick in my mind.

I was playing with some friends during the lunch break at school, when I noticed a couple of the older boys talking to a girl of thirteen called Belinda Moley. Although she had always ignored me, I had become quite interested in her over the previous few weeks as I noticed her budding breasts pressing against her dress. The two boys, fourteen year-old twins Freddy and Jacob Jones, were standing close on each side of Belinda and the furtive way they were talking to her made me uneasy. Belinda didn't seem impressed by what they had to say and started to walk away, but, standing either side of her, the twins each grabbed an upper arm and, after saying something more, seemed to march her away into a small copse on the edge of the school yard. Intrigued, I followed.

The copse was quite deep with the trees close together, which made it impossible to see more than a few yards in and so they disappeared from view shortly after entering. I crept after them, but couldn't tell which way they had gone until I heard voices not far off. I followed the sound and saw the three of them together under a widespread oak.

Belinda was standing with her back to the tree with Freddy and Jacob standing each side of her still holding her arms. 'I don't want to,' she complained.

'We don't care what you want,' grinned Freddy, 'If we want to feel your tits and fanny, we will.'

His brother laughed and grabbed one of Belinda's breasts. She struggled and fell to the ground. The twins knelt beside her, lifted her skirt and started to feel between her legs.

I moved closer and said, 'She doesn't want you to do that and so you should stop.'

I'd taken them by surprise, but their nervousness evaporated when they saw who it was. Freddy dismissed me with, 'You're just a kid, Kidd, fuck off.'

They both laughed at his weak joke and continued with their ham-fisted fumbling.

'If Belinda wants me to go, I will,' I persisted, 'But I don't think she does, so I'm asking you to stop and, if you don't, I'll make you.'

This was the first time I had put Asuka's training into practice. I was prepared to fight, but I was going to give them every chance to do the right thing first.

Freddy decided to assert himself. Walking towards me, he asked rhetorically, 'What the fuck do you think you can do, chicken shit?'

As soon as he was close enough, he swung a round house right at my head. I had trained for this moment from the age of six and so I dealt with it easily by swaying away from the punch, allowing his fist to pass in front of my face. I grabbed his wrist in my right hand and pushed his arm up to unbalance him before sweeping his legs from under him. With his legs in the air, Freddy's back took the full force of his impact with the ground. He gave a grunt as the wind was driven from him and he lay unable to move as he gasped to regain his breath.

Jacob gave a shout and rushed at me with his arms out, apparently intending to use his extra size and weight to push me over. I stood waiting and, as he got to me, pushed his hands to each side, grabbed the front of his shirt and fell backwards into a roll. His momentum took him over me. I brought my feet up under his hips and, when he was immediately above me, kicked my legs up straight and hard, flipping him up as he passed over me so he turned a full circle in the air before landing with a bump on his back, Just like his brother before him, Jacob was winded and struggled to recover his breath.

I turned to Belinda. She was now standing and straightening her dress. To my surprise, she said, 'I suppose you want to see my fanny now.'

To a boy of twelve this was an exciting prospect. I didn't want her to think I was like the Jones twins, but neither did I want to miss the chance of seeing something that had been in my thoughts quite a lot over the last few weeks and so I replied, 'Only if you want to show me.'

With a toss of her head, she said, 'Well I don't,' turned and strutted away without another word.

So ended my first lesson on the fickleness of women.

When I got back to the playground, Belinda was talking to a couple of her friends. They didn't say anything to me, but looked across at me a couple of times and giggled. She seemed none the worse for her experience.

The Jones twins returned about ten minutes later. They were a little subdued, but appeared otherwise unscathed. As far as I know, they didn't tell anyone what had happened. They certainly didn't discuss it with me. They just avoided me for the rest of the time we were at school together

When I told Asuka about the incident, he didn't comment. He simply nodded sagely, which I took to be his seal of approval.

*

Meg died shortly before my thirteenth birthday. She hadn't been injured and didn't seem unwell beforehand. She was simply not there waiting to come to bed with me one evening and, when I went to look for her, I found her lying on her side in the barn as though she were asleep. I knelt next to her and felt her. She was starting to get cold and I realised she had died. I lifted her big ugly head and cuddled her to me, covering her face with my tears.

We buried her the next morning. Tor carried her to where I wanted her buried. I dug her grave myself and placed a layer of hay on the bottom. Tor laid her gently on the bed of hay. I placed more hay over her and then filled the hole. We all stood around her grave for a few minutes. Gramps tried to comfort me. 'She had a good life with us and died peacefully, no creature can ask for more. Ve don't know how old she vas because she vas fully grown vhen ve adopted her. I think she had a good, long life.'

By an extraordinary coincidence, later that day another dog came into our lives. It was as big as Meg, but, where Meg was ugly, ungainly and had a tatty coat, this dog was elegant, well proportioned and had a soft, medium length coat. It was obviously a bitch because she was heavily pregnant.

She wandered into our yard and stood there. I walked towards her.

'Careful,' warned Tor, 'We don't know if she is aggressive and she might have rabies.'

I watched her as she sat and then laid down with her head on her paws. Saying, 'She doesn't look either of those things to me, Tor,' I walked over to her slowly and held my hand out. She wagged her tail, lifted her head and licked my hand. 'Obviously very dangerous,' I commented sarcastically.

She turned out to be a very gentle and loveable dog. We had no idea where she had come from and decided she could stay with us until someone claimed her. In recognition of the way she came into our lives, we called

'Wander'.

That night, she had her puppies. We had bedded her down in the barn. First thing the following morning, I rushed out into the barn to see how she was and found three large, healthy puppies suckling contentedly. Wander was happy for us to hold them and so we soon discovered there were two girls and a boy.

Over the next few weeks, the puppies' growth was astonishing. They got big and strong and were walking in almost no time. The boy puppy was particularly adventurous. His urge to explore took him everywhere and I seemed to be constantly rescuing him and taking him back to his mum. Because he looked more like a wolf with each passing day, I called him Lupus.

The puppies were weaned after a couple of months. No one had claimed Wander and she had become a member of the family. Lupus and I had become good friends and so Gramps found homes for the two bitches, but gave Lupus to me.

After his sisters had left, Lupus and I became even closer. We were together the whole time I wasn't at school. He had even taken Meg' place on my bed each night. On the days I went to school, Lupus sat on the porch and watched me go. When I came home, he was sitting there and galloped to me as soon as Asher and I rode into view.

By the time he was six months old, Lupus (who had become a tall, gangly dog), caught up with me shortly after I had left home and kept pace all the way to school. I made half hearted attempts to send him home, but I was too pleased to have him with me to actually make him go.

Miss Sharp wasn't impressed. 'I'm not having that animal in my classroom,' she asserted. 'If he won't go home, he can wait outside while you have your lessons, Jimmy Kidd.'

Lupus followed me to the schoolroom door where I told him to sit and stay. I only just had time to sit at my desk before he started barking. He kept it up for several minutes before Miss Sharp told me to, 'Stop that dog from barking.'

I went to the door and told Lupus to be quiet. He started barking again as soon as I shut the door.

'He might be better if you let him sit under my desk,' I suggested.

As she couldn't think of a better solution, Miss Sharp agreed. I opened the door, called Lupus in and told him to lie under my desk. He laid there quietly for the rest of the lesson.

During the breaks, all the kids in the school wanted to play with Lupus. He enjoyed running around with them, but I noticed he wouldn't stray far from me, which pleased me. He didn't disturb any of the lessons for the remainder of the day.

The following day, Lupus followed me again. Miss Sharp gave me a disapproving look, but didn't comment when he took his place under my desk. From then on, Lupus came to school with me each day. This cemented our relationship and we became genuinely inseparable.

By the time he was one, Lupus had grown into a big

dog who stood more than three feet at the shoulder. He was still leggy and rangy, but over the following year he became well muscled and deep-chested. Most people thought he looked more wolf than dog. I had to agree; his ears stood up from his head, his pointed muzzle and his brown coat did give him a wolf-like appearance, but to me he was beautiful. His look also belied his character which was gentle and loyal. He was never aggressive except when his family was threatened.

*

On the morning of my thirteenth birthday, I came down for breakfast to, once again, find everyone standing around the breakfast table. The memory of my eleventh birthday made me look immediately at my place.

My eyes nearly popped out when I saw what was there. On the table in front of my chair were a Winchester rifle, a box of .44 shells, several neatly folded clean rags and a can of oil.

I couldn't have been more surprised. 'Can I touch it?' I asked.

Gramps smiled and said, 'Yes. It isn't loaded, but treat it with respect all the same.'

I did more than that; when I picked it up I treated it with reverence. Like my knife, it was very old with a stock that was worn and had seen better days. The barrel looked old, but I could see it was perfectly true when I sighted along it. I opened and closed the lever and pulled the trigger. The action was smooth and I realised that, in spite of its age, this was a good gun.

'You must learn respect for guns and how to use them properly,' said Gramps. 'Lessons will start after breakfast.'

That meal was probably the longest I have ever had. It seemed to take forever. My gaze was repeatedly drawn to my gun and I couldn't wait to fire it.

Breakfast finished at last. Gramps said, 'Now you will learn about guns.'

I didn't shoot that day. I sat at the table opposite Gramps as he dismantled the gun, explaining at each stage what he was doing and the function of each part. He polished each component before reassembling the gun and passing to me. 'Now you take it to pieces, Yimmy.'

I tried to remember what Gramps had done, but I was too excited and got myself in a complete mess. Gramps put it together and passed it back to me. Realising I was not going to be allowed to shoot until I had mastered disassembling and reassembling, I calmed myself with a deep breath and resolved to concentrate.

On the fourth attempt, I got it right. By the sixth attempt, I was confident i knew what I was doing. Gramps must have felt so too because, he finally conceded, 'Okay, you now know how this gun works and how to look after it. Tomorrow you can learn how to fire it.'

I was horrified. Wait another day! It was more than I could bear, but when I looked outside I saw the light was fading and it was too late to start now.

Having suffered the longest meal of my life at

breakfast, I then had to endure what seemed to be an interminable night. It ended eventually. Everyone realised how keen I was and they were kind enough to hurry breakfast.

So, after what seemed like an endless wait, I was standing about 100 paces from the house facing the wilderness with my own gun in my hands. Gramps took it from me. 'Before ve load, ve vill learn how to stand, hold the gun, aim and pull the trigger. Vhen ve are standing, ve haf our legs about shoulder vidth apart to give us a good, solid base. Ve hold the stock tight against our shoulder to visthstand the recoil and hold the barrel about half vay along. Our left elbow is low under the barrel to support it. It is not pushed out to the side. Ve sight along the barrel placing the little pip at the end in the V of the back sight. The target must be just above the little pip. Ve don't pull the trigger, ve squeeze it gently.'

He passed the gun to me. As I held it up to shoot, I repeated each of his instructions as I carried them out, starting with planting my feet for a solid base and finishing with squeezing the trigger.

'Okay,' he said, 'Let's see how you get on. Shoot at that old tree twenty paces away that's about two feet wide.'

He had shown me how to load the Winchester and so, on his instruction, I pushed fourteen rounds into the long magazine that ran underneath the barrel. I looked at him. He nodded to indicate I could now shoot. I held the gun to my shoulder, forgot everything he told me and missed the easy target by a mile.

When he stopped laughing, he said, 'Okay, you just got excited. Now, take a few moments. Think how Asuka has taught you about being calm. When you are ready, try again.'

I hadn't thought about applying Asuka's control techniques to shooting, but realised Gramps was right. I took a whole minute to allow all the excitement to leave my mind,. I then brought the rifle to my shoulder, paused as I aimed at the tree and then pulled the trigger. My bullet clipped the edge of the trunk. So, although this was an improvement on my first effort, it was still a poor shot given the size of the target and its nearness. 'Much better,' Gramps encouraged me. 'This time concentrate on squeezing the trigger even more gently.'

I took my second shot following his instructions and hit the tree dead centre. I resisted the temptation to whoop with delight because I didn't want to lose my composure.

'Vell done,' enthused Gramps, 'Now try the next tree.'

This was about the same size, but twice as far. I followed exactly the same procedure as the previous shot and missed the target by such a wide margin we couldn't see where the bullet landed.

'It's your breathing,' explained Gramps. 'It moves your chest up and down, which throws off your aim. Breath in, let out half your breath, hold it and then squeeze the trigger.'

I did exactly as he said and hit the new target dead centre. I took several more shots with the same result. I was following Gramps' instructions to the letter, and the more I shot, the more I felt at one with the gun. After about forty shots, everything from the way I stood, to how I breathed, which seemed so unnatural to begin with, became second nature, an innate part of my shooting. The Winchester seemed an extension of my body. Shooting it was instinctive, an unconscious reflex like breathing.

As my confidence grew, I looked for more challenging targets. I moved on from simply shooting at the trunk of the tree to aiming at branches. I searched out smaller and smaller branches and each time I hit the target. After I had emptied the Winchester for the fourth time I looked around me. Gramps had a slightly stunned look on his face. Behind me, Tor and Asuka had stopped their work and were watching. Asuka spoke first, 'Before you reload, let me have a look at that tree.'

He walked over to the tree and studied it carefully. He pointed to the trunk and asked, 'Can you see that knot?'

I replied, 'Yes.'

Gramps and Tor said, 'No.'

Asuka came back to us and instructed me to, 'Reload and put as many bullets as you can in the knot.'

I pushed another fourteen shells into the magazine, put the Winchester to my shoulder and fired 14 times in quick succession.

'Let's have a look,' suggested Gramps.

We walked to the tree. The area immediately around the knot, which was about one inch across, was shattered. Asuka calculated that six of the shots had hit the knot while the other 8 were within a radius of two inches. 'Not bad for a beginner,' remarked Gramps.

I did not have time to practise shooting on school days, but on Fridays, Saturdays and Sundays, I shot as often as possible. Each member of my family gave me their views on shooting animals. They expressed themselves in different ways, but they agreed that killing for fun was wrong. A real man would only kill for two reasons: for food and to protect himself, his property and those close to him. I took this to heart and only shot game when Granny ordered it for the pot. At other times, I made targets of trees and pebbles. My favourite practice routine was to set up a target, start shooting at about 50 paces and then increase the distance by intervals of ten paces until I missed. I was aware that ammunition was expensive and so I didn't ask for bullets, but Gramps bought me a box from time-to-time and so I was able to keep up my practising..

*

Smalltown was, as its name suggests, small, but they had an annual fair that attracted a lot of people from outlying areas. It allowed those who would otherwise not see one another to get together, swap ideas, compare animals and have some fun. Showing animals was most important, as ranchers and farmers could keep up with developments, find new breeds and market their stock. Of secondary importance, but still a lot of fun, were competitions that included running, wrestling and shooting. One of the competitions was rifle shooting and Tor suggested I

43

should enter. The idea of a 13 year old competing with adults who had shot all their lives seemed silly and I thought he was joking.

'If that's how you feel, you have nothing to lose, Jimmy, so why not try?'

With no weight of expectation, I decided it would be fun to try and I might also learn something by competing with the best shooters in the area.

On the day of the fair, I made a special effort to clean my Winchester before we all set off for town. With it tucked under my arm and a box of shells in my hand, I strutted around the fair taking in the atmosphere as people called good naturedly to one another. I enjoyed the unaccustomed noise and bustle until it was time for the contest. Asuka came with me just in case the judges thought I was too young to take part. In the event, they didn't question me, but I was reassured by his presence.

There were about thirty people lined up to take part. They talked confidently of previous successes and looked as though they were experts. Asuka could see I was overawed. 'This is the same as karate, Jimmy,' he reminded me. 'You can never discover how good someone is from what they say. Look into their eyes for the truth. Some of them are frightened. See the way that man is chewing his nails? That one is constantly fiddling with his collar, that one keeps checking his rifle and that one has nervous eyes that are constantly darting around. If you stay calm, you will shoot your best. If someone beats you, it is because they are better than you, but at least you have the satisfaction of knowing you could not have done better.' He patted me on the shoulder and went to the spectator stand to join the others.

The competitors were separated into three groups of ten. The first group took up their positions in a line while the rest of us waited a safe distance behind them. Fifty paces in front of each shooter was a target with a number of concentric circles, the outer blue one was ten inches in diameter, the white one six inches and the inner red one three inches. Group one was given the instruction to load five bullets. When they were ready, they raised an arm. When all ten had their arms aloft, they were told to start firing. They then had a minute for their five shots.

There was a staccato of shots. I looked at the targets. My first impression was how bad many of them were. Some missed the target altogether while others only clipped the edge of the blue circle. They all finished within the minute. Most had improved on their first shot, but I was generally unimpressed except with two who had hit the centre five times. My overriding thought was that at least I wasn't going to be last!

We had been told that the first two in each group would go through to a final together with the next best four scores. The two winners strutted off to the finalists' holding area, those who had a good score waited nervously to see it they qualified and those who had no chance melted into the crowd.

I was in the third group and so I watched the second follow the same procedure as the first. The results were much the same, but this time there were three who had maximum scores. The judges decided on the two winners by those who had the most shots closest to the absolute centre. They went into the finalists' enclosure while the third confidently waited close by.

It was my turn. The stewards took us each to our appointed places. I was roughly in the middle of the line. I rested my Winchester in the crook of my arm and waited for instruction to, 'Load five rounds,' which soon came from the judge.

I took five bullets from the box in front of me, cradled the Winchester against my left forearm and pushed them into the magazine with my right thumb. This familiar movement calmed my nerves and, when I lifted it to show I was ready, I was pleased that my arm was steady.

On the instruction to commence firing, I took a deep breath in and out before lifting my rifle to my shoulder. I breathed in, let out half the breath as I sighted along the barrel.

From when I first started shooting, it had never been my habit to take a long time over aiming. I realised that holding the rifle in the aim position was tiring and the longer you held it, the more I shook, so I rationalised that there was no point in waiting once the target was in my sights and had always fired as soon as I had a bead. I saw no reason to change my routine and so I fired 5 times in quick succession. I was certain I had hit the bull with each shot.

The others finished shooting and the stewards recovered the targets. One other competitor also had five shots in the centre and two had four dead centre with one clipping the white. I was sent to the finalists' enclosure together with my joint winner, who grinned and said, 'Good shooting, youngster.'

There were six finalists when I went into the enclosure. The man from the second round who had five bulls, but lost on his centering, joined us at once After carefully checking all the other targets, the judge decided the two who had just missed out from my group plus one other were the best first-round losers. One of the stewards asked us our names, which he wrote on a scrap of paper and took over to the announcer. As we were taking our places, our names were shouted out by the loud-voiced announcer. When he called my name, I could hear Gramps, Granny, Tor and Asuka cheering. It wasn't the loudest cheer by a long way.

The procedure was the same. After we had shot, the targets were taken to the judge. Eight of us had all five shots in the bull. Of those, two shots were slightly off centre. They were unable to separate the remaining six and so it was announced we would shoot again, but this time the distance would be sixty paces.

Six of us had our names announced again as we took up our positions. My family cheered me again. We took our shots and waited for the judge to consider the targets. He determined that there were three that were as good as one another and would have to shoot again. I was one of them. Our names were announced again. This time there was more of a buzz when my name was heard. My young age made me a bit of a novelty.

Much to my surprise, I was enjoying myself. I had already proven I was one of the best and anything more would be a bonus.

The target was taken back another ten paces, so it was now eighty paces away. We shot again and the judge studied the targets. It was announced that it was still impossible to separate two competitors and so they would have to shoot again. They then broadcast the names. I was one and the man who had won through with me in my group was the other.

We were taken to the firing points. The target was moved back to 100 paces. The judge decided that this time we would shoot one after the other, which he thought would make it more exciting. We tossed to determine who would go first. I won the toss and, as I turned to him to tell him he could shoot first, I noticed for the first time my opponent looked unsure

He wasn't actually nervous, but he seemed to lack the confidence he had shown when he had slightly patronisingly congratulated me after the first round. I realised he hadn't been expecting to see me at the last and, with sudden insight, I realised he wasn't expecting to shoot at such a small target over this distance.

I stepped back to give him room. The judge gave the order to load and then to shoot when he was ready.

He raised his gun, took careful aim and shot - dead centre! He lowered his gun took a deep breath, raised his gun, took careful aim and shot - dead centre!

He lowered his gun, shrugged his shoulders, took a deep breath, raised his gun, took careful aim and shot - dead centre!

He lowered his gun, rolled his shoulders, took a deep

breath, raised his gun, took careful aim and shot - dead centre.

He prepared for his fifth and final shot by moving his head from side to side, rolling his shoulders, taking a deep breath and raising his gun. He was being careful and took much longer with his aim. I thought about what Gramps had said about the effects of fatigue; he was taking too long. He fired just before his minute was up and hit the white.

He had just missed a three-inch centre at 100 yards with one of five shots. I recognised that, although not perfect, it was still exceptional shooting. He turned to me looking slightly forlorn. I said, 'That's pretty good shooting, mister.'

He looked at me for a moment. Realising I was sincere, he responded, 'Thanks, kid, do you think you can do better?'

With a grin I replied, 'I don't know, but I'm certainly going to try.'

I went to the firing position and waited for the judge's instructions. On the command to fire, I raised the Winchester to my shoulder, breathed in, let out half my breath and then fired five times in quick succession.

There was silence as the sound of the shots died away. The steward shouted, 'Five dead centre.' The shocked crowd didn't respond until Tor started shouting over and over, 'Jimmy Kidd, Jimmy Kidd, Jimmy Kidd …'

This seemed to break the spell as the crowd took up the call. They cheered and shouted. The man I'd beaten clapped me on the back and said, 'Well done. Jimmy

Kidd is a name I won't forget in a hurry.'

At that point, Tor and Asuka came running over. Tor lifted me onto his shoulders. They took me back to Granny and Gramps, who were grinning with pleasure and couldn't have looked prouder. Together, we went to the front of the crowd, who cheered again as the judge presented me with a trophy and the largest amount of money I had ever seen. I kept the trophy in my room, but gave the money to Granny and Gramps.

4

Mortifer

Religion hadn't played a big part in my life. My parents had taught me to pray and so I said the Lord's Prayer each night before I went to sleep. Granny always muttered a few words of thanks before each meal. But these were more from habit than conviction; we barely considered God at these moments and didn't give him a thought at other times ... until the Reverend Preston came into our lives.

Father Archibald Preston was an imposing man. Tall and wide with a great shock of black hair and the most impressive black beard I have ever seen. He would never go unnoticed in a crowd, but his deep, booming voice made him impossible to ignore.

As soon as he arrived in Smalltown, he stood in the middle of the street and condemned all and sundry as sinners who would burn in hell unless they followed him to redemption. Such was his impact that within a couple of months of his arrival he had convinced, coerced, browbeaten and bludgeoned the inhabitants of the town and surrounding farmsteads to build a church. It was a simple, log structure, much like many of the other buildings. It was furnished with wooden benches, which he called pews, and could hold a congregation of about fifty. As soon as it was finished, he went around inside and out throwing drops of water over the walls and floor declaring the building to have been consecrated by holy water and that it was from henceforth a house of God. My immediate reaction was that, as he had collected it in a bucket from a nearby horse trough, I couldn't see how there could be anything special in the water and that, if it made the building holy, the town must have had the holiest horses in existence.

For the next few weeks, we all attended a church service each Sunday. This comprised singing some hymns and kneeling to pray, but most of the time was taken with the Reverend Preston's interminable sermons, which confused rather than enlightened me. To start with, I couldn't understand why God had spoken so often and freely to people in ancient times, but had not spoken directly to anyone recently.

I also wondered how someone who said that humility was a virtue could be so vain that he insisted on us getting on our knees to tell him how great and almighty he was.

Similarly, why did someone who preached forgiveness threaten such dire punishments if we didn't follow his rules? He also seemed to have got his priorities wrong because, if the Reverend Preston was right, we would suffer the most painful punishments for simply not praising Him, praying to Him or respecting the Sabbath. Even in my short life, I had seen much worse and so I wondered why a God, who was supposed to be merciful, could get so worked up about pretty minor transgression, but be so tolerant of much worse.

Furthermore, I wondered about his inconsistencies. For instance, why did he feed the 5,000 when I have heard there are many thousands who have died of starvation when their crops failed? After all, the 5,000 were there for a sermon, there was no real need to feed them. They would have only missed a picnic lunch, there was no suggestion they starving.

Also, why did Jesus convert water to wine when the wine ran out at a wedding? The guests had already drunk all the wine, which suggests excess. Why go to such lengths to provide more alcohol when the Reverend Preston called drink 'evil'?

For several weeks I tried to balance these doubts in my mind with the absolute conviction of the Reverend and the way in which other members of the congregation seemed happy to accept what he said. The problem was resolved a couple of weeks later.

When the Reverend Preston asked for volunteers to make decorations and artifacts for the church, Gramps agreed to make a polished wooden cross to place on the altar. When it was finished, he asked me to deliver it so that it would be in place when the congregation assembled for the next service. I put it in a shoulder bag, picked up my Winchester, leapt onto Asher's bare back and set off at a fast lope with Lupus in close attendance.

When we arrived, I decided that it wouldn't be right to take a rifle and a dog into a church and so I rested my Winchester against the wall next to the door and told

Lupus to sit and wait.

As I was about to enter, I heard raised voices and felt it best to keep a low profile in case I interrupted something important. Slipping silently through the door and staying in the shadows at the back of the building, I could see two people at the front by the altar. One was the Reverend Preston and the other was a tall, skinny, weasel looking man who was waving a pistol in the reverend's face.

'Repent, my son,' said the reverend, 'Put down your gun and let us kneel and pray for your eternal soul.'

'To hell with your prayers, just tell me where you keep the silver,' was the response.

'Oh, you poor, misguided soul,' oozed the vicar, 'This is a new church and the people here are very poor, so there is no silver. Let us see this as an opportunity for you not to gain worldly wealth, but as an opportunity for you to seek redemption.'

'Bollocks,' was the unequivocal reply. 'Give me the silver or it will be the worse for you.'

The reverend put his hands together, closed his eyes and said, 'Ever merciful God, show this poor sinner the error of his ways and let him see the light of your goodness.'

'Fuck your God and fuck your light, all I want to see is your silver.' The weasel man was at least consistent.

The reverend changed tack. 'This poor sinner is beyond saving, Lord. I beg you to bring down your wrath and smite him.'

Tapping Preston on his head with his pistol barrel to

emphasise his point, the weasel shouted, 'I'll bring my fucking wrath down on you if you don't give me the fucking silver.'

I'd heard enough to realise the situation was getting dangerous and slipped out of the church to get my Winchester. When I returned, the reverend was on his knees, firstly begging God to strike the sinner down and then making a direct plea to the weasel, 'Please don't hurt me. I'm a simple man serving God as best I can in this poor outpost. If there were any valuables, I would give them to you, but there are none.'

This display of grovelling cowardice brought the reverend to a new low in my estimation and I felt nothing for him but contempt.

The weasel was similarly unimpressed, 'Fucking pleading will get you nowhere. Get off your fucking knees and show me the silver or I'll put a bullet through your elbow and I'll shoot out all your joints until you give me the money.'

Although I no longer had any respect for the reverend, I realised he was the innocent party and that effective and decisive action was required. As Preston continued with his pleading, 'Please, I implore you …..',

I raised my rifle to my shoulder and shot the weasel through the head.

At such a short range, his head did not slow the bullet significantly. It made a neat entry hole in his left temple and exited his right in a small explosion of blood and brains. It didn't even knock him sideways, he just collapsed in a heap in front of the kneeling, so-called holy man.

In such a confined space, the sound of the Winchester was like a thunderclap. Still on his knees, the reverend looked at the crumpled body in front of him and, as the reverberations died, put his hands together and cried, 'Thank you God for sending your thunderbolt to smite this sinner and save your faithful servant.'

I walked down to the aisle saying, 'It wasn't God and his thunderbolt, it was me and my Winchester.'

Preston got to his feet and watched me walk towards him. Recovering remarkably quickly, he boomed, 'My son, let us fall to our knees and thank the Lord for sending you to save me.'

Taking the cross from my shoulder bag and holding it up, I replied, 'It wasn't the Lord who sent me to save you, it was Gramps who sent me to give you this.'

He used the stock response, 'The Lord moves in curious ways his wonders to perform. Let us give thanks together.'

Feeling annoyed, I continued, 'Bollocks, the Lord had nothing to do with it.'

He lifted his hand and pointed at me, 'Blasphemer, get on your knees and beg forgiveness.'

Shouldering my rifle, I pushed his outstretched arm to the side so I could get close. He was at least a foot taller than me and so I had to lift my head to look him in the eye. I wasn't unnerved by his size as I could see in his eyes that he lacked the courage and conviction of his words. Tucking the cross into the belt of his cassock and getting right into his face, I couldn't keep the contempt from my voice, 'There is no God. If I hadn't come, if I didn't have my Winchester and if I couldn't shoot straight you would now be writhing in pain with bullets through your elbows and knees. There was no God protecting you any more than there was a God protecting my parents when they were tortured to death. They were good people who cared for me, worked hard and didn't hurt a soul. If anyone deserved protection, it was them, but here was no one there to save them. You were just lucky that I was here to rescue your cowardly snivelling hide. You certainly don't have it in you to save yourself.'

I reflected that this was probably the longest speech I had ever made. I'd finished and so I turned on my heel and started to leave.

'Who's going to help me clean up this mess,' he snivelled peevishly.

Not pausing, I called out over my shoulder, 'I've done the difficult bit, you can sort out the rest. If you haven't got the stomach for it, ask your God to send someone who has.'

With that, I left, vaulted onto Asher and rode home slowly so that I could think. Lupus followed without being called.

I was certain I had done the right thing, but I couldn't immediately think how it fitted in with my philosophy of killing. It was not gratuitous, as I had made sure it was a quick kill and, if I hadn't killed him, the weasel would have killed Preston. The dead man had felt no pain and I suspected he had moved from life to death without even realising.

However, I couldn't see how this fitted into only killing to protect myself, my property and anyone close to me. I was in no danger as I could have slipped away without anyone realising I had even been there. There was no property to protect because, as Preston had said, the church didn't have any. Even if it had, it was not my property. Preston was not anyone close to me. I had never liked him and had started to despise him before I shot the weasel, as I recognised him for what he was: a snivelling coward who hid behind the persona of a blustering windbag.

However, in spite of his shortcomings, he was the victim. In the end it came down to a choice of me killing the weasel or letting him kill Preston. I rationalised that, if he was prepared to kill Preston, the weasel would probably be prepared to kill others. On the other hand, being the contemptible coward he was, Preston probably didn't have the guts to kill anyone and so I had probably saved many lives by taking one. It made things more complicated, but I decided that by adding weak and vulnerable people to the list of those I should protect, I would not be compromising my principles.

It also dawned on me that until that moment, I was a victim like everyone else who had to accept the randomness of death. Now I had a measure of control. In situations like that, I could decide who died. I had become what my favourites, the Romans, would call a mortifer - a killer, a bringer of death!

As soon as I got home, I called my family together and told them what had happened. Tor immediately said

I had been right. Asuka was his normal taciturn self and nodded his approval. Gramps was upset and Granny was horrified, but they said I had done the best I could in the circumstances. I explained my rationale of protecting the weak. This seemed to make it easier for them to accept and closed the subject by saying the most important thing was that I was not hurt.

Sheriff Brand called in later that day. I told him exactly what had happened. He said that the Reverend Preston's version was similar, but varied in that he claimed to have confronted the would-be thief and that, with the help of God's goodness, he had used the power of his own personality and was about to convince the intruder of the error of his ways when I shot him. He had conceded that I might not have known he was about to overwhelm the poor soul with the strength of his character because I may not have heard the conversation and the thief had a gun in his hand. I should, therefore, be given the benefit of the doubt and treated leniently.

I was most indignant. I told the sheriff I had heard every word and that Preston was on his knees begging for his life when I shot the thief, who had threatened to shoot Preston through the elbow to make him talk.

The sheriff gave me a long, hard stare and then smiled. 'I'm inclined to believe your version, Jimmy. I've a colleague who knows Preston of old. He reckons he's a windbag and a fraud who would run a mile from a fight. Even if that's not so, the thief was a piece of low life by the name of Sellars. He had a reputation for stealing from churches and was suspected of murdering a couple of vicars by shooting them through the joints and leaving them to bleed to death. So I reckon you, young Jimmy, have done us all a favour and probably saved a few lives into the bargain.'

I thanked the sheriff and reflected on where God might have been while the other preachers were shot and left to bleed to death.

The whole family agreed we would no longer attend church. Granny, Gramps and Tor because they didn't believe Preston was the right man to lead the congregation. Asuka because he had his own beliefs. I went along with this decision, but kept my reasons to myself for fear of upsetting Granny and Gramps. I sat quietly while Granny said grace before each meal, but stopped offering prayers of my own.

*

I was about half way through my fourteenth year when our best mare was due to give birth. When walking by the mare's enclosure, I noticed she had gone into labour. I got a head collar, led her into the birthing stall in the barn and went to find Tor.

We watched her for a long time. With all her previous foals, she had stood up for the duration of the delivery, but on this occasion, after standing to begin with, she laid on her side.

'This doesn't look good.' Tor was talking to himself rather than telling me what he thought. However, shortly after lying down, two feet appeared. 'At least this is not a breach birth,' Tor breathed with some relief.

We waited, but the foal made no further progress. Tor knelt down next to the mare and inserted his hand into the birth canal. 'The foal is in the right position, but it's very big and seems to be stuck. We need to help her. Come here, Jimmy.'

I knelt next to Tor. He pushed his hand in again and instructed me, 'You pull the feet while I ease the head out.'

As I started, he guided me, 'No, not straight out, pull the feet down towards the mare's legs.'

I pulled, but nothing happened. There was not much for me to hold and the legs were slippery. Tor was patient as I changed my grip to get a better hold and gave a good pull. Tor eased the head forward at the same time. I felt some movement. The front legs came out followed by the head and then the rest of the body in a sudden rush of fluids.

It was a colt and he was the biggest new-born foal we had ever had; it was no wonder he needed help to negotiate the birth canal!

In addition to his size, he was one of the strongest I had seen and was on his feet more quickly than most. His mother seemed to recover quickly. She was able to stand as the colt was finding its feet and was in position for him to take his first feed of colostrum, which was any newborn's most important feed as it contained not only nourishment, but other stuff that would help to stop the colt getting ill.

As we washed our hands under the pump, Tor said, 'I was worried for a moment, but I think they're going to be okay. That colt is a little monster! Can you check them a few times before you go to bed, just to be sure?'

I was pleased to be given the responsibility and went to see them four times before going to bed. Each time they were standing quietly with the foal either suckling or standing contentedly by its mother. I stood each time admiring the colt, who I felt was the most handsome foal I had ever seen. Some people commented later to the effect that his bay coat was common and uninteresting as he did not have white socks or a star on his forehead and that having nothing more than a brown coat with black main and tail was boring. To me he was beautiful.

I woke early the following morning, dressed quickly and rushed to the barn to check the mare and colt were before breakfast. Everything had changed. The colt was standing in the corner of the pen. The mare was lying in the middle. The straw bedding all around her was soaked in blood.

I ran out shouting for Tor, who came quickly and confirmed my worst fears: the mare was dead! He checked her over and told me she had haemorrhaged. I didn't know what that was and so, with tears running down my face, I asked him to explain. He told me that it was when a major blood vessel breaks resulting in massive bleeding that leads to death. He guessed that the unusually large foal had damaged a vessel on the way out, but only slightly so that we did not see the bleeding, as it was mixed with the amniotic fluid and afterbirth. The damaged vein had gradually worsened in the night until it had burst causing catastrophic bleeding and death.

The loss of our best mare was sad and a serious blow to the business, but there was nothing we could do for her. We now had to do the best we could for her son.

On the rare occasions a mare had died while giving birth, we had been able to foster them onto another mare who had a newly born foal of her own. Previously, this had always been shortly after the birth and Tor was worried that, as the colt had been born hours before and had already suckled on its mother, it might not accept another mare or she might reject him.

Together, we introduced the colt to one mare after another, but none of them wanted to have anything to do with him. Indeed, some were so aggressive that we feared for his safety.

Tor looked dejected. When I asked him why, he said, 'If the colt can't feed, he will starve to death. It would be better to shoot him before he starts to suffer.'

'No,' I cried in horror, 'I won't let you! We must get advice. Someone will know what to do.'

Tor nodded his agreement, but I was sure he was just humouring me and planned to shoot the colt after I had gone to bed.

We had a family meeting and Granny came up with a plan. 'Our sons' vives had babies vithin a few days of one another. The first had so much milk that she nearly drowned her child vhereas the other's breasts were almost dry. The first offered to suckle them both, vhich she did successfully for a few days. This pleased us all except the second mother who felt she vould not bond with her baby. The problem was solved when they bought a bottle that had a soft end like a nipple. The plentiful mother squeezed half her milk into a bowl, vhich we then transferred to the special bottle. The second mother vas then able to hold her baby as she drank from the bottle through the special nipple.'

'How does that help us save the colt?' I asked.

She continued, 'I'm sure the nursing mares can each give a little milk vithout harming their foals. Ve can then put it in the bottle to feed the colt.'

With that, she got up, went to a kitchen cupboard and got out a clear glass bottle that had a soft end shaped like a nipple.

'It won't hurt to try,' said Tor.

'I'll do it now,' I said excitedly.

'You vill need a clean bucket to collect the milk, Yimmy. Keep it covered until you need it and then transfer some of the milk to a jug so you can pour it into the bottle. Before you feed it to the colt, make sure it is warm enough. Body temperature vould be best, you could varm it under your arm.'

We had six nursing mares at the time. I squeezed a little milk from each of them to give me what I judged would be enough milk for a day. It was still warm from the mothers and so I filled the special bottle and took it to the colt.

Tor and Asuka had taken him to a clean pen so that he didn't see them dragging his mother's body away and clearing up the bloodied straw. He was standing in the corner looking very dejected. I approached him slowly talking to him all the time in a very calm voice. To begin with, he turned away. Eventually, he let me get to his head. I continued to talk soothing nonsense and stroked his head and neck trying to simulate his mother licking him. He seemed to get calmer. I slowly brought the bottle to his mouth. He didn't know what to do. All his instincts told him that, in order to feed, he needed a large, four footed creature with teats under her belly. This little, two footed beast was friendly enough, but was all wrong when it came to feeding.

I stroked his nose, put my hand under his chin, lifted his muzzle and dribbled some milk over his lips. He licked his lips and lifted his head. I dribbled some more milk, he licked again. We did this several times and then I presented the bottle's teat to his lips. He licked it. I dribbled some more milk and he licked it again. This time, while his tongue was out, I pushed the teat into his mouth. The milk taste and the shape of the teat were familiar. Instinct took over and he started to suck. As the milk flowed into his mouth, he became more enthusiastic. He started sucking and didn't stop until the bottle was empty.

From that point on, we didn't look back. To start with, the colt had to be fed every two hours. First thing each morning, I collected milk from the mares. This lasted the whole day. Each evening I did the same. I kept the next feed's bottle in bed with me and somehow was able to rise every two hours. On school days, Tor, Asuka or Gramps gave the three feeds while I was at school. I rushed home each day to take over and on Fridays, Saturdays and Sundays I gave all the feeds.

The colt grew well. Tor remarked early on that he had 'Bucked up very well'. From then on he was known as Buck.

After a couple of months, the feeds became less frequent and at five months Buck was weened. By that time, we had bonded; Buck, Lupus and I became the three amigos. Lupus came with me wherever I went. Buck followed me around whenever I was home, but had to stay behind when I went elsewhere. On those occasions, he grazed with the other youngsters, but always ran to the gate when he saw me. I would let him out and we would stay together, Buck moving with us and grazing as he went along.

One day, Gramps sent me on an errand. I mounted Asher and was leaving with Lupus when Buck cantered up to the fence. He called to us. I waved and shouted I would be back later. Buck turned ran a few strides away from the fence, turned back, cantered up to the fence and jumped it. It was an enormous jump for a colt of his age, but it was an indication of the horse he was to become. From that day on, Buck joined us wherever we went and not once did he stray.

Buck grew into a fine young horse. Standing at just under fifteen hands, he wasn't as big as might have been expected from such a big colt. Instead, he was finely built in line with his Arabian ancestry. He had a chiselled, dished head and matured from a leggy and rangy youngster into a well muscled, but athletic horse with strength and, above all, outstanding speed and stamina.

From the time he was eighteen months, Asuka started

checking his joints to see when we could back him. He paid particular attention to the knee joints, which had to be fully matured to ensure carrying the weight of a rider didn't damage them. Asuka wouldn't pass Buck as ready to ride until he was over two years old. His style was to take things very slowly. Buck had not needed even a head collar until then because he just stayed with me. So we had to be very careful when it came to tack. First of all, we got him used to a head collar. Then we placed a blanket on his back and walked him around. He took to that easily and so Asuka tried him with some weight by laying on his belly across Buck's back. Buck kicked up his heels and flipped him off.

'Very aptly named,' Asuka remarked as he picked himself up and tried again. Same result. After the third time, I asked if I could try. I stood next to Buck, patted his back, jumped up and down twice and, on the third jump, laid across his back. He just stood there. Asuka picked up the lead rope attached to the head collar and encourage Buck forward. He walked forward as steadily as you like.

Asuka scratched his head, 'Well, would you believe it, a one man horse.'

The next stage was to sit on Buck's back, which I did by squirming around from a laying position, swinging my leg over and sitting up. He stood perfectly still. Over the next few days, I rode Buck without a bridle or head collar and nothing but a blanket as a saddle. When teaching me to ride Asher, Asuka had taught me how to control a horse using my heals, calves, thighs and seat.

He said that the best horses needed nothing more. I didn't believe him until I rode Buck.

From the beginning, he responded to my legs and seat. Within a few weeks, I could move up through walk, trot, canter and gallop and, much more surprisingly, come back down through the paces to halt. Although I thought about what I was doing to begin with, after a couple of months the whole process became instinctive.

It had always felt wrong when I put a bit in a horse's mouth, but I understood the need in every other horse I had ridden. It didn't seem necessary with Buck and, when I mentioned this to him, Asuka said that I could use a bitless bridle. This comprised cheekpieces, a noseband, a loose throatlash and reins that ran from small rings attached to the nose band where it joined the throat lash.

Although I used nothing more than a blanket during the early schooling, Asuka suggested I should use a saddle as this would give me a stable seat, which would be better for both horse and rider during long rides and when we had to make quick changes in direction. We couldn't afford a new one and so Asuka adapted an old saddle. He repaired it and then re-flocked and adjusted it so that it fitted Buck perfectly. My tack was worn and scruffy, but perfectly functional.

When I started riding Buck frequently, I introduced him to the farrier on one of his visits to the homestead. He cleaned and trimmed Buck's hooves and passed them as in good condition. I asked him a question that had puzzled me for some time, 'Why do we put iron shoes on horses?'

'It's been done for a long time. Why should you question it?' was his response.

'Well, wild horses aren't shod and their feet seem to be fine. I know they are not carrying a rider, but they walk and run over the same surfaces.'

With a wry smile, he explained, 'You're right, the main reason people want their horses shod is because they always have been. I reckon it's a good idea in towns and on other roads that are cobbled or have a stone surface, but it's probably not necessary out here. I don't argue with customers who want their horses shod because it's the way I earn a living and if I didn't do it, they'd go elsewhere. Buck here has a fine set of feet and he would probably be better off without shoes, provided you look after his hooves.'

'Can you show me?' I asked.

At his next few visits, the farrier showed me how to trim hooves. He even took me on his rounds one day so I could see him work and, under his careful supervision, I did some trimming.

One day he said, 'You're not bad, young Jimmy. You may not be a farrier yet, but you can trim a hoof. Here's a present for you.'

He handed me a small, rather tatty bag. It contained a curved trimming knife and a hoof file. 'That's my old set. They wouldn't last long with the use I give them, but, if you look after them properly, they should last you years.'

I thanked him profusely and, from that day on, I cared for Buck's hooves.

*

Like all pupils, I left school at the end of the term during which I had my fourteenth birthday. For the next year, I helped around the homestead. I mucked in with all the chores, but Buck was my special responsibility.

On my fourteenth birthday, I came in for what had become a biennial ritual. There were four expectant faces around the table and there, laid out in my place, was a Colt .44 and cartridge belt with a holster.

'You must learn to use this properly and responsibly, Yimmy,' warned Gramps as he wagged his finger at me. 'After breakfast, I will teach you how to care for it. Later this morning, sheriff Brand is coming over to teach you to use it.'

I was ecstatic! I was pleased with my Winchester, but the gift of a pistol showed me they thought I was growing up and could be trusted.

As with the Winchester, after clearing the breakfast things, Gramps and I sat at the table. He dismantled the Colt, cleaned it, reassembled it and passed it to me. It was also old and worn, as were the cartridge belt and holster, which I could see Granny had repaired and re-stitched extensively. My experience with the Winchester stood me in good stead and so I completed the task without Gramps's help, albeit very slowly. He made me repeat the exercise several times until I became adept.

After what seemed an interminable wait, Sheriff Brand appeared late in the morning. After greeting the others, he turned to me, 'Big day for you, young Jimmy. We know you're good with a Winchester. We're now going to see if you can handle a pistol, but, most of all, you are going to learn to use it responsibly.'

Of course, I agreed with an energetic nod. I would have agreed to almost anything to bring forward the moment I was going to shoot my own pistol, but I meant it, nevertheless.

The sheriff took my pistol and led me out to the back of the house where we could shoot safely. He looked it over, making sure it was unloaded before listening to the clicks as he pulled the hammer back and squeezed the trigger. He checked the cylinder and barrel. 'It's an old gun, but is well made and has a good few years left in it,' he concluded

The lesson started with gun unloaded. I stood next to him on his right while the sheriff held the gun out so I could see it. 'It's a double action, which means you have to pull the hammer back all the way. This rotates the cylinder so that there is a live shell under the hammer and cocks it ready to fire. When you pull the trigger, the hammer is released and it comes down hard on the back of the shell making it fire.'

Holding my gun in his right hand, he pulled the hammer back with the thumb of the same hand. It clicked twice and stayed in place. He pulled the trigger and the hammer came down as he had explained, but only made another click as it fell on an empty chamber. He repeated the procedure a couple of times and then passed the pistol to me.

I weighed it in my right hand to get the feel, held it out in front of me and pulled the hammer back. It needed a firm pull, but was smooth and locked into place without trouble. I pulled the trigger and the hammer fell.

'So far, so good,' said the sheriff. 'So you don't spray bullets around, you have to aim. Hold the pistol out in front of you and sight along the barrel.'

I cocked the gun, held it arm's length, sighted on a tree in the distance and pulled the trigger. I was reasonably confident I had the hang of it, but the sheriff made me do it over and over until my arm and thumb ached.

Finally, he said, 'That's enough. Now you can learn to load.'

He took the gun from me and pulled the slide to the side to give access to the cylinder. Taking one shell, he pushed it into the first chamber, rotated the cylinder, left the next chamber empty and then put a bullet in each of the remaining four chambers. 'Did you see I didn't load the second chamber?' he asked.

I nodded and he continued, 'That empty chamber is now under the hammer. It's called a "safe load" because these single action pistols have a tendency to go off when they are given a jolt, so you always keep the chamber under the hammer empty.'

'But that means you have fewer bullets,' I protested.

'That's true, but you are far less likely to get into trouble by having to reload after five shots instead of six than you are of having your leg shot off by an accidental discharge when you have a full load.'

I was convinced by this graphic illustration and resolved to always have a safe load.

The sheriff unloaded the pistol and passed it to me.

He then gave me the five bullets. For a few moments I felt as though I was juggling too many things. I eventually worked out that by cradling the pistol in my left hand and keeping the bullets in the palm of my right hand, I could feed one bullet at a time into the fingers of my right hand and put them in the chamber. I remembered to leave the second chamber empty and to keep the pistol pointed away from us both.

The sheriff nodded his approval. 'Okay,' he said, 'Time for your first shot. Just as when it was empty, hold it up, sight along the barrel at that tree over there,' (he pointed), 'Cock and fire.'

I lifted the pistol. It was noticeably heavier now it was loaded. I cocked and fired. I was pushed back and my arm was thrown up by the recoil. I don't know where the bullet went.

I gave the sheriff an apologetic look. His only reaction was, 'Try again.'

I lifted the gun and this time braced myself so the recoil didn't have the same effect. I saw the bullet kick up some dirt behind and slightly to the right of the tree.

I dropped my arm to rest it, rolled my shoulders, tried again and was rewarded by a satisfying thump as the bullet hit the tree.

I tried with the remaining three bullets with mixed success. 'You're doing fine,' the sheriff encouraged me. Take a short rest then reload and try again.'

I did, but with the same level of accuracy.

The sheriff decided I'd had enough for the first day, 'Okay, we'll call it a day. Practise on your own for a short while each day and I'll come and see how you are getting on next week. Little and often is best.'

For no more than thirty minutes at a time, I practised twice a day for the next seven.

To begin with, I was discouraged by my lack of progress. I remembered how shooting the Winchester had become second nature within a short time, but I didn't seem to have the same aptitude with the Colt. I told myself it was because I was young, the Colt was heavy and I was having to hold it out with one hand. I said this more to console myself rather than believing it, but, by the fourth day, the pistol was sitting more comfortably in my hand, it didn't seem so heavy and I was hitting the tree at twenty paces every time. I moved further away and found my accuracy reduced with distance until it reached only about fifty at forty paces. Discouraged again, I thought about it. I rationalised that, unlike the Winchester which seemed an extension of my body, I wasn't comfortable with the Colt and holding it at arm's length was both tiring and made it more difficult to hold steady. If I really was an intuitive shooter, I needed to find a way that was more natural to me.

The next day, I tried holding the pistol a little in front of me at just above waist height. It was easier to hold there, but I couldn't sight along the barrel and so I had to aim instinctively looking at the target and aiming the Colt in the same way I would point with my finger. Everything fell into place. My accuracy improved and I could shoot for longer without getting tired.

When the sheriff came and we went to what had

becoming my firing range, he stood me 20 paces from the target. I said, 'Come with me,' and walked away, doubling the distance.

He followed and, as soon as he was standing next to me, I raised the Colt to just above waist height and fired 5 times in quick succession, hitting the target each time. He looked at me, smiled and said, 'Some improvement since last week, then.'

With that he swivelled and drew his Colt from the holster on his hip and shot five times faster than I thought was possible, hitting the tree with every shot. He was able to fire so much more quickly than me because, instead of pulling the hammer back with the thumb of his right hand, he brought his left hand across the top of his pistol and pulled the hammer back by moving his open left hand parallel with the barrel and using the heel of his hand to pull the hammer back between each shot.

I stood open-mouthed. Realising I was in awe of his shooting, he said, 'It's not as difficult as it looks and there are many gunfighters who are better and faster than me.' I passed this off as false modesty and asked him if he would teach me.

'Okay,' he started, 'It's called fanning. What you do is keep the trigger pulled so the hammer will come forward to strike the shell as soon as you let go.' With his gun still empty, he showed me slowly by raising his gun, pulling the trigger and then fanning the hammer. 'You try.'

I didn't need further encouragement. Making sure I was aiming at the target, I lifted my Colt and copied his action.

'You'll shoot quickly like that, Jimmy,' he laughed, 'But you won't hit anything you're aiming at. When you fan, you are pulling your pistol all over the place, so your bullets are going to go everywhere but where you want them. Firstly, you must make sure your fanning hand is coming back straight in line with your arm. That way, you won't pull off to the side. Secondly, you must push the barrel down slightly as though you are aiming below the target. That will stop you shooting high.'

I thought about what he said and tried again. Pulling in line with my arm wasn't difficult, but I found it hard to get the downward pressure right; I was either pushing too hard, which would have made my shot go low, or not hard enough, which would have made it too high. He didn't have to tell me, as I could feel when it was wrong. I practised for ten minutes before I felt I'd got it right.' I then loaded my gun and tried for real.

Once again, having bullets instead of empty shells changed the balance of the gun and it took me several goes before I was anywhere near right.

The sheriff brought the session to a close with, 'Carry on with your practise, I'll see you next week.'

Shooting an hour each day used a lot of shells and I was worried Granny and Gramps couldn't afford it. The problem was immediately resolved that evening. At our meal, Gramps said that Abe Smithers, who owned the livery stables in Smalltown, needed help three days a week. Gramps said that, as I had left school and was nearly grown up, perhaps I could do the job. It didn't pay much, but it would give me some money of my own.

So, from then on I worked for Mr Smithers for five hours a day on Mondays, Wednesdays and Fridays. It was dogsbody work (mucking out, taking care of the horses on livery, etc.), but it was work I knew, it paid enough to buy shells and left me time to do my chores around the homestead as well as time for training with Asuka and shooting practise. Each work day, I vaulted onto Asher and Lupus, Buck (who hadn't been backed by then) and I set off for town.

Now I no longer had to worry about how many shells I used and I was getting stronger, which meant I could practise with the Colt for longer each day. When the sheriff came for my next lesson, I was able to fan the Colt and hit the tree at 40 paces every time.

No comment, just, 'Okay, time to move on to the next stage.'

For the first time, we took my battered old holster with me. I'd put shells into the belt the night before and I could not have been more proud of the whole rig. With the gun in the holster, the sheriff buckled the belt around my waist. He took it up to the last hole, but it was still too big and the weight of the gun and shells pulled it over my hips and it fell to the ground, causing much hilarity. 'Some gunfighter you are with your belt around your ankles.' We took the belt to Granny, who punched a couple more holes in it.

Buckling my belt, the sheriff explained, 'Adjust your belt so the handle of the gun is level with your wrist when you stand naturally with your hands by your sides. This is the best height, close enough to your hand to draw quickly, but not so low it gets in the way when you walk and ride. Right, now check your gun is empty and place it in your holster.'

I followed his instructions. He continued, 'Remember, you don't have to draw fast on every occasion and you should never rush. Draw slowly and smoothly, making sure you lift your hand so the gun is clear of your holster before you point it forward, otherwise the barrel with catch on the front of your holster.'

I did as I was told, pulling the gun smoothly and making sure it was clear before bringing it up to the firing position and cocking with my thumb. I replaced the gun and repeated the procedure several times. As I was doing so, I realised that, if I moved my hand back slightly as I was drawing, I could bring the barrel up sooner. I put in a safe load and drew again slowly and smoothly, shooting once at the target on each draw. Although painfully slow, my accuracy was good.

After five shots, the sheriff said, 'Good! Don't load yet, just try it faster and this time fan to get off five shots quickly.' I did as he said, but rushed and caught the barrel in the holster. 'Being smooth is even more important when drawing fast. Now try again.'

I did it half a dozen times and was reasonably pleased with my efforts. The sheriff couldn't have been displeased because he told me to try with the gun loaded. I did and hit the tree 5 times. The sheriff drew and shot, also hitting the tree five times, but he was noticeably faster. He ended the lesson with, 'This week, practise your draw, but your target is not going to be in one place like a tree. From now on, set up cans or stones on a fence. Put them a foot apart and shoot them off.'

He went over to an old, dilapidated fence we didn't use any more, placed 5 small rocks on the top rail, came back to me, reloaded, put his gun in his holster, drew and shot them all off the rail in quick succession.' Once again, I was in awe, but resolved to do my best to emulate him.

The following week, I practised at every opportunity. I pulled together everything I had learned from my mentors. Asuka had taught me that, whatever I was doing, my performance would improve if I remained calm and the more stressful the situation, the more important relaxation became. The sheriff had shown me that smooth movements would improve my speed and accuracy. I applied these principles whenever I practised. By the end of the week, I was able to draw and move my Colt to cover all the targets, fanning the hammer and releasing it as I lined up with each one. I felt confident that, at least, I would not embarrass myself in front of the sheriff.

For the next lesson, the sheriff brought tin cans to use as targets. He explained that they were used in competitions because they were more uniform in size and the bullets would not ricochet off them in an unpredictable way. He set up five cans on the old fence rail and we walked thirty paces away.

'Okay,' he said, 'Let's see what you can do.'

I rolled my shoulders, drew and fired, knocking each of the cans off the fence.

Without speaking, he went over to the fence and lined up five more cans. 'Try that again, but this time don't draw until you hear me say 'go'.' I reloaded, re-holstered my pistol and waited.

After a few seconds came the command, 'Go.' I drew, fired and knocked off all five cans.

I expected the sheriff to set the cans up to show me how it should be done properly. I felt I had improved significantly, but I didn't think I had achieved the level of speed and fluency I had seen from him. To my surprise, he just said, 'Nothing more I can teach you, Jimmy.'

I thought he had decided I would never be good and didn't want to waste any more time with me. I was disappointed, but resolved to carry on practising. I may never be as good as him, but at least I would be the best I could be.

*

Having won the rifle-shooting competition at the fair in my first year, I had won it more convincingly at my second attempt because the man who had pushed my out to 100 paces wasn't there. I planned to defend my title and was surprised when the sheriff suggested I should enter the pistol shooting competition, which was exactly as I had practised with the tin cans. Although I didn't think I was good enough, I agreed.

The pistol competition had been won for as long as I

could remember by a tall man by the name of Billy Moynes, who I would guess was now in his late twenties. He was the epitome of smooth and I had never seen him miss.

The rifle shooting competition was first. There were far fewer entrants than previous years. I was told that many had dropped out as they were sure they couldn't compete with me and there weren't enough good shooters who were attracted by the prospect of beating me. In the event, I won easily.

I went over to the collecting point for the pistol shoot to find there were only five competitors. I guessed it was for the same reason: very few thought they had a chance of beating Billy. In this competition, we shot in pairs. Each shooter had five cans lined up at twelve-inch intervals thirty paces away. The judge would fire his gun in the air as the signal for them to draw and shoot. The winner was the one who knocked off most cans. In the event of them both hitting the same number of cans, the one who completed five shots first was the winner.

In order to get down to a final two, they had to put three byes into the draw, which meant the first round involved just one shoot-off. I got a bye. Billy had to shoot in the first round.

They lined up. The judge fired the start gun. Both competitors had five hits, but Billy finished before his opponent had fired three times. I admired his smooth draw, but noticed he paused momentarily before each shot.

There were now four of us left. Our names went into

the hat and I was drawn against Billy. As we took our places, he glanced across at me and his already sky high confidence seemed to lift another few notches as he realised his opponent was a fifteen-year-old boy. Even so, he wasn't unkind or condescending, he just said, 'Good luck, kid,' and turned to face his targets, waiting for the starter's gun.

It struck me that, just as when I had first entered the rifle shooting competition, I had nothing to lose. Here I was up against the person who had been champion since I had been coming to the fair. No one expected me to win, all I had to do was my best. I smiled to myself and relaxed as I waited for the signal to start.

The gun fired. I drew on the 'B' of 'Bang!', shot all my cans and turned to look at Billy. He was just knocking down his second can. He finished, hitting all five, and turned to me. 'How many times did you shoot?' he asked.

I nodded towards the fence that had held my cans. He saw there were none left standing. 'I only heard one shot. It sounded long and loud, but I couldn't distinguish the individual shots.'

I was too elated at my success to reply.

The final was a formality. From the other semi final, I knew that my opponent was much slower than either Billy or me. I cleared my five cans and turned to see my adversary was just pulling the hammer back on his first shot. Flustered, he only hit two of the five cans.

My family clustered around me slapping me on the back in congratulations. The sheriff came over grinning. I said, 'When you left after the last lesson, I thought you were giving up teaching me because I was no good.'

'Just my way,' he explained. 'In fact, you were so good I knew there was nothing more I could teach you. I have to admit I was also more than a little scared that shooting against you, I would look silly. You have to remember, I'm the sheriff.'

Billy came over and greeted me with, 'Well done, kid.' He took my hand and pumped it up and down by way of congratulations. 'I knew someone would beat me someday and I'm glad someone as good as you came along to do it. I watched you shoot against the other guy. Your hands moved so fast, I could barely follow them. You don't take any time to aim, you just move along the targets shooting as each one came into line and you're so fast that I couldn't hear the individual shots, it was just a blur of sound.' Still grinning, he walked off shaking his head.

5

Manhood

Although I now had a reputation as an all-round shooter, I was still only fifteen, a naive Jimmy Kidd who lived with his family and had a part time job at the local livery stables. Each working day, I rode Asher to the stables with Lupus and Buck in close attendance. Buck and Asher grazed while Lupus generally stayed with me as I went about my work.

One day, Belinda came in with her father, who had business with Abe. They went into Abe's office, leaving me alone with Belinda.

Belinda had ignored me at school after the incident with the Jones twins. This hadn't been long because, being a year older than me, she had left shortly after.

She wasn't exactly pretty, but she wasn't too tall, her hair fell in pleasing blond ringlets and her body had realised the promise it had shown about three years before.

She giggled a little and said, 'Hello, Jimmy.'

'Hello, Belinda,' I replied uncertainly.

'I hear you are quite the hero now, having won all the shooting competitions at the fair.'

'I don't know about hero, but I did win.'

'I know,' she continued smilingly and doing something strange with her eyes and lashes, which I didn't understand, 'You were a hero once.'

I guessed what she meant, but decided it best not to say anything.

She continued, 'I should have thanked you after you saved me from those horrible boys, but I was confused. You see, although I didn't want them to see me, the thought of showing you didn't seem so bad. Would you like me to show you now?'

'Only if you want to show me.'

She laughed as she realised we were reprising the conversation we'd had all those years ago. Looking at me slightly sideways, she whispered, 'I would now.'

Taking my hand, she led me towards the ladder leading up to the hay loft. I followed her up. She went to the very back and laid down. Not knowing what to do, I stood and looked at her. She giggled and patted the hay, indicating I should sit next to her.

As soon as I sat, she lifted her skirt. To my surprise, she wasn't wearing underwear. What I saw didn't appear to be attractive at first sight, but it was strangely exciting. There was a clump of hair that seemed to cover most of the top of a cleft that disappeared between her legs.

As I watched, she lifted her hips slightly and opened her legs. 'You can touch, if you want.'

I put my hand on the hairy part. She giggled, 'Not like that,' and picked my hand up in hers, turned it and used my middle finger to rub up and down the cleft. She then pushed my finger between her legs and pushed it up into a moist opening.

From our horses, I knew about mating and assumed it was similar between people, but I wasn't sure where a woman had her entrance.

She moved my finger in and out and up the cleft a few times and then murmured, 'You do it.' I carried on, noting her reaction.

She seemed to get most pleasure when I touched a fleshy part near the opening and when I pushed my finger inside and pushed it up. She lifted her hips and moaned and so I stopped, thinking I had hurt her. 'Don't stop.' Her voice had a note of urgency.

I carried on enjoying it without understanding why. She gasped and moaned a little more and then put her hand in her mouth, which I assumed was to muffle the sound so as not to attract attention. She then seemed to spasm, closing her eyes, shaking her hips and moving them up and down. After a good many seconds, she stopped moving, opened her eyes and, with a wicked grin, said, 'Your turn!'

I laid on my back, undid my belt and pulled my pants and trousers down. My cock was engorged and was pushed up over my tummy. She sat up and exclaimed, 'It's so big and why is it lying on your tummy, I thought it would stick straight out?'

I was too excited to talk properly, but managed to say, 'That's the way it goes when it gets big. It can be pulled up.'

She didn't need a second invitation. She leaned across

and grabbed my stem with her right hand and lifted my cock off my belly. It was obviously the first time she'd felt one because she exclaimed, 'It's so hard and big, I can't hold it with just one hand.'

She moved her left hand across and grabbed my knob end.

That was too much and I ejaculated. She found that hilarious as well and giggled as I shot gouts of semen from the end of my cock. Most of it went on her hand, but some shot off to make a few damp spots on our clothes.

When I finished spurting, she let go and dried her hands on several handfuls of hay. Neither of us knew what to say and so we went back down the ladder. At the bottom, we removed the hay from each other's backs.

Her dad came out of the office a few minutes later. Seeing us where he left us, he quipped, 'I hope you two have been behaving,' and gave Abe a knowing wink.

Without further comment, he strode out of the barn and Belinda followed him.

I was confused. I'd enjoyed my first fumbling attempts at sex, but the process was so strange and messy that I didn't know why. Belinda seemed to have a good time too, but she didn't actually say so. Finally, I didn't know if I was going to see her again and, if I did, how long it would be. Was I going to have to wait another three years?

I needn't have worried. A few days later, Belinda's dad came for another meeting with Abe and Belinda came with him. As they went into Abe's office, Abe called out to me, 'Show Belinda around.'

After they had gone, Belinda looked at me and, without saying anything, started climbing the ladder to the hayloft. I followed and found her lying at the back. I sat next to her, as I had before, but she put her hand behind my neck, pulled my head down to hers and kissed me on the lips. She pulled her head away and said, 'I'm not your gran, relax! Haven't you heard of French kissing?'

'No.'

'We open our mouths a little and play with our tongues.'

She pulled my head down again, put her lips to mine and pushed her tongue in my mouth. It struck me as disgusting and delightful at the same time, but much more delightful as I got used to it and started to use my tongue to play with hers.

We practised this for a while getting used to one another's mouths and discovering the best way to do it and what was most pleasurable.

After a while, she took my hand and placed it on her breast. It felt firm and squishy through her dress and seemed a perfect fit for my cupped hand. I experimented, squeezing it and pressing it gently. She sighed as she kissed me, which I took as a sign she was enjoying it. She then lifted her skirt. I took this as a signal that she wanted me to touch her as I had before and dropped my hand. She lifted her hips and opened her legs. I used my fingers as I had before, stroking near her entrance and pushing my finger inside her.

She laid back with her eyes closed, obviously enjoying the sensation and then turned on her side, undid my belt and the top of my trousers and pushed her hand inside, grabbing my cock. She kissed me again and pulled her hand up and down my cock while I continued to finger her. It didn't last long as I came quickly. As I was coming, I continued to finger her. She groaned and did the jerking and hip pumping thing she did before. It occurred to me that perhaps girls have similar sensations to boys and enjoy sex as well.

We lay there for a while facing one another with our hands on each other's most intimate parts. Eventually, she pulled her hand out of my trousers, sat up and dried it on some hay. I sat up, did my trousers up. We went down the ladder quickly and cleaned the hay off one another. We sat on a bale of straw, she looked at me and said, 'I don't want you to think I'd do that with any boy, you are the only one.'

It occurred to me that she must have learnt French kissing from someone, but said, 'I didn't think you did that with everyone.' I needed to know and so I asked, 'Did you enjoy it too?'

'Of course I did, you silly goose,' she replied, 'I wouldn't do it if I didn't think it was fun. Dad won't be coming here much more, but I will slip over when I can.'

I didn't have time to do anything other than nod because her dad and Abe were coming out or the office. They finished what they were saying before Belinda's dad turned to us and said, 'Hope you had fun and didn't get up to any mischief.'

He gave Abe a knowing wink and roared with laughter at his own joke. Belinda and I ignored him.

True to her promise, Belinda came every few days. We slipped up to the hayloft without anyone seeing us and continued with our explorations. Things developed to the point that I was caressing her bare breasts, which she enjoyed and I thought was great. I was also able to last longer before I came, which was a bonus as it prolonged the enjoyment and I loved the sensation of her rubbing her hand up and down my cock. However, we didn't get beyond heavy petting.

We couldn't have kept it secret forever and taking longer as we became more experienced only increased our chances of being discovered.

As we came down from the hayloft one day, Belinda's dad was waiting for us. 'I wondered why you kept slipping off to the stables, you little slut,' he shouted as he slapped Belinda's face.

Indignantly, I cried out, 'Don't hit her!'

'Okay,' he countered, 'You're the one who deserves a good slapping for leading her astray.'

With that, he swung a punch at my head.

He blamed me and, realising that fighting her dad would only make matters worse, I ducked under his punch, ran out of the barn, vaulted onto Asher's back and, with Lupus and Buck in close attendance, raced home.

I didn't tell anyone. When I returned to work, I expected all hell to break loose, but Abe carried on as if nothing had happened. I didn't see Belinda again. Her dad sent her to something called a finishing school in a large city. Years later, I heard she had become quite a lady and married a wealthy banker. I wonder if she ever told him about her dalliance with a stable boy?

*

The years from then until my eighteenth year were the most carefree of my life. I lived in a home in which we each had a deep affection for one another, I loved working with horses at home and at Abe's and I continued with my karate training and shooting practice. Lupus was my constant companion, but Buck was the greatest revelation. He developed into what Asuka described as the best horse he had ever seen. His speed, stamina and agility were unique. Moreover, I was the only one he would let ride him; I felt this was a great privilege.

I matured physically, growing to just under six feet tall. My shoulders grew wide, but I didn't become bulky. I was strong with a hard, lean body and muscles like rope. My black hair was straight and would have fallen down my back and in my face if Granny had not trimmed it regularly. With the exception of my bright blue eyes, my colouring was dark and so it was strange that my beard was weak, making shaving unnecessary. I didn't look like anyone I knew and so I asked Granny, 'You, Gramps and Tor have white skin and blue eyes, Asuka has darker skin and he has brown, smiley eyes. I have the darkest skin and the bluest eyes. Why don't I look like anyone else?'

'We all inherit our looks from our biological parents,' she explained. 'People from different parts of the world look different. Gramps, Tor and I come from Europe, which is why we look like one another. Asuka comes from Asia where they have darker skin and smiley eyes. Your mum came from Europe and you inherited your blue eyes from her. I don't know where your dad came from, but I think it was somewhere down south. He had dark hair and olive skin, just like you. He didn't have to shave and so I wouldn't be surprised if you don't either.'

'So,' I was articulating my thoughts, 'We all inherit things from our parents and the way we look depends on which part of the world our ancestors come from.'

'That's about it.'

'It's strange that the Commancheros look like me. They are the most hateful people in the world. You, Gramps, Tor and Asuka look nothing like me, but you are the most lovely people I know.'

'That's an important lesson, Yimmy, and it's a good thing you have learnt it while you are still young. You can never tell what people are like from the way they look. Black, red, yellow, brown or white skin; blue eyes or brown eyes; curly, straight, blonde, brown, black or red hair; long noses or flat noses; we all look different, but these things tell you nothing about the person inside. You have to find that out by learning their character.'

'That was enough for me. Up until then I had not judged people by their appearance because I knew no different. From then on I didn't judge them by the way they looked because I knew if didn't matter.

92

My idyllic life came to an end unexpectedly and abruptly.

I woke up one morning to hear Granny sobbing. The sound was coming from her bedroom. I knocked on the door, but there was no response and so I opened it quietly and stepped in. Granny was in bed with her head and arms across Gramps, who was lying on his back. I went across to them, stroked Granny's hair and felt Gramp's cheek. He was stone cold!

The doctor said he had died of a heart attack in the night. He tried to console us by saying he probably hadn't felt a thing.

Granny didn't recover. Each day she spent longer in bed until, eventually, she didn't get up at all. I left my job in the livery stable so I could concentrate on helping Tor and Asuka with the horses as well as care for Granny.

I took her meals into her and sat with her as she pushed the food around the plate. I said she should eat to regain her strength, but she said she wasn't hungry. She got weaker with each passing day. I still took food to her, but I usually just sat watching her sleep and stroking her hair. One day, she opened her eyes and smiled at me, 'You are a good boy, Yimmy, you know Gramps and I love you like a son.'

I nodded, too choked up to speak at first, but eventually managed to whisper, 'I love you too, Granny.'

'Gramps and I agreed you should inherit the homestead and the horse business. When I'm gone, it will all be yours.'

'Don't talk like that, Granny,' I pleaded, 'You are just

upset at the moment. You will regain your strength.'

But she didn't. Just a few weeks after Gramp's death, I went into her room to find her lying in bed lifeless. The doctor said she had died of a broken heart because she couldn't live without Gramps. I think he was probably right.

In spite of our grief, we carried on running the homestead and business. We knew it was what Granny and Gramps wanted. We didn't discuss it, but Tor and Asuka accepted me as the boss, although they had been doing their jobs for so long, they needed little or no bossing.

A couple of weeks after we had buried Granny, sheriff Brand paid us an unexpected visit. I invited him into the house and asked him if he would like a drink. Obviously on edge, he waived away the offer and launched into the reason he had come.

'You know that, as there is no lawyer in Smalltown on account it is so small, I deal with the occasional legal matter that comes up from time-to-time?'

I nodded.

'And you know that Granny and Gramps wanted you to have their homestead?'

I nodded again.

'The trouble is,' he went on, 'They didn't make it legal. You see, you are no kin of theirs and so, in order for you to inherit, they should have made a will to say so. Maybe they didn't know this or maybe they just didn't get around to doing it, but the fact is they did not leave a will.'

He looked at me for a reaction and, as I didn't have one, he continued, 'This means that all they owned must pass to their closest relatives. As you know, their sons were killed and their grandchildren were taken back to Germany and so we can't trace them. The closest relative we can find is Gramps' brother, who, together with his wife, live a couple of days' journey away. They have written to me to say they will be here by the end of the week.'

There was nothing I could say and the sheriff had nothing to add and so he left.

I went out and discussed this unexpected turn of events with Tor and Asuka. 'That's not fair and not what Granny and Gramps wanted,' was Tor' reaction.

'I know it's not what they wanted,' I agreed, 'But, fair or not, it's the law and there's nothing we can do about it. Anyway, if you think about it, we won't be any worse off. I expect Gramps's brother is just as much a gentleman as he was and, if that's so, he would have married a lovely lady. Although it won't be the same without Granny and Gramps, it will be a bit like the old times.'

We decided to make the best of it and so, when the new Schmidts pulled up in their buggy, all three of us were waiting outside the house to welcome them. Without any sort of greeting, Mr Schmidt, a skinny little, clean shaven man with a bald head who looked nothing like his brother, jumped down and ordered, 'Take all our belongings into the house and then take the buggy to the barn and take care of the horses.'

Before we could move, Mrs Schmidt, also small and skinny with the sharpest features I've ever seen, which were accentuated as her hair was pulled back severely from her face into a tight bun on the top of her head, added, 'And be careful. The cost of any breakages will be deducted from your wages.'

Although taken aback, we all three set about unloading the buggy. Tor then drove it around to the barn while Asuka and I carried the boxes and cases into the house. Mrs Schmidt had already conducted a search of the house and directed us as to which box and case should be taken to which room. Walking into my room, she crooked her finger to indicate we should follow.

'Whose room it this,' she asked without any preamble.

'Mine.'

'And where do you sleep?' She addressed her question to Asuka, who pointed to his room across the hallway.

'And Tor sleeps in the room next to Asuka's,' I volunteered.

'Did you hear that, Nathan?' she called to her husband. As he joined us, she continued, 'The hired hands have rooms in the house.'

With a look of horror that I don't think was feigned, Nathan responded, 'That won't do, it's just not the done thing. In any case, we will need these rooms for when we have guests staying over. We will have to build a bunkhouse. In the meantime. they can organise a corner of the barn to bed down.' Turning to Asuka and me, he went on, 'Collect all your stuff and take them to the barn and tell that great oaf to do the same once he has finished tending the horses.'

Stunned, we did as we were told.

Later that evening, we were sitting in the barn discussing this major turnaround in our fortunes. Tor was the most upset and reflected on our new circumstances, 'This is a very bad turn of events. Granny and Gramps will be turning in their graves at the way they are treating us. They wanted you to have the homestead, Jimmy, not his miserable brother and his sour faced wife. I don't think I can stand it. I'm going into town for a drink.'

He went out, saddled his horse and galloped off towards town.

Asuka and I discussed the matter well into the night, but were unable to come to a conclusion.

The next morning, we were surprised to find that Tor had not returned. Worried, we saddled up and, together with Lupus, set off for town to pull him out of whatever gutter he had spent the night in and get him sobered up.

We found him before we got to town. We saw his horse first of all standing by the side of the track grazing. When we got closer, we saw Tor's body lying in the grass. He was dead, apparently having fallen from his horse. We picked him up and took his body to town. The doctor confirmed Tor had broken his neck and Carl, the barkeeper at the saloon, told us that Tor had been drinking all night and couldn't walk straight when he left. He and other people in the bar had suggested he stay the night, but he had insisted on riding home.

It was then that I resolved never to drink alcohol. If it rendered Tor, one of the best riders I had known, so incapable that he fell off his horse and broke his neck during a gentle ride home, it must be bad. I didn't ever want to have my faculties diminished to that extent and so I decided total abstinence was best.

Asuka and I arranged Tor's funeral and went home. When we explained what had happened to Tor, their reaction was, 'Stupid idiot! He should have realised our job is difficult enough without reducing our staff by a third. You two will just have to work harder.'

There really was no answer to such selfish insensitivity and so Asuka and I went to the barn without comment.

For years, the only difficulties we'd to deal with were routine problems inherent in horse breeding. The deaths of Granny, Gramps and Tor plus the unwanted intrusion in our lives of Mr and Mrs Schmidt had come hard on the heels of one another. We thought life couldn't throw anything more devastating at us, but we were wrong - we were hit by another bombshell!

In all the time I had known him, Asuka had not received a letter. Two days after Tor's death a letter arrived for him. He read it in the privacy of an open field. Several hours later, he came to me.

'Do you know that I left my country because of an argument with my father?' he asked.

I told him that I didn't and so he continued, 'He wanted me become a Shinshoku priest. He had always planned that I would become a karate champion and then devote myself to the priesthood. When I told him I couldn't because my faith was not that strong and I preferred to work with horses, he disowned me and banished me from his house. This is why I left Japan.'

Overcome by the memory of the loss of his family he paused for a while before going on to explain, 'I have not thought of this for many years. I now find the memory very sad.'

He broke off again. I was unused to him being emotional, he was a man who advocated and displayed control at all times. He quickly regained his composure and went on, 'The letter was from my mother. She says my father is very ill. He will die in a matter of months and his dearest wish is that he and I should be reconciled before his death.'

I waited for him to go on. 'I must go back to him, Jimmy. I can't live with the thought of him dying wishing that we were father and son again.'

I understood and asked him when he wanted to leave. His reply was simple, 'Tomorrow!'

Early the following morning, we were standing together outside the house. His horse was saddled and he had packed his few meagre belongings in his saddle bags. I didn't know what to say. He held out his hand. I took it. Looking at me as though he wanted to imprint a picture of me on his mind, he said, 'It has been a privilege to watch you grow, Jimmy, and has been a privilege to have made a small contribution towards making you the fine young man you have become.'

This was too much for me. The tears ran down my

cheeks as I dropped his hand, threw my arms around him and told him, 'You have played more than a small part in making me what I am, Asuka. I will never meet another man like you and I shall always cherish the years we spent together and thank you for all you have taught me.'

Overcoming his natural reserve, he returned my embrace. We stood there for a while. He then let me go, mounted, turned his horse and galloped out of my life.

Lupus was by my side throughout. I whistled for Buck. He cantered to the edge of the field, jumped the fence with ease and came over to us. Realising I was upset, Lupus jumped up to put his paws on my shoulders. Buck rested his head on my chest and I held them both close. They were the only two left from my childhood. We put our heads together, as I sobbed my heart out.

Recovering slightly, I walked into the barn for privacy and sat at the back to reflect on my future. Lupus came in and laid beside me while Buck chewed on the hay.

I couldn't see a future at the homestead and decided to leave. It would not have occurred to me that Lupus and Buck would not be with me wherever I went. My only possessions were my knife, Colt and Winchester, as they were presents, and a few clothes. I reckoned the old saddle was mine by virtue of having been the only one to have used it since I had lived there. There was an equally decrepit set of saddle bags in the tack room, which I reckoned no one could begrudge me. I got all my possessions together, put my few pieces of clothing in the saddle bags, tacked up Buck, vaulted into the saddle and, with Lupus close behind, walked up to the door of the house.

Mr and Mrs Schmidt must have been watching me because they came out as I approached. 'What do you think you're doing?' asked Mr Schmidt.

I replied, 'Now that Tor and Asuka have gone, there is nothing for me here.'

'What do you mean 'Asuka's gone'?' Mrs Schmidt's voice was a screech.

'He's had to go home,' I explained.

'How do you think we can cope?' Mr Schmidt complained peevishly. 'It's going to be difficult enough since the big fellow killed himself and now he's left without even the courtesy of a *goodbye*. How will we manage with just you?'

It occurred to me that they hadn't even bothered to learn Tor's name and their lack of compassion at his death was the final straw. 'I suppose Asuka decided you set the tone of our relationship when you didn't even have the courtesy of a hello when you arrived. You haven't even bothered to remember Tor's name, let alone grant us the courtesy of recognising our grief at having lost our friend. We don't owe you anything and now you're going to have to manage without us.' That was all I had to say and so I turned Buck to walk away.

'You can live in the house and we'll increase your wages.' Mr Schmidt was becoming desperate.

I just waived and continued.

'You useless bastard,' his voice increased in volume and pitch, 'We don't need you.'

'Loser!' Mrs Schmidt added to the vindictive outpouring.

If ever there was doubt, it was now gone. Turning Buck to face them, I grinned and gave a sarcastic wave. I made him rear and, when his front hooves were at their highest, turned him in a spin that had us facing away from the house and set off at a collected canter, showing off by changing legs on every other step. I then gave a whoop and released him into a gallop. With Lupus keeping pace, the three amigos were headed for town.

6

Profession

Abe took me back on. I worked seven days a week for a wage that bought my food with a little left over plus Buck's feed and a corner of the barn for me to bed down. My routine was to go to the saloon each morning for breakfast and again in the evening for my main meal. Carl, the barkeeper and manager, gave me water and as many cups of coffee I could drink.

I fell into a routine of bedding down Lupus with Buck before walking down the road to the saloon for my evening meal. I would settle in the back corner next to the bar so I could see the whole room. I got to know a few people at the stables and in the bar. They would acknowledge me and some would exchange a few pleasantries, but I wasn't good at small talk and so the conversations didn't last long. I enjoyed watching people coming and going, eating and drinking. I watched them chatting with friends or playing cards for money, but the main attraction was Josie Greenall.

In her mid to late twenties, Josie was petite and pretty with long, straight brown hair. She wore it in a pony tail that waived appealingly as she walked. Together with her long fringe, lovely smile, engaging personality, there was no doubt in my mind she was a significant asset to Carl's business as she went about her duties of serving at table and at the bar, cleaning, cooking and chamber maiding.

Sheriff Brand would often come in for his evening meal. He would acknowledge me along with a number of other acquaintances with a nod and a smile before sitting at his usual table where he could see the rest of the room and the door. This meant he had his back to me. He would order his food. Josie would serve it to him together with a cup of coffee. His habit was to take his time over the coffee after he had finished eating and then leave with a general 'good night' to everyone.

He had just started his coffee one night when a stout, desperate looking man came in. He looked around, walked over to the sheriff, drew his pistol and pointed it at him. The sheriff looked up and said, 'Take it easy stranger.'

Snarling, the man pointed with his gun, 'I'm going to kill you. You put my brother in gaol where he died.'

'I don't know who you are and I don't know who your brother was, but I'm sorry for your loss,' the sheriff tried to defuse the situation. 'I may have arrested your brother, but I would have had good cause. He would have stood trial and it's the jury who found him guilty of whatever he was charged and the judge who sent him to gaol.'

'I know all that, you arsehole,' the man was far from soothed. 'I aim to kill you and then kill the judge.'

The sheriff was losing control of the situation. He had

his hands on the table, so he couldn't get to his gun easily, which put him at a distinct disadvantage. Everyone else had left or dispersed to the sides of the room. I got up and took a couple of steps towards the man. Seeing me out of the corner of his eye, he warned, 'Stay out of this, boy. This is between me and the sheriff. I don't want to hurt no one else.'

Ignoring the implied threat, I told him, 'I can't let you kill the sheriff.'

'You can't,' he sneered. 'What the fuck can a kid like you do to stop me?'

'If you put your gun away and walk out, I'll do nothing. If you make a move to pull that hammer back, I'll kill you.'

He sneered again and moved his thumb over the hammer of his gun.

My bullet travelled in an upwards trajectory from level with my hip. It made a small hole just above the juncture of his eyebrows and continued upwards to exit via a large hole high up at the back of his head. It left the building by punching a small hole in the wooden wall just below the ceiling. The impact with bone and wood had deprived it of much of its momentum. Air resistance continued to degrade its progress and gravity pulled it in a parabola to plop innocuously in the dust of the road. Its progress through his brain caused massive trauma and its kinetic energy pulsed outward through brain tissue only to be reflected back by the inside of his skull. The resultant catastrophic damage meant all brain function ceased as the bullet was leaving the building. No longer receiving messages to make the micro adjustments required to remain standing, basic physics asserted itself. The gun he was holding was sufficient to tip his weight in front of his centre of gravity and he fell forward onto the table between him and the sheriff.

I removed the spent cartridge case from my Colt and was about to replace it with a live round when the sheriff surprised me.

Standing up and looking at the dead man, the sheriff turned to me and shouted angrily, 'You damn fool, Jimmy!'

I knew he was taciturn and I hadn't expected effusive thanks, but complaints and criticism were not what I expected. At my quizzical look he continued, 'That man had his gun out. He had the drop on us both, but you still aimed for his head, just about the smallest target on him. If you'd missed, we'd both be dead. You should have shot him in the chest, which you had far more chance of hitting.'

Deciding this was no criticism at all, I finished reloading, put my pistol in my holster and looked up at him. 'I considered that, but decided a body shot was more of a risk. He was less likely to die immediately and could have got a shot off before he fell. I reckoned a head shot was more certain and a quick death is more humane.'

Having made my explanation, I went back to my stool, sat down and finished my coffee.

The sheriff looked down at the body for a minute or so and then came over to me. He put his hand on my shoulder and said, 'I'm sorry, Jimmy, I shouldn't have spoken to you like that. Of course, you were right. If I was as good as you, I would have chosen a head shot. You saved my life - thanks.'

I nodded acknowledgement. He turned and went out to make arrangements to remove the body.

The following day, the sheriff sent a message to say he wanted to see me. I couldn't see how anything had changed since he told me I'd done the right thing, but I still felt apprehensive as I stepped into his office. Looking up from his seated position behind his desk, he blew out his cheeks, pushed his hat to the back of his head and started by saying, 'There was more to that fellow you killed than we thought.'

He waited for me to comment. I had nothing to say and so he continued, 'Turns out, he was a murderer and a thief and there was a reward for him dead or alive.' He opened a desk drawer, took out a small bundle of notes and laid it on his desk. 'So that's yours.'

I was astonished. All I could do was stare at the money. It may have been a small pile, but it was more money and I had ever had before. Regaining my voice, I said, 'I don't know what to do with that amount of money, sheriff.'

'Well, young Jimmy, I suggest you learn.'

'I've no where to put it. Could you look after it for me?' I asked.

Pausing for a moment to think, he agreed, 'Okay, I'll keep it until you decide what to buy.'

With that, he put it back in his desk drawer and closed it. I thanked him and left.

For a while, a few men came up to me, shook my hand and said I'd done the right thing. Although there weren't many, I knew it was the talk of the town because regulars would point at me while talking to newcomers. Like all things, it was only a matter of weeks before the excitement died down and I went back to being an observer in the corner by the bar.

Amongst the people who came to the saloon were professional gamblers who would drift into town, take the local amateurs for as much money as they could and then move on to further victims in the next town. These men were usually very courteous as they fleeced the locals, but there was one exception.

He was a big, brute of a man. His voice was loud at all times and he would often shout at others around the card table if they annoyed him. He once slapped a man across his face with the back of his hand because he wasn't quick enough to make his bet. On another occasion, he kicked the chair from under a man who was leaning back on its two back legs sending him sprawling on the floor and telling him to sit properly if he wanted to play cards with him. He even beat someone senseless with his fists because he said he needed to go home to get money to pay his debts. The bully justified this by saying that, if a man was gambling, he should carry the money needed to meet his losses.

I wasn't impressed, but didn't do anything, reasoning that his victims were men and should be able to take care of themselves. They must have known what he was like after he'd been there for a few days and didn't have to play with him. Neither was he a threat to their lives, so I reckoned it was none of my business - until the day he went too far.

I'd noticed that the bully had the habit of patting Josie on the bottom when she served his drinks. I don't suppose she liked it because she kept away from him as much as possible, but she tolerated his attentions with a girly giggle because he was a good customer who spent a lot on drink.

One evening, the brute clicked his fingers at her indicating he wanted her to refill his glass. As she was doing so, he patted her backside a little harder than usual causing her to jump and spill some drink from the bottle onto the table, some of which ran onto his trousers. Jumping up, he shouted, 'You clumsy bitch.'

Josie turned saying, 'I'm sorry. I'll get a cloth.'

He called out, 'Don't turn your back on me when I'm talking to you, you bitch,' grabbed her pony tail and pulled.

Josie fell back, sitting on the floor with a bump.

'I'll teach you to be clumsy,' he screamed at her and proceeded to drag her across the floor by the hair.

This was too much. I had to stop it. A couple of large strides brought me up behind the brute. I grabbed him by his shoulders and hurled him with all my might across the room. He fell over backwards and slid into the bar. As he did so, his gun fell out of his holster and skidded to the end of the bar, where Carl picked it up.

Looking up at me, the brute said, 'Brave, aren't you. standing there with that gun on your hip while I'm lying here unarmed.'

Without saying anything, I drew my gun and passed it to Josie for safekeeping. With a grin, the brute got to his feet and launched himself at me.

As he got to me, I stepped to the side, caught him by his lapels, turned him and, using his own momentum, gave him a push. He staggered backwards and then fell, landing in a tangle of arms, legs, chairs and tables. Many of the onlookers laughed.

Unhurt, but enraged, the brute leaped to his feet and charged again. I executed the same manoeuvre, sending him lurching in the opposite direction so that he ended up on the floor propped up against the bar.

He may have been furious, but he was still thinking. Realising that the charge was not a tactic that was going to work, he raised his fists, adopted a boxer's stance and shuffled towards me. As soon as he was close enough, he threw two quick, straight lefts followed by a right hook. I swayed away from the punches and moved to my right. He followed and repeated his attack. I noticed that, as he threw the right hook, his left fist moved to his left and he raised his chin, exposing his throat.

When he attacked in the same way again, I stepped inside his straight left, blocked his right hook with my left and hit him in the throat with my right in a spear fist. My intention was to hit him just hard enough to end the fight by bruising his larynx, making him stop while he recovered his breath. Unfortunately, I hadn't allowed for the fact that his weight had been thrown forward in the act of throwing his hook and so the impact with his throat was much greater than intended.

He stepped back clasping his throat with both hands. Endeavouring to take a breath, he realised that air would not pass through his crushed wind pipe and his eyes opened wide with terror. Falling to his knees, he tried harder to breath and, unable to speak, he put his hands out to me in a gesture of begging for help. No one could do anything to mend his shattered throat. Within a minute, he had fallen on his side, jerked for a short time and then laid still.

Unsure what had happened, everyone stood in silence staring at the brute's dead body. By coincidence, the sheriff arrived at that moment for his evening meal. Seeing everyone gathered around the prone figure, he asked, 'What's going on here?'

Carl was the first to recover. 'It wasn't Jimmy's fault,' he explained, 'Grover kept trying to hit him. Jimmy kept getting out of the way. He only hit him once.'

There was a lot of muttering as the others in the room agreed with Carl's assessment, but the sheriff hadn't finished. 'So, what started it?' he asked.

Carl had become our spokesman, so he continued, 'Grover was pulling Josie across the floor by her hair and Jimmy stopped him.'

'Stopped him by killing him?' The sheriff wasn't ready to give it up yet.

'No,' Carl exclaimed, 'He just pulled him off. Grover lost his gun in the fall,' Carl held it up for the sheriff to see, 'When Grover asked Jimmy if he was going to shoot him. Jimmy gave his gun to Josie to show he wasn't going to shoot an unarmed man. Grover decided he would teach Jimmy a lesson and attacked him. As I said, Jimmy just kept getting out of his way until he realised Grover wasn't going to stop when he hit him the one time.'

The sheriff looked at me. 'That's right, sheriff,' I agreed. 'I only intended to incapacitate him, but he was coming at me so hard it increased the power of my punch.'

The sheriff seemed to accept this. He said he would sort out the details after his dinner. In the meantime, he detailed a couple of the bystanders to take the body to the undertakers. Wagging his finger at me, he warned, 'Don't let this become a habit, Jimmy.'

He went to his table. Josie came up to me, slipped my gun into my holster with her left hand, put her right hand on my chest, got on her toes and gave me a peck on the cheek. Looking deep into my eyes, she said, 'Thank you, Jimmy.' Then, with her mouth close to my ear, she whispered, 'Stick around. I'll thank you properly after I've finished work.'

I did and saw for the first time how Josie and Carl wiped down and cleared away after their customers had left. They had nearly finished when Carl said, 'Okay, Josie, I'll finish off here, you can go to bed now.'

Josie came over to where I was sitting, took me by the hand and led me to the stairs, saying as we went, 'Thanks, Carl, see you in the morning.' Carl replied, 'Sure. Goodnight Josie, goodnight Jimmy.'

She took me up to her room. We went in, she closed the door, stretched, went over to her bedside table, picked up a bottle of wine that had been opened and poured herself a glass. After a couple of sips, she indicated her glass, 'I'd offer you one, but I've never seen you drink, so I assume you don't.'

I shook my head and then, recognising the ambiguity (was I indicating that I don't drink or that she was wrong in thinking I don't drink}, I added. 'No, I don't.'

Amused at my confusion, she smiled, put her glass down, came over to me, put her hands around my neck and kissed me. I put my hands behind her waist, pulled her into me and gave her my best French kiss. She pulled away, raised her eyes to suggest surprise and then clamped her mouth on mine.

We enjoyed exploring one another's mouths for a while and then she dropped her hand and felt my erection. Giving it a squeeze, she commented, 'This feels promising. I'd better take a look.' She dropped to her knees, undid my belt and pulled my trousers and pants down to my ankles. Seeing my cock standing proudly against my belly, she continued, 'Promise fulfilled. You're more than just a pretty boy with blue eyes, Jimmy Kidd.'

She put her hand behind my cock, pulled it forward slightly and then ran her tongue along its length from my balls to my bell end. She then pulled my cock down and, holding it in place, put her mouth over it.

I was shocked, but loved it. Firstly, she just ran her tongue over the end. Then she moved her head back and forwarded rubbing my cock between her tongue and the roof of her mouth. I had never had such a pleasurable and intense sensation. Within seconds, I lost control and came in her mouth. My first reaction was worry because I thought she wouldn't like having semen in her mouth, but she didn't stop. In fact, when she realised I was coming, she increased the intensity of the stimulation with her mouth and tongue. I looked down to see she had what appeared to be a satisfied look on her face with her eyes closed. Accepting this at face value, I gave full vent to my orgasm.

After I had finished, she got up, went over to her bedside table and swigged down two large mouthfuls of wine. Putting the glass down, she started to undo her dress. I didn't move. After a moment, she looked up at me, 'What are you standing there for, Jimmy?' she asked. 'That was the *hors d'oeuvres*. It's now time for the main course. Take your clothes off and get into bed.'

With that, she pulled all the covers off the bed and continued to undress.

Not wishing to look stupid by shuffling across the room with my trousers around my ankles, I stripped where I was, walked over to the bed and laid down on my back with my hands behind my head. My cock had lost much of its vitality, but I felt something of a stirring as she finished undressing and stood next to the bed naked. She took the bow from her hair letting the pony tail fall away. She shook her head making her hair cascade below her shoulders and frame her face. At that moment, she was the most beautiful girl in the world.

Lying next to me, she laid her head on my shoulder and stroked my chest. I let my hand fall over her shoulder and played with her hair. This was bliss, I was in heaven.

I don't know how long we enjoyed this gentle caressing, but I became aware of her hand moving down my chest. She paused at my belly, moving across it with a gentle massage. The effect was so profound that, when her hand arrived there, my cock was well on the way. She continued caressing until it was engorged and then rolled onto her back, pulling my head over and down to her mouth. Our kissing was as passionate as before. Remembering how much Belinda enjoyed it, I let my hand touch her breasts, stroking and fondling them gently. She stopped kissing and whispered, 'Harder.' I increased the pressure, squeezing her nipples as firmly as I dared. I noticed her breasts were smaller than Belinda's and not quite as firm, but they were still wonderful to hold and her nipples swelled up delightfully.

Putting her hand on the top of my head, she pushed it down to her breasts. I kissed, nibbled and sucked her nipples to the accompaniment of her soft moans of pleasure.

Drawing on my experience with Belinda again, I let my hand drop as I continued to let my mouth play with her breast. I ran it over her stomach to the top of her legs. She opened her legs wider and lifted her hips. I let my fingers slip a little way inside before withdrawing and caressing the entrance. Her little moans grew into large groans.

She pushed me on top of her and opened her legs

wider so that I was lying between them. This was new territory for me and I wasn't sure where to go from here. I needn't have worried because Josie grabbed my cock and laid it at her entrance. Putting her hands behind me and pushing on my bottom, the whispered, 'Push it in all the way.'

I pushed my hips forward and was rewarded by my cock sliding inside her well lubricated pussy. I pushed a little harder and drew a satisfied sigh from Josie. She got her hands in front of my hips and pushed me away, withdrawing my cock a little. She then lifted her hips further and thrust forward, taking my cock deep into her again. I repeated this on my own initiative and she responded by matching my movements. Our thrusting increased in urgency until we were both writhing and pumping uncontrollably, as our mutual orgasm took control.

Sated, at least for a while, we fell back and lay side by side holding hands. She reached down, pulled the bed covers over us both, snuggled into my side and we both fell asleep.

I was awoken by a strong sensation in my cock. After shaking the sleep from my eyes, I realised that Josie had pushed the bed covers off and was now lying with her head on my stomach sucking my cock. It was still mostly flaccid, but as she continued to work her magic, it came to attention with a vengeance. She knelt up, took hold of my cock and, while giving it a bit of a tug, admired the results of her efforts. Apparently pleased with what she saw, she straddled me, kneeling up and holding my cock at her entrance. As soon as she was sure it was lined up, she sat down, pushing my cock deep inside. Pushing with her knees, she lifted herself slightly before coming quickly back to sit on me. She kept this going mercilessly. In an effort to gain some control, I lifted my hands only to find I was holding her breasts, which seemed to encourage her. I eventually caught her arms and pulled her towards me. She fell forward, her breasts crushed on my chest. I put my arms around her to hold her there. She clamped her mouth on mine in the most passionate of kisses and started to rut, thrusting her hips up and down so my cock came in and out of her pussy with the maximum possible friction. For the second time, our bodies were racked by the deepest, most intense orgasm.

After the first night, the white hot intensity of our love making cooled to red hot. From the second night on, we made love just once per night. Over the ensuing weeks, I learnt how to give pleasure as well as take it, how much greater gratification could be gleaned from taking time and the intense pleasure of holding the moment just before orgasm for a prolonged period.

I loved Josie, but I soon came to realise I was not in love with her. Our relationship was one dimensional, comprising nothing more than enjoying one another's bodies. In the absence of anything more fulfilling, that was fine with me and she seemed equally at home with the arrangement. Each evening I would sit at the bar taking in the goings on around me. She would get on with her work. We barely exchanged a word. Just after closing time, we would walk hand in hand up the stairs to her room.

This happy routine was shattered by two tough looking men who burst through the swing doors of the saloon, looked around and then one of them shouted, 'Who's the bastard that killed our brother?'

The room went quiet. The talkative one took the opportunity to explain, 'We're the Grover brothers and we're here kill the bastard that killed our brother.'

The room emptied.

With nowhere to hide even if I wanted to, I stood up and said, 'It was an accident. I stopped him from knocking a girl around and he went berserk. He kept coming for me swinging. I only hit him once and I only intended to put him down for a while, but he ran into my punch and it killed him.'

'Bollocks,' was the unequivocal response. 'Jack was a fighter. A little runt like you couldn't have killed him in a fair fight.'

Not wanting to risk the damage that a gun fight might cause, Carl risked poking his head just above the bar to explain, 'The kid's right. I saw it all and it was just as he said.'

'Shut the fuck up, bar-keep. Don't put your nose in where it's not wanted. We're going to kill this little runt.'

There was no suggestion of compromise in his voice, but I decided to have another try. 'Look, I'm sorry about your brother. I really didn't want to kill him and there's no need for anyone else to die because of a mistake.'

'You're not going to squirm your way out of this one,

runt. As you're the one about to die, you're bound to say that.'

It was near the point of no return. Explaining what happened was not going to help. Perhaps I could convince them that a gun fight was not in their best interests and their sense of self preservation would prevail. From my exploits at the fair, I had a reputation with a gun. If they knew who I was, they might back down. I tried it, 'I'm Jimmy Kidd. If you turn around and walk out, this will be over. If either one of you goes for his gun, I'll kill you both.'

They laughed. Not the reaction I was hoping for. They obviously hadn't heard of me. They took a step away from one another and their hands moved together.

An accomplished gunfighter could draw and fire in 750 milliseconds. An effective gunfighter could perform at his best in the most stressful confrontations. Those who couldn't were the first to die. These two were experienced and accomplished killers, winners of many previous gunfights. Their confidence was rooted in their numerous successes, but they weren't complacent as they increased the distance between them to give me two, wider spaced targets while they went for their guns with their normal breathtaking speed.

I had the experience of only one previous gunfight, but I had the benefit of training to deal with stressful situations from the age of six and of shooting in competitions where I was yet to meet my equal. I also had the arrogance of youth.

Asuka had estimated my reaction time was about

twice as fast as average. The muzzle velocity of a well made and maintained Colt with the best ammunition is 1,000 feet per second. The loss of speed over the twenty feet that separated me from the Grovers was negligible. The combined time it took me to draw and fire plus the time my bullet took to travel to the head of the first was 440 milliseconds. It took me a further twenty milliseconds to traverse and fire at the second and so his brain stopped 460 milliseconds after I had drawn. To the observer, they fell together and neither achieved more than sixty-one percent of their draw, which meant my bullets had entered and exited their heads before they had cleared leather. Having started the move in perfect synchrony, they finished it in the same way by falling back and hitting the ground together.

Having been warned him of a developing fight, the sheriff was on his way when the shots rang out. He arrived to see the Grovers fall. From my trademark neat holes in their foreheads and blood spilling from the back of their heads, the sheriff only needed a cursory glance to realise they were dead and that I had killed them. Looking across at me as I was reloading, he asked, 'You can't claim an accident this time. I suppose you're going to tell me you had no choice?'

Carl appeared from behind the bar. 'That's right, sheriff. These two are the Grover brothers.'

'Any relation to the Grover Jimmy killed with his fists?'

'His brothers,' continued Carl, 'They came in asking who killed their brother. Jimmy explained it was an accident, but they didn't believe him. He tried warning them off by suggesting he could take them both, but they didn't believe him and went for their guns.'

Waving his finger at me, the sheriff concluded the conversation with, 'This is becoming too much of a habit, Jimmy.'

He arranged for the bodies to be removed. I helped Josie and Carl clear up the mess and people drifted back. I sat on my usual stool. No one came to congratulate me this time.

At the end of the evening, Josie did not take my hand, she went upstairs without a word. I followed her into my room. As she undressed and got into bed, she said, 'You can sleep here, but I'm not in the mood for anything else.' She turned away from me. No kiss, not even a , *'Good night'*.

The next day I got another message to go to the sheriff's office. He was sitting with his feet on the desk apparently deep in thought. He steepled his fingers and gave me a long, cool look over the top before taking his feet off the desk, opening the draw and taking out three small bundles of notes.

Without any sort of preamble, he started straight in with, 'You've done it again. The two Grovers you shot yesterday were the bad sheep of the family. They were wanted dead or alive for a whole string of felonies including rape and murder.'

Pushing the piles of notes forward one at a time, he continued, 'That's the reward for Smithers, who you shot protecting me. That's for Grover number one and that's for Grover number two.'

'I don't want it, sheriff.'

'Too late for that, Jimmy. My problem is that the body count has risen by too much since you moved to town.'

'I don't go looking for trouble.'

'I know you don't, Jimmy, you just sit there on that stool in the saloon and it comes right in to find you.'

'What can I do?'

'The thing is, Jimmy, you've got a talent. In fact, I have never seen anyone as fast as you or who could shoot as straight.' He held up his hand to stop me from interrupting. 'The way I see it, if trouble is always going to find you, you might just as well use your talent to your advantage.'

He went to another drawer in his desk and pulled out a bundle of posters. 'These are flyers for wanted men. Each one of them is a bad lot and they each have a price on their head. With your abilities, you are ideally suited to work as a bounty hunter. You would be using your talents, you would earn a good deal of money and you would be doing the community a service.'

I raised my eyebrows and gave a little sideways nod of my head to indicate I was thinking about it.

'There is one thing further.' He continued, 'Your pistol and rifle were the best in their day, but they're old now. Their parts must be worn and one day they may fail when you most need them. When your life depends on it, you need to have the best equipment. I suggest you go over to Bigtown where there's a first class gunsmith. Take this cash and buy yourself the best guns money can buy. While you're at it, you could buy that horse of yours a decent saddle, the sort of quality he deserves.'

I suddenly had a lot to think about. I got a chair from the other side of the office, pulled it up to the desk and sat down opposite the sheriff with my feet out in front of me and my hands crossed over my chest as I thought it through.

I concluded that there really was nothing for me in Smalltown and, although I couldn't know what I could achieve elsewhere, at least there might be possibilities.

My mind made up, I looked up and smiled, 'Thanks, sheriff, I'll do what you suggest. I'll settle things here with Abe and Josie and be on my way tomorrow morning. If you look after my money until then, I'll call for it before I go.'

'Wise decision,' was the sheriff's judgment. 'One more thing. There is no official position of bounty hunter, but I'll write a letter for you to show anyone who questions you. I will say that I have known you since you were a young boy, that you are an honest and upright citizen trying to rid society of the anti-social elements and that you are acting, if not with my authority, then at least with my blessing. This will convince people who know me (and there are quite a few) and having a letter signed by a serving sheriff might carry a little weight with some of the others. I'll have it ready for you when you collect your money.'

I thanked him and left.

I went first to see Abe. He wasn't happy that I was leaving without giving notice, but I emphasised the sheriff's wish for me to leave soon, which calmed him a little.

I went to the saloon to have my dinner as usual. It was never busy early in the evening, so I took the chance to pull Josie aside.

'The sheriff wants me to leave town,' I blurted out without any preamble. 'Those Grovers I killed had a reward on their heads, too, and he suggests I use it to buy new guns and then earn a living as a bounty hunter.'

She didn't comment, so I continued, 'I'm leaving first thing in the morning.'

Again she remained silent, as she looked at her feet. Eventually, she looked up. Her eyes were moist with tears. She took my head in her hands, pulled my face down to hers, kissed me long and hard on the lips, turned and walked away..

I had my dinner, as usual As soon as I had finished, I called Carl over, shook his hand, said, 'Goodbye,' and left before he could reply.

I slept in the barn that night and rose at dawn. I packed my few meagre belongings into my scruffy old saddle bags, tacked up Buck and, together with Lupus, walked over to the sheriff's office. He was waiting for me and came out with my money, a bundle of wanted posters and the promised letter in an envelope. I pushed them all into one of the saddle bags and turned to find him holding out his hand, which I took in a firm grip and shook with all the sincerity I could muster. He put his left hand on my shoulder and, looking me straight in the eye, said, 'I don't say this to many men, Jimmy, it's been a real pleasure knowing you. I wish you all the very best for the future.'

With that, he let go of my hand, walked into his office and shut the door.

I watched him go, vaulted into the saddle and set off at a slow walk. We ambled the whole length of the street, such as it was. It was deserted. I had lived in and around the town for my whole life, but there was no one to say goodbye or to wish me luck. As we passed the last house, I put Buck into a fast lope, Lupus barked with excitement at the sudden change of pace and I left Smalltown with the only real friends I had in the world.

*

It was generally reckoned that the journey from Smalltown to Bigtown took the best part of two days. With just two twenty minute breaks for rest, water and feed, we arrived early in the evening of the same day.

I found the livery stables and arranged for Buck's stabling. I untacked him, rubbed him down and made sure he had enough feed and water. I collected my saddle bags and Winchester, but left Lupus as company for Buck, as his wolf-like features disturbed and upset some people.

I made my way to the hotel, booked a room and left my Winchester and saddle bags there while I had a meal.

The saloon was bigger, but not otherwise dissimilar to its counterpart in Smalltown. I told the barman I would like a meal and a bath. He suggested I should go down to the barber's to order a bath and then come back for my dinner. By the time I finished eating the tub should be filled with hot water.

I had my evening meal sitting on the stool in the corresponding position to my normal seat in Carl's bar and then went to the barber's for a good wash and soak.

After I had dried, I changed into my spare clothes. They were badly worn, but they were clean. Feeling much better, I threw away my dirty old clothes and, after checking on Buck and Lupus, went to bed.

I rose early the following morning, went to the livery stable, fed Buck and asked the owner if he had any food for a dog. He sold me a side of meat that he had for his own dog, half of which Lupus wolfed down in next to no time.

Leaving Buck to his hay, Lupus and I went back to the hotel. The kitchen was now open and so I ordered breakfast. Lupus received a few wary glances, but he sat quietly beside me as I ate my egg and bacon. I finished my coffee quickly and went to my room to collect my Winchester and saddle bags.

I was waiting outside his shop when the gunsmith arrived to open up. I followed him in and responded to his enquiring look, told him, 'I'd like a replacement for this Winchester.'

'From the look of that gun, not before time, young man. I've got exactly the gun for you right here.'

Ignoring his condescension and insult to the gun that had served me so well for nearly six years, I followed him over to a display case. He pulled out the most beautifully ornate gun I have ever seen. Elaborate carving on its stock was of a hunting scene, but the side that would rest against the cheek was smooth. The metalwork was silver-coloured and that, too, was decorated with patterns etched into the casing and barrel. I took it from him, checked it was unloaded and then worked the lever and pulled the trigger several times getting a feel for the mechanism and listening to its action.

I passed it back to him, 'The action is stiff, it catches in several places in its movement and the trigger needs too much pressure to squeeze off accurately. I'm not interested in pretty, I want a tool that works well and will last.'

Giving me an appraising look, he revised his opinion, 'Sounds as though you know your guns.' Without further comment, he took me over to a locked case, unlocked it and opened the doors to reveal two guns of the highest quality. There was a complete absence of decoration. In its place was a walnut stock that was finely made and well polished and blued metal work that indicated the finest workmanship in the most subtle way.

He took one out and offered it to me. I ignored the proffered gun and picked up the other. I repeated the test on that, swapped it for the one he was holding and tested that one. I could find nothing wrong with either. 'Do you have anywhere I can try them?'

'I've got a small range out the back. Bring them with you.'

I followed him. He was right it was small, only about thirty feet long. At the far end were bales of straw piled five high and two deep to catch bullets. There were a range of targets from man sized down to black circles that were much smaller than any target I had seen previously.

The gunsmith offered me some shells from a box he had brought with him. I loaded one of the Winchesters, sited down the barrel at a target with a number of roundels and fired. I looked up to see a hole slightly high and to the right of the centre. I adjusted the sites and fired again. Dead centre. I shot off the remaining twelve rounds in quick succession, grouping the shots within an inch of one another around the bull. The rifle felt perfect. It fitted like the most comfortable pair of old shoes and behaved like an extension my body.

I tried the other Winchester in the same way. It performed perfectly, but did not feel the same. The difference was intangible, but my preference was clear. I concluded, 'I'll take the first one. Can I clean it and set it up first?'

We swapped guns and he led me back into the shop. Pointing towards a work bench set in the corner, he said, 'Help yourself.'

On the bench and hanging on racks next to it were all the tools required to maintain a gun. I set to and disassembled the Winchester. Starting with fine files, working through increasingly finer grades of abrasive paper and finishing off with the finest wire wool, I removed all the minute machine marks on the workings of the gun, leaving them smooth and shiny. Making sure all the metal filings were removed, I cleaned each part thoroughly and reassembled the gun. In the hour it took me to do this, a number of customers came into the shop. They glanced at me disinterestedly, made their purchase and left. In between customers, the gunsmith watched me closely.

I finished and asked, 'May I try it again?'

He nodded and we went out to his yard. I pushed fourteen cartridges into the magazine and sent each one into the centre of the smallest target in quick succession. The gun that seemed faultless when I first tried it had improved. It was now silky smooth and perfect.

The gunsmith had been standing behind me. Holding the Winchester out, I said, 'I'll take it and would like a Colt to go with it.'

He turned and walked back into his shop and opened another locked cupboard to reveal a rack of six beautifully made Colts. 'You're obviously a man who knows his guns.'

Stepping aside and indicating with his hand that I should choose for myself, he continued, 'These are six of the best Colts in the country.'

His dropping of the prefix '*young*' before the word '*man*' did not go unnoticed.

I walked past him and took them out one at a time. Ensuring they were unloaded, I held the mechanism close to my ear and cocked and pulled the trigger of each one several times. Choosing two that operated more smoothly than the others, I asked, 'Can I try these?'

We went back to the shooting range. He held one of the new guns while a loaded the other, tested the balance now that it held a full load and, holding it slightly in front of me and just above waist height, I fired off five shots slowly and deliberately using the thumb of my right hand to cock the hammer. I swapped and went through the same procedure with the gun he had been holding. As with the Winchesters, they were both wonderfully balanced and beautifully smooth, but the second had that intangible edge. Turning to him, I said, 'This is the one, but would you mind if I clean it and set it up?'

'Be my guest.' We returned to his shop.

An hour later, I had completed a service similar to the one I had carried out on the Winchester. Once again, when he wasn't busy, the gunsmith watched my every move.

We returned to the shooting range. I asked him to hold my old gun. I loaded the new Colt, placed it in my holster, turned, drew and fanned off five shots into the centre of the target.

He nodded appreciatively, 'Fast and accurate.' We went back into the shop.

I laid my old Winchester and Colt on his counter next to those I wanted to buy. 'What would you allow me on my old guns against these two?' I asked.

I didn't really want to lose them because of their sentimental value, but I realised that, now I had two guns of the highest quality, I would never use them again and they would become nothing more than ballast taking up space I didn't have.

He looked at me for a while and then asked, 'You're Jimmy Kidd, aren't you?'

I nodded. He continued, 'I should have guessed after you shot the Winchester, but it only dawned on me when you got off five shots that not only all hit the target, but were so fast I couldn't hear each one separately. You've won all the shooting competitions at the Smalltown fair, haven't you?'

'Rifle for the last five years and pistol for the last three,' I corrected him.

With a snort, he continued, 'I can't sell those old guns of yours because they are too old and worn. My reputation wouldn't be enhanced if they were to blow up in someone's face.'

This was an exaggeration. They were sound, just worn out. They might fail at some time, probably would, but they weren't going to explode. I let it pass as an irrelevance and waited for him to go on.

'In spite of that, I might be able to give you something for them if you agree to let me use them to promote my business.'

'How?'

'What I have in mind is to have them mounted in a display and then have a sign saying something like '*Josia Smithers gunsmith to Jimmy Kidd winner of Smalltown fair shooting competition. These are the guns he used to win five years in a row.*''

I couldn't see how that would help him sell more guns. In fact, I found the idea funny, but decided that if that's how he wanted to spend his money, I wasn't going to get in his way.

We agreed a price for the two new guns less an

amount for my old guns. Mr Smithers obviously felt he could make more money from me. Before I settled with him, he suggested, 'You need a new belt and holster to match the quality of the gun it holds. That old one not only looks shabby, it is likely to fall to pieces at any moment and you'd lose that fine new Colt.'

His point was valid and so, when he pulled out a couple of belts and holsters, I had a careful look at them.

They were both beautifully made of the best quality leather and prepared by the finest tanners. 'They were made by leather workers who specialise in making holsters, not your normal run of the mill saddler or boot maker.'

I didn't know if that was true, but I could see that whoever had cut and stitched them was an expert craftsman. Neither of them was ornate and so they matched the guns. I couldn't choose between them until I tried them on and found that one sat a little more comfortably than the other. I agreed that the only place for my old one was with the rubbish and so he took it away after I had transferred all the shells to my new one.

Buckling it on, I was about to ask how much, when he said, 'And finally, you'll need a proper holster for that fine new Winchester.

I had not previously bothered with a holster for my Winchester, always carrying it as I rode, but I could see the advantage of having both hands free. I agreed and, of course, he had the finest possible example. It was about as well made as the holster I had just bought for the Colt and so I agreed.

By the time I had settled my account, I'd been in his shop for four hours, but it was still only midday. As I left, Mr Smithers called after me, 'Thanks for your custom, Mr. Kidd, it was a pleasure to serve you. Please come again.'

Quite a reversal from his patronising greeting.

On a buying spree, I decided to skip lunch and went over to the stables to collect Buck. I needed to replace his old saddle, but I wanted to make sure the new one fitted and so I led him to the saddlers with Lupus dragging behind.

Leaving Buck at the hitching rail, I went into the saddlers with Lupus. My new Colt was in my new holster on my hip, my new Winchester in my hand and my old saddle bags over my shoulder. The proprietor looked up. I got straight to the point, 'I need a new saddle for my horse. He's outside.' From my experience in the gunsmiths, I decided to refine my requirements, 'I don't want anything fancy, just something of the highest quality.'

'Nice to have a customer who knows his mind,' was the friendly reply.

Walking to a rack of saddles, he continued, 'I think you'll find what you're looking for over here.' I chose a couple of the sort I liked and thought would fit Buck. We took them outside and tried them on him.

Thirty minutes later, I left having chosen a saddle that was comfortable for me and was a good fit for Buck. The saddler agreed to adjust the flocking so that it fitted Buck perfectly and for him to attach my new rifle holster to the rear of saddle so I could draw it easily with my left hand. In addition, I ordered a new bitless bridle, a new sheath for my knife, a new belt for my trousers and a new set of saddle bags. They were all to be ready for me to collect by lunchtime the following day.

Realising I'd forgotten something, I went back to the gunsmith's. Mr Smithers was surprised to see me so soon, but didn't seem disappointed. I bought a new gun cleaning kit and four boxes of .44 shells.

Then on to the general store where I bought two completely new sets of clothes. I put on one and asked the owner to dispose of my old clothes. I tried a pair of the riding boots with high heel that I'd seen others wearing, but the leather was hard and they hurt my feet, so I bought a pair of moccasins like those I had always worn.

It was then mid afternoon so we went back to the stables. I spent some time handling and admiring my new guns. Buck was happy munching hay, but Lupus became bored with lying watching me and started to nudge me to play with him. I made a ball of rolled up straw bound together with lots of bail twine and threw it for him. He chased after it and brought it back. It didn't take long for the game to degenerate into a scuffle with Lupus hanging on to the ball while I tried to wrestle it out of his mouth. My new clothes became very dusty. Although the youngest, Buck retained a mature demeanour, watching us fooling about with disdain, as he munched his hay.

When evening came, I gave Buck his oats and fed Lupus the remainder of the meat. As usual, Buck took his time while Lupus wolfed his down. I left them together so they could be company for one another and returned to the hotel.

I had my evening meal sitting on my favoured stool. Took my time over a couple of cups of coffee as I engaged in one of my favourite pastimes: watching people. I went to bed early.

The following morning, I didn't rise early and so the bar was in full swing serving breakfast. Nevertheless, I went down to the stable to check on Buck and Lupus. I bought some more meat for Lupus and gave them both their breakfast before returning to the hotel for mine.

I finished eating quickly, collected my pile of wanted posters and Sheriff Brand's letter and went to the local sheriff's office.

The sheriff was at his desk when I walked in. He looked up and greeted me, 'What can I do for you, young fella?'

'I'm Jimmy Kidd. This is a letter of introductions from Sheriff Brand.' I passed the letter to him as I was speaking.

He read it and laid it down on his desk. 'So, you're Jimmy Kidd, the one who has won all the shooting competitions. What can I do for you?'

I ignored the exaggeration this time and passed him the bundle of wanted posters. 'Can you tell me where I can find any of these?' I asked.

He saw what they were at a glance, but before looking through them he said, 'So, you want to be a bounty hunter. Probably think you can make a lot of money, but shooting at someone who's shooting back is a different proposition to shooting at targets.' It was a statement, but he gave me an enquiring look.

'I've some experience of that, too,' was the only explanation I offered.

He implied *I guess it's your business* with a shrug and looked through the posters.

When he'd finished, he had selected four. Holding them out to me, he said, 'I only know these four. They're a nasty bunch of thieves, murderers and rapists who generally hang out together. They hole out in Dusty Canyon, about four hours ride from here.'

'If you know where they are, sheriff, why haven't you arrested them.'

'I tried once,' he chucked wryly, 'But anyone approaching Dusty Canyon can be seen for miles off. They have a couple of them watching at all times and, by the time you get there, they are hiding high up in the best shooting positions. I lost two good men when I tried to get them. Since then, no one is interested in trying.'

'How do I find Dusty Canyon?'

'Leave town on the south trail. After about six miles, there is a fork in the road, take the right one. After about an hour you'll see the canyon ahead, It rises out of the plain, which is flat as far as the eye can see, except for the canyon. At that point, you still have two hours of riding. They will see you coming when you are still an hour out, which gives them plenty of time to organise a warm reception.'

With a, 'Thanks, sheriff,' I gathered up my posters,

making sure I kept those he'd chosen separate from the others and started to leave the office.

'Give it up, Jimmy Kidd. You might have a reputation with a gun, but you'd be pushing your luck.' I gave him a wave and left.

He came to the door and shouted after me, 'If you're intent on going, make sure you have plenty of water with you. It's as hot as hell and as dry as a bone out there.'

I took that as a piece of good advice.

I went back to the stables for Buck and Lupus. It was too early to collect my new saddle and so we wandered over to the general store together. We got a few strange glances. I suppose the townsfolk were used to seeing a man with his dog walking at his heel, but seeing a dog and a horse that followed without being led was less common.

I bought two water canteens and then went back to the hotel to collect my old saddle bags. Buck and Lupus waited for me by the hitching rail.

The saddle was perfect. I fitted the new bridle, strapped on the saddle, vaulted up and galloped up and down the main street to make sure it was secure

Returning to the saddlers, I put the Winchester in its new holster and transferred the contents of my old saddle bags to the new.

Finally, I made sure my knife fitted its new sheath and threaded it onto my belt.

Happy with my purchases, I paid the saddler and noticed the large roll I'd had when I arrived in town just two days before was very much smaller, but still sufficient for my immediate needs.

I bought some oats for Buck and some beef jerky for me to last our journey. I expected Lupus to catch game for himself and I would be able to supplement the jerky, but, although I hoped I would find some grazing, I couldn't depend on it.

I fed and bedded the two of them down, had my dinner and went to bed early. The following day was going to be a big one.

The next morning I was up early again and followed my usual routine of seeing to Buck and Lupus first and then having my breakfast, which I finished quickly before collecting my belongings from my room and settling my bill. I filled my canteens, saddled up and checked all my new equipment was stowed safely. We then headed south out of town at a steady lope.

The sheriff was right in every regard. The land was arid, flat to the horizon and scorchingly hot. I sweated profusely even though I was riding steadily. So as not to over exert him, I kept Buck to an easy lope and stopped whenever I felt he needed a rest and a drink.

As predicted, we hit the fork in the trail at six miles and went right. The land remained unremittingly flat and it didn't take much to raise a plume of dust, which would make it easier to see out approach. Dusty Canyon loomed above the horizon an hour after we had forked right. I wanted to find a way of approaching without being seen and so I stopped there to survey the scene.

The canyon appeared to be a deep gulley between two massive rocks that rose starkly from the surrounding plain. As the gang was using it as more of a fortress than a hideout, I assumed it was wide at the mouth and narrowed towards the back. The rock to my right seemed to be steep on both sides, but the one on the left appeared to have more of a slope on its outer edge. Taking the sheriff's word that I could not be seen at this range, I turned left off the trail and travelled at right angles to the canyon until I could no longer see the entrance. I then stopped and waited.

It was getting into the afternoon and the sun was past its peak, but it was still hot and there was no shade. Lupus was panting all the time. I gave them both some water and took a drink myself. I'd used one canteen and so I didn't want to go more than one more day without refilling.

I knew there was a new moon that night, but even that might throw too much light for an invisible approach. I reasoned that there would be enough star light to see my way if I took it slowly and I would have to do so anyway so as not to kick up a cloud of dust.

While waiting for sunset, I reviewed my plan. I knew the canyon was 2 hours ride away when approached directly, but I had ridden to the left for 30 minutes and I wanted to get level with the canyon at this distance before approaching it . I reckoned that a combination of approaching from an unexpected direction, the extra cover gained from coming from the side rather than the front and the fact I would be there in the early hours of the morning when the guards would be at their drowsiest gave me the best chance of success. I calculated that two and half hours riding equated to six hours walking. Allow another 30 minutes to get into position, I would have to leave at 10:30 pm to be there at 5am.

I removed Bucks saddle and bags to allow him to cool as best he could and settled down to wait.

At 10pm I tacked up Buck and then started walking with him and Lupus. Having given my eyes a chance to adjust to the lack of light, I could see well enough. The massive rocks of the canyon stood out as shadows against the clear, starlit sky and I was able to see them well enough to keep them over to my right until I was alongside them. I then turned right and walked towards the nearest rock being careful not to make a noise or to stir up any dust.

We reached the base of the rock without causing an outcry. It loomed massively above me. I untacked Buck, gave him a drink and a feed, hid his tack as best I could, picked up my Winchester and set off with Lupus.

This rock may have been less steep than the other, but it was still a difficult climb in the half light while trying to be quiet. I assumed the guards were towards the entrance to the canyon. I didn't want to disturb them because I reckoned there would be one on one side and another on the other. It would have been difficult to take out one without disturbing the other and so I wanted to take the other two first, as I reckoned they would not be on the lookout and, if I was very lucky, would still be asleep. To avoid the guards, I slanted my climb to the left so that, when I got to the top, I would be nearer the back of the gulley than the entrance.

This worked well so that when I looked over the rim, I saw further along there was a shack with another building, which I assumed was a stable. There was the first glow of dawn. I wanted us to be down at the shack before daylight and crept as quickly as possible along the ridge with Lupus immediately behind me. The inside of the canyon sloped more gently than the entrance and I was able to angle my approach so that I arrived level with the shack as I reached the canyon floor.

I listened carefully. No sound. I edged over to check the outbuilding. It was, as I thought, a stable and there were four horses in four stalls. They looked at me expectantly hoping for an early breakfast.

The saddles were over a fence rail, each with a rope over the saddle horn. I took a couple of them and cut them into 16 lengths each about three feet long. Leaving them there and resting my Winchester against the wall, I told Lupus to stay and crept out to the shack where I waited in the shadows by the only door.

After only a short wait, I heard some movement within and some coughing and farting. The door opened slowly and a man walked out rubbing the sleep from his eyes. He was completely oblivious of my presence. Keeping still, I let him walk by me and then swung my left hand to chop the back of his neck.

As he fell unconscious, I caught him and carried him to the stables where i used two of the lengths of rope to bind his hands in front of him and his legs. I found an old rag, stuffed it in his mouth and tied it in place as a gag. I told Lupus to guard him and reckoned that, being confronted by a 'wolf' when he woke up was enough to keep him quiet and still.

I returned to my position by the door. My waiting was rewarded a little later.

The other occupant woke and, finding his companion gone, started a rant to the effect that his friend was a lazy bastard who always took a shit in the morning leaving him to cook the breakfast. He burst out the door shouting obscenities. I hit him in the same way, took him to the stables and tied him up like his friend.

This was the first chance I'd had to look at them. They looked every inch the desperados described in the wanted posters. Men who lived a life of hedonism without even knowing the word. Their record suggested they took what they wanted when they wanted it without regard to anyone else. They would inflict pain for their own pleasure and kill as the mood took them.

Whatever their attitude when they had the advantage, they were chastened by their present circumstances. I encouraged the belief that it would be in their best interests to remain quiet because the 'wolf' didn't like noise of any sort and would not have any hesitation in silencing them. Leaving them safe in Lupus's tender care, I picked up my Winchester and laid down next to the barn door, which I left open just a little so I could see the approach to the shack.

My wait of an hour and a half was rewarded when one of the others came striding up the gulley. As soon as he was close enough, he shouted, 'You fucking, lazy bastards should have relieved us more than an hour ago.

I've had to leave Bill up there on his .....' His voice tailed off as he went into the shack and found it empty. Coming out, he looked around and yelled, 'Where the fuck are you? If you've fucked off somewhere, I'll fucking kill you.'

As I hoped, he decided to look in the stables. I stood up and moved into the shadows. He pulled the door open and stepped in. I rabbit punched him as I had the others with exactly the same result. Two minutes later, he was trussed up like his friends and I was back in my position.

It took nearly two hours for the next one to come. He was obviously a conscientious guard because he must have been tired from his all night session, but had stuck to his post until he was certain no one was coming to relieve him.

He was far more cautious. This was understandable, because two people may have overslept, but when the man sent to find them hadn't returned, it suggested something more sinister. Although he crept forward with his gun at the ready, his options were limited. He still had to check the shack and the stables. Having established the shack was deserted, he edged his way towards the stables and crept in. Unfortunately for him, my plan was well rehearsed and he ended up trussed up in exactly the same way as his colleagues.

I saddled one of their horses. After ordering Lupus to guard my prisoners with elaborate and gruesome instructions on what he should do if they moved that were for their benefit rather than his, I vaulted into the saddle and galloped off to get Buck.

On my return, after unsaddling Buck and the one I had borrowed, I fed all five horses and made sure their water trough was full. I then went into the shack and found a large quantity of bacon, a few eggs and some beans. I cooked it all and went back to the stables where I fed most of the bacon to Lupus and was pleased to see my prisoners watching in horror as he tore it to pieces.

After breakfast, I collected all the canteens from the shack and filled them and my two canteens from a spring that was bubbling nearby. I then saddled all the horses, picked the prisoners up one at a time, laid them belly down across their saddles and, using the last eight lengths of rope, tied their wrists to the stirrup on one side and their ankles to the stirrup on the other. This would make the ride back to town excruciatingly uncomfortable for them, but I reasoned it was the surest way, as I was certain they would try to escape if I let them sit properly and, having not slept for more than twenty four hours, I couldn't be sure of maintaining the required level of concentration for the whole journey. My only concession was to remove their gags, which I regretted immediately as they all started either pleading with me to have a little pity or threatening me with all sorts of unpleasantness if I didn't release them. This would have been very trying if they kept it up for the duration of the journey, so I called Lupus over to the one who was shouting the loudest, grabbed a handful of his hair, pulled his head up so it was in line with Lupus's jaws and warned, 'My dog doesn't like that noise. If you keep it up any longer, he's likely to do something about it.' The one who had Lupus

144

in his face shut up immediately and the others got the idea pretty soon after. There were no more complaints.

I created a train by tying the reins of three horses to the tail of the one in front and leading the foremost by his reins as I rode Buck. We set off to involuntary moans of discomfort, but none of them had the courage to complain.

I didn't have time to go at a leisurely pace and so, although I knew it would mean my prisoners would arrive a little bruised and battered, I maintained the fastest pace possible given the baking conditions. I stopped frequently to water the horses and pour water into the mouths and over the heads of my hapless prisoners, but made no further concessions even when they begged to relieve themselves. As all they did was wet their trousers, it may have occurred to them that missing breakfast had its advantages!

My unusual caravan attracted a lot of attention as we entered town and there was a large crowd gathered when I dismounted outside the sheriff's office. He came out to see what the fuss was about and raised an eyebrow when he saw how I had transported the prisoners. 'They're moving and making too much noise to be dead, so why are they riding like that?'

'I had to catch them and truss them up one at a time. As they were already tied up nicely, it was easier to load them onto their horses like that rather than untie them. Anyway, considering the murder and torture they have inflicted on their victims, I didn't have a lot of sympathy for them and reckoned it wouldn't do any harm to give

145

them a taste of their own medicine. I thought they might prefer that to being dead.'

We cut them loose from the stirrups and they slid off the saddles. None of them was in any condition to stand, let alone put up any resistance, and so we untied them and supported each one into the gaol at the back of the sheriff's office.

The sheriff took the wanted posters and identified each of the prisoners before confirming I was entitled to the reward. 'I don't keep that sort of money here,' he informed me, 'And I won't be able to get it until tomorrow afternoon. You'll have to come back then.'

I nodded, shouldered my way through the crowd and took Buck and Lupus to the livery yard. After brushing him down and checking his hooves, I fed Buck and made sure he had enough water. I then went to the owner and bought some more meat for Lupus. Leaving them both to their feed, I took my guns and saddle bags, ordered a bath at the barbers, booked a room in the hotel and went down for a meal.

As on the occasion when I shot the man who was threatening the sheriff in Smalltown, very few people spoke to me as I ate my evening meal. However, it was apparent that word had spread, as there were several groups in earnest conversation and a good number of looks in my direction. As I soaked in my bath later in the evening, I wondered if I would recognise the story after it had been told and retold so many times.

I collected my money the following afternoon. As the sheriff did not know of any other felons I might be able to apprehend, I left Bigtown.

*

In the months that followed, I earned my living as a bounty hunter. I generally managed to get the drop on the men I apprehended and I was able to bring them in alive. There were some who were more difficult and I had to kill them. In accordance with the principles I agreed with Granny and Gramps when I first had a gun, I only confronted villains and I always gave them a chance to surrender. Over time, my reputation grew and most surrendered when I introduced myself.

My success created a problem: I was accumulating too much cash to carry around. A sheriff who I had a few dealings with suggested I should deposit most of it in a bank. I couldn't see how that would work because, even if I trusted them, I moved from town to town and my money would be difficult to get because it would be in banks all over the territory. He explained that I should choose a big bank with branches in most towns. On my first deposit, they would 'open an account' for me, which meant they would keep a tally of my money in my name. I would have an account number that only I knew. If I went to a new town that didn't know me, I just had to let them know my name and account number. They would telegraph their head office where they kept all the records to confirm my details and find out how much money I had in my account. I could then withdraw what wanted up to the total in my account. This may take a day or so, but it would be a small inconvenience when compared to the risk of losing it all on the trail.

I followed his advice. I opened an account, but kept a careful record of my deposits and withdrawals. The first time I checked, I was surprised to find I had more in my account than expected. The bank clerk explained that this was my interest. Apparently, the bank combined my money to other people's to make large sums they lent to companies for them to finance their businesses. These companies paid the banks a fraction of the loan as interest and the bank paid its depositors a smaller fraction. The difference between these fractions was the bank's profit. It seemed a good idea.

*

About eighteen months into my career, the three of us went to a new town. At the sheriff's office, I discovered the bank had been robbed earlier that day by three men who escaped with all the money the bank held, but not until they had killed a couple of the bank's employees and the sheriff. The town was outraged and the bank offered a reward for the apprehension of the thieves with a bonus if the money was returned. I re-provisioned at the town's store and set off in pursuit.

The thieves had a start of several hours on me, but from previous experience, I knew that, after an initial mad dash, they would settle into a steadier pace. There were few horses of Buck's quality and his steady pace was considerably faster than most. The trail they had taken had little use and several miles out of town I picked up the tracks of three horses. I calculated it would take me three days to catch up with them.

On the evening of the third day, I had closed the gap to a couple of miles. I had seen no indication that they were aware of being followed, but I didn't want to risk stumbling upon them in the dark and so I set up camp, resolving to take them the following day. To avoid attracting attention, I didn't light a fire, eating cold jerky, which I shared with Lupus. Shortly after dark, I rolled up in my blanket with my Winchester for company and fell asleep.

I awoke to a low, rumbling growl from Lupus. I grabbed my Winchester and rolled away from my blanket into the cover of a low bush. Lupus followed and lay a few feet away from me.

Shuffling around to look back at my camp site, I could see nothing but the bushes on the other side silhouetted against the starlit sky.

The silence was suddenly shattered by the crack of several guns being fired repeatedly. There was just enough light for them to shoot by and I could see my blanket jumping and bucking as it was hit by a fusillade of bullets. I had to admire the persistence and thoroughness of my would-be killers as they continued to shoot long after they would have killed anyone in the bedroll.

Eventually, silence returned. I didn't move a muscle. After a while, I heard rustling. A man moved into the clearing. From my prone position, his torso was silhouetted against the sky. He stood with his rifle at the ready looking at my blanket and then around generally.

As nothing had happened to him, his colleagues gained the courage to join him. There were now three silhouettes. The more bold of the three crept over to my blanket, gave it a kick and looked around in horror as he realised it was empty.

This was my moment. I fired three times in quick succession. Because of the poor light, I took Sheriff Brand's advice for the first time and aimed for their torsos. I was rewarded with three grunts as three bodies fell to the ground.

As far as I knew there was no one else in the area and so I assumed these were the three I had been following. Not wishing to present my silhouette to anyone still able to shoot, I crawled over to where they had fallen. The first two were dead. The third was bleeding profusely. He hadn't long to live, but I wasn't going to take any chances and so I rose to a squatting position to remove the Winchester he still grasped in his right hand.

As I did so, I was startled by a menacing growl just in front of me and looked up to see Lupus jumping over my crouching body. Behind me, I heard a thump followed by a shot and a scream.

I turned to see Lupus on top of a fourth man who was on his back screaming in terror and trying to fend him off with his hands. It was futile. Lupus had him by his throat, from which he tore great chunks of flesh, silencing his victim within a few seconds and killing him only shortly after. Next to the dead stranger was a pistol that had just been fired. My first concern was for Lupus, but a thorough check showed he had not been injured and so I assumed the shot had been involuntary and not aimed.

Reconstructing the scene, I could see the stranger creeping up behind me in order to get close enough to be sure of a kill with his first pistol shot in the dark. He would have succeeded but for Lupus's intervention. I'd made a bad mistake and was rescued by my clever, faithful dog.

Recovering my composure, I started wondering where the fourth man had come from. He most certainly hadn't travelled with the other three because I had followed only three tracks, but he was obviously with them, nonetheless. If there was one more than expected, then there could have been even more, I quickly made sure all the camp intruders were dead and then moved to a defensive position off the side where I could cover all approaches and waited for dawn.

Shortly after daybreak, Lupus gave a warning growl. I placed my hand on his shoulder to keep him quiet. Before long, I heard a horse's hooves and what sounded like a man walking. Whoever it was, they weren't trying to creep up on me. I saw some movement just beyond the outer bushes and then a man shouted, 'Ahoy the camp, I wish you no harm. I'm coming in with my hands up to show you I am unarmed. Please don't shoot.'

I didn't answer and he didn't move.

After a while, he called again, 'Is there anyone there? Did you hear me? If so, please let me know that you won't shoot me on sight.'

I called just loud enough for him to hear, 'Come in. I won't shoot provided you don't make an aggressive move.'

With an, 'I can promise you that,' he walked into sight.

He was a fit looking man in his early forties, I guessed. He moved with an assurance I hadn't seen in many men, especially when they were as vulnerable as he was at that moment. Following him was a fine looking sorrel horse.

I remained hidden and called out, 'Who are you, what are you, why are you here and what do you want?'

He kept his hands up, but chuckled as he said, 'That's a lot of questions on first acquaintance. My name's Jake Cody. I guess you would call me a Commanchero hunter. I'm here because I have been asked to catch that fella your dog killed last night. I want to take him back to collect the reward.'

There was something about this man I liked. It may have been the way he was so relaxed when I could have killed him in an instant. It may have been his direct manner. Whatever it was, he could have tried to ambush me, but had chosen to take the greater risk of walking into my camp with his hands up and so I decided to give him the benefit of the doubt. I walked out of my hiding place with my Winchester by my side in my left hand. My right hand was poised by my Colt. Giving him the benefit of the doubt did not mean trusting him.

He smiled and dropped his hands. I had my Colt out and cocked before they reached his sides. 'Easy,' he reassured me, 'Not only have I no wish to hurt you, I'm not so stupid as to go up against Jimmy Kidd.'

For reasons I couldn't understand, this made me laugh. It broke the tension. I replaced my Colt and relaxed, although not completely, there were still some unanswered questions.

'How do you know who I am and, if you are after this fella, why have you only just made an appearance?'

'A young, lean guy with the bright blue eyes who can draw a Colt faster than the eye can follow, there's not many matching that description. As for this fella, I've been trailing him for a week. He has been on his own all that time except last night, when he met your three. Incidentally, what are they to you?'

'They robbed a bank and killed three people. I'm after them for the reward. Go on.'

'I couldn't get close enough to be sure, but I reckoned they were old friends. Anyway, I was unexpectedly having to deal with four instead of one and so I moved back a mile or so to make camp and consider my options. All that shooting woke me and so I moved in cautiously to see what was happening. I got here just in time to see your dog tearing the throat out of my man and decided you and the dog would be too jumpy to approach in the dark and so I waited until it was light. You know the rest.'

'Which direction were you travelling when you were trailing him?' I wanted to know why they were both unexpected.

'From the south.'

That explained why I had not seen their tracks because I had travelled from the east. His story was plausible and so I decided he was probably okay.

We searched the bodies and laid them in a line. Their guns and ammunition were all they had that was of value or interest to either of us. I needed to find the stolen money, but didn't trust Jake enough to tell him about it and so I said we had to go to their camp to get their horses so we could transport them. I saddled Buck and we set off, leaving Lupus to guard bodies from scavengers.

Jake remarked on Buck's quality. I was interested in his armaments. Like me, he had a Winchester in a saddle holster and a Colt on his hip, but, in addition, he had two further Colts that lay either side of his horse's withers in special holsters mounted in front of his saddle. I could see that he could draw these easily when riding, but wanted to know why he carried them like that or even needed them at all.

He started his explanation, 'If you're fighting Commancheros, you often have to do so from horseback. There is little time to reload and it's usually at close quarters. So, you need more weapons. Pistols are best because they are quick to draw when mounted in front of the saddle like this, they are less unwieldy than a rifle when riding and one in each hand gives you greater fire power.'

'And when they're empty?' I asked.

'The fight rarely lasts long and you have your sidearm as a backup. You can then pull your Winchester, which is sometimes handy at the end of the fight to pick off those at a distance as they are running away. It also has the advantage of fourteen shots. Battles are short; I've never needed all the twenty-nine shots I have available. There is one thing you need in addition to two extra pistols and that's a horse that can be manoeuvred at speed without the reins.'

Unable to resist showing off, I dropped Buck's reins, held my hands at shoulder height, pressed my heels to his sides and immediately broke into a gallop. After fifty yards, I stopped him, span in a complete circle and galloped on another fifty yards. We then turned through 180 degrees and galloped back, this time moving from side to side as though weaving around poles. I galloped past Jake, turned again, galloped up and fell into a walking pace alongside him.

'As I said, a fine horse!' was his only comment.

Their horses were tethered in their camp. Saddles and bags were piled neatly under a tree. Three of them were stuffed with money. Although I tried to keep it hidden, Jake saw it. 'It's the bank's money and I'm taking it back,' I said defensively.

'I guessed as much and I wouldn't have expected anything less of you,' was all he said.

We saddled the horses and led them back to my camp. We helped one another lift the deadweight of the bodies onto the horses and tied their wrists and ankles to the stirrups in the way I had with my first capture in the gulley. The only difference was, these bodies were dead.

As we mounted, Jake said, 'If you don't mind, I'll ride with you. It doesn't matter where I take my man because the local sheriff can telegraph through to their H.Q. with details of my capture and they will authorise my money.

Also, you don't know if they were expecting more friends and you might appreciate the help.'

I agreed, but resolved to ensure he rode in front of me. I didn't have to worry about the nights, Lupus was always on the alert. I liked this man, but I didn't know him. The mistake I'd made in missing the fourth man made me even more wary than usual, I wasn't going to get caught out again.

Over the three days of our return journey, I relaxed as I learnt more about Jake. His wife and child had been killed by Commancheros and he had been hunting them ever since. He'd caught up with and killed the group that had murdered his family, but by then he'd seen enough of their atrocities to have an ingrained hatred of them and decided eliminating as many as possible was a public service. So he'd made a career of it.

'How about you,' he asked, 'How did you get into this line of work.'

I wasn't ready to tell him the whole story. I just told him the part where Sheriff Brand had suggested bounty hunting was a good use of my abilities. The closest I got to telling him about my parents was, 'I can tell you that I have no love for Commancheros. I wouldn't mind partnering up with you for a while.'

He just nodded and said, 'We'll see.' It was apparent I did not have the monopoly on caution.

When we got back to town, two men with four bodies attracted some attention. The crowd around the sheriff's office became quite large when word got around that I had been sent out to find the bank robbers and recover the money.

Jake and I left the bodies on the horses, but took the saddle bags stuffed with money into the office. The newly appointed sheriff arranged for the bodies to be identified and then taken to the undertakers. He then sent a messenger to the bank to ask the manager over to check the money.

Thirty minutes later, the bodies had been identified from their wanted posters and the bank manager had confirmed all the stolen money had been returned. I was pleased because I was now due one of the biggest rewards I'd collected. I thought a little reminder wouldn't hurt, 'That's good because it means I get both rewards, one for the robbers and one for returning the money.'

The bank manager became evasive and, looking at the sheriff for support, said, 'Now look here, young man, that offer was made on the understanding it was going to take weeks, if not months, for it to be tracked down. No one can expect to receive that sort of money for less than a week's work.'

I was not impressed and summed up my feelings, 'That's total bullshit! There was no mention of the time it might take when you offered the reward, you just wanted your money back. On top of which, if it had taken more than a week to track it down, they would have spent most of it on gambling, drink and women, so you wouldn't have got it back. Finally, I've been shot at and had to kill four men to get this back. If you think it's easy, you can do it next time.'

As I finished speaking, my face was close to his and the threat, although unspoken, was apparent in my every gesture.

Turning to the sheriff, he whined, 'Are you going to stand by while he threatens me like that?'

The sheriff's reply was laconic, 'I didn't hear a threat. I just heard someone talking a lot of sense.'

Realising he was not going to get any support, the manager retreated, 'I didn't mean to suggest the money should not be paid as promised, I was just pointing out that I need to obtain the necessary authorisation, which may take a day or two.'

The sheriff concluded the discussion, 'Well, I'm glad we understand one another. Would you like someone to escort you to the bank with all that money? I'm sure Mr Kidd here would be only too pleased to help.'

'That won't be necessary. I'll arrange for one of my staff to accompany me.' He apparently didn't have any inclination to continue our conversation.

'And just so we understand one another,' interjected Jake, 'Will you confirm you will have the full amount due, including the money for my man, here in the sheriff's office the day after tomorrow at, shall we say, noon?'

Having been outmanoeuvred, the manager agreed and scuttled off to get a couple of his clerks.

7

Transition

Jake and I fed and bedded down Lupus, Buck and his horse, Jacob, at the livery yard, booked a bath each at the barber and checked into the hotel. After our evening meal, we took our clean clothes with us and went for our baths. I was still young enough not to feel the effects of a long ride, but Jake sighed as he sank into the hot tub to soak his 'old bones'.

We luxuriated in the hot water in companionable silence. I thought Jake was sleeping, but he was probably just thinking because he suddenly opened his eyes and said, 'Were you serious about joining me to run down Commancheros?

I nodded.

'Okay,' he continued, 'Tomorrow we'll get what's needed to bring you up to the required fire power and then do some training.'

We didn't discuss it any more, just finished our baths, dried, put on our clean clothes and went back to the hotel, where we arranged for our dirty clothes to be laundered before going to bed.

As usual, the next day I was up before breakfast to see

to Lupus and Buck. I also fed Jacob. Lupus then came back with me to the hotel, where we met Jake in the bar and had breakfast.

The town was big enough to have a good sized gunsmith and so we headed there to buy a couple of Colts. We had to drop into the bank beforehand for me to withdraw the money to pay for them, which was annoying, as the following day the reward money would give me several times the amount required and I would have to deposit most of it.

The gunsmiths was empty when we went in except for a fat little man with a bald head, who I assumed was the proprietor. He looked up and squinted at me in a way that suggested his eyesight wasn't good. I placed my Colt on his display counter and asked, 'Do you have a couple of Colts of this quality?'

He picked up my pistol and looked at it carefully. Saying, 'Not exactly the same, but not far off,' he walked over to a cabinet, unlocked it and stood back. I replaced my Colt in my holster and looked at the six Colts on the racks in the cupboard. They were all similar to mine inasmuch as they were unadorned, but looked extremely well made with handles of polished wood and blued metalwork.

I took them down one at a time, made sure they were unloaded and checked their mechanisms by listening to them as I cocked the hammer and pulled the trigger. I chose three and asked if I could try them. The proprietor nodded and led us through the back door to his range. It was similar to the one in Bigtown with targets mounted on straw bales at the far end. I asked the proprietor to hold my Colt, took one of his, loaded it and put it in my holster. As I turned to face the targets, Jake caught my arm, 'Hold on,' he said, 'We know you're lightening fast and never miss, but you already have your fast draw gun. These are for a completely different sort of fighting.'

He took the gun out of my holster and put it in my right hand. He retrieved my Colt and put it in my holster. He then took one of the other guns from the confused looking shop owner, loaded it and put it in my left hand. 'Now,' he went on, 'You have to be able to use both hands. Fire the guns alternately aiming at different targets with each hand. Concentrate on your left hand because that's the one that's likely to go haywire.'

I did exactly as he asked, firing each gun in turn until they were empty. As he suspected, the bullets from the gun in my right hand were grouped closely in the bull of the target. The shots from my left hand were hardly grouped at all. They were all on target, but were scattered around the bull.

He gave me a meaningful look. I was unused to being so wayward with my shooting and so I was looking for something to blame other than me. In a disgruntled voice I said, 'I'll do it again with the guns swapped.'

I reloaded and made sure the gun that had been in my left was now in my right and vice versa. Concentrating on my left hand, I shot again - with the same result. Jake could see I was likely to keep on like this and so he interrupted, 'Okay, practice will sort that out. The important thing is, do you like them?' They were good, but it was sensible to try the third. I did and settled on the first two. Turning to the gunsmith, I told him, 'I'll take these,' and then asked, 'But can I set them up before we go?'

He agreed, led us back into the shop and pointed out his workbench. I set to with the files, abrasive paper, wire wool and oil. When I'd finished, I took them outside to try again. I wanted to compare them with my original Colt and the only way to do that was to draw and shoot. I tried each one in this way. They were good.

As I was paying for them, the gunsmith said, 'I can see you are a man who knows his guns. Do you also shoot a rifle.'

Thinking he was looking for another sale, responded, 'Yes, I have an excellent Winchester.'

'And what is the effective range of your Winchester?'

'I can hit what I aim at up to 200 yards, 250 if the light is good.'

'And what after that?'

'The accuracy falls off.'

'What would you say if I told you I had a rifle that is accurate up to at least 800 yards?'

I realised that far from deflecting him, I had fallen into his trap, but I was intrigued and so I guardedly responded, 'I might be interested to see such a gun.'

'I've got a Martini Henry over here.'

'Hold on a minute,' Jake interjected, 'I've tried these and they have a maximum range of 1,900 yards, but only an effective firing range of 400 yards.'

Unperturbed, the gunsmith went on, 'That's the

standard model, take a look at this.' He went over to another cabinet and unlocked it. The rack inside contained five Winchesters and one breech loading rifle with a long barrel. He took it down to show us.

'The first, and most important, thing to notice,' he explained, 'Is the elongated barrel. There is a man I know who modifies these by replacing the barrel with one that's three inches longer and with special rifling. Also, and like you did with those pistols, he strips them down and tunes them by removing all the machine marks and other small manufacturing imperfections. It's chambered for .303 British Mark VII cartridge because English powder is the finest and purest, giving the bullet a more complete and cleaner impulsion which does not foul the mechanism so quickly. Also, their bullet has the truest flight. The maximum range is only marginally improved, but if anyone cannot hit the target at least 800 yards, it's a reflection on the shooter, not the gun.' Having completed his speech, he passed the gun to me.

I took it and was immediately impressed. As he had said, it was finished to the highest standard. Surprisingly, the extra long barrel did not spoil the balance and it sat very comfortably when raised to the firing position. It had a lever like the Winchester. When pulled down, it cleared the spent cartridge just like the Winchester, but, unlike the Winchester, it did not inject a live cartridge when returned. Instead, you had to push the live cartridge into the breech while the lever was down, returning the lever pushed the cartridge into place and cocked the gun. The disadvantage of having to reload after each shot was offset by increasing the effective range by a factor of four.

The other difference was the rear sight. Instead of a simple V rear sight, it has what the gunsmith described as a ladder aperture sight. This comprised a simple V when shooting at close range, but it had a hinged piece that laid along the barrel when not in use and could be hinged up when needed. This was a piece of flat metal that stood about two inches from base to tip. It had a slot in which a moveable V sight could be moved up and down and had various distances etched into the side. The greater the distance, the higher you placed the V. This had the effect of making the shooter raise the barrel to line the front sight up with the V. It was necessary to aim above the target at long range because, as the bullet lost speed over a greater distance, it would drop from its original trajectory. The further the target, the higher you had to aim and, therefore, the higher you had to raise the rear V sight in the slider. Without the ladder sight, you would have to aim for a point above the target and, as the target would have dropped out of view, it was difficult to maintain the alignment.

I was impressed and told the gunsmith so, but had to voice my main concern, 'This looks very good and sounds plausible, but we only have your word that it does what you say.'

'A reasonable reaction, but I'm so confident I will let you borrow it for the rest of the day. If it isn't as good as I have said, you can return it and I won't even charge you for the shells.'

Jake asked the obvious question, 'Why should you trust us.'

'You've got a reward to collect tomorrow, so I don't think you'll leave town.'

The price was very high, but I could afford it and, if it was as good as he said, it would be worth it. I paid for the Colts and walked out with them, the Martini Henry and a box of .303 shells.

From the gunsmith's we went directly to the general store and bought a 4 x 4 sheet of ply, a tin of white paint, a tin of black and a brush. We painted one side of the ply white and left it to dry.

We then went to the stables, collected our horses and rode to the saddlers. We showed the saddler the way in which Jake's two Colts were mounted each side of Jacob's withers in front of the saddle and asked him to make a pair for me. I explained I would like the leather strap that ran across the withers to have ammunition loops and that the holsters should be stabilised by strapping them to the saddle. He took measurements and I left the new Colts and my saddle with him. Riding Buck bareback, we went back to see if the paint had dried.

It had and so we marked the centre of the board, hammered a nail part way in, tied a piece of string to it with a pencil on the other end and marked out circles diameters of two feet six inches.one foot six inches, one foot and four inches. We painted the centre circle black and disposed of the rest of the paint and the brush.

We took our freshly made target out of town a couple of miles and found a wide, open space with just a few trees. I dismounted under the shade of one while Jake galloped off to what he estimated was half a mile, rested the target against a large rock and came back. He pulled a telescope from his saddlebag and stood just behind me.

I laid down with my legs apart, raised the ladder sight, and set it to what I thought was the right mark, took aim and fired. Jake looked through his telescope before reporting, 'Bottom edge of the board, slightly right of target.'

I pushed the V sight up the ladder, aimed and fired again. 'In line, but still to the right,' was the verdict.

I shot twenty rounds, which gave me a good feel for the gun. My accuracy improved to the point I could hit the black spot with most shots. We decided the modified rifle was everything the gunsmith claimed, went back into town, drew more cash from the bank, paid for the gun, the shells we had used and another five boxes. I then took the Martini Henry to the saddlers and arranged for him to make a special saddle holster for it and attach it to the right side of my saddle. I knew this would mean I had to lift my knee higher when mounting and that, with the two new Colts and rifle, Buck would be carrying more weight, but I reckoned we could both cope.

The following day, we collected our reward money, deposited most of it in the bank, collected my modified saddle and set off to start my training.

*

We were travelling to meet one of Jake's contacts who he believed knew the whereabouts of a group of

Commancheros. Travelling hard, we would have completed the journey within three days, but we took our time and made a couple of detours to give me time to learn how to fight from horseback.

Jake said I had to start by strengthening my weak left hand. He did this by periodically pointing at targets like a tree or rock. I would have to draw the pistol from the left side of my saddle and shoot at it. The objective was to be smooth and accurate rather than fast. It took me several days to reach the required standard before he allowed me to move onto the next stage.

This comprised riding through trees using just my legs to guide Buck around the trees while using other trees as targets. I had to use both Colts, shooting left and right alternately. The riding came easily and I mastered the shooting without too much trouble.

We continued our journey, arriving at our destination, a small town I hadn't heard of, after eight days of travel.

We went to find Jake's informant, who we found propping up the bar in the saloon, as expected. Jake took him to one side, plied him with drink as money and was rewarded with the whereabouts of a band of Commancheros together with a detailed route to follow to their hideout.

We set out the next day, travelling initially through grassland that had been well grazed. The weather was warm, but not so hot that there was a haze. The view to the horizon was uninterrupted, which meant it would be impossible for us to be ambushed, but also meant we could not approach undetected.

We had been told the journey would take three days. Midway through the second day, the terrain changed. There was less grass and we had to weave around large boulders. Trees were becoming more frequent and, late on the second day, we passed a large wood about 250 yards to the right.

Jake was riding about a horse's length in front of me and slightly to my right. I became aware of a change in his demeanour. He was more alert and looked intently at the woods to our right. He suddenly threw himself off Jacob, dragged his rifle from its holster, gave Jacob a slap on the rump that made him gallop off around the bend to the left created by the rocks, and ran hell for leather for the rocks to our left. I had no idea what had prompted this behaviour, but decided it was best to follow suit and ask questions later. I had just sent Buck after Jacob and was running for the rocks with Lupus when I heard gun shots and was aware of bullets pinging off the ground all around me.

I jumped for cover behind the rocks and hunkered down to avoid the bullets. For the first time since the age of five, I was genuinely and deeply afraid. I had faced gunmen before, but on those occasions I was in control. I was now pinned down by an unknown number of gunmen and I had no idea of where to go or what to do.

Jake was by a rock about five yards to my left. He raised himself over the rim of the rock and started firing deliberately. Slightly reassured that he seemed to know what to do, I raised up to copy him. Before I got off the first shot, he shouted, 'No! Wait until I reload.' I sank down to the safety at the base of the rock and watched him.

Dropping down, he called to me, 'Reloading!' I lifted up to the rim and sighted down my Winchester. I could see flashes against the darkness of the trees and copied Jake by taking carefully aimed shots. As I did so, I was aware that our adversaries were not as controlled. I could see about eight separate flashes, but most of their shots were going high, with the others going wide. Although we were outnumbered, I gained in confidence as I realised our shooting was more effective.

After my fourteenth shot, I dropped back and shouted, 'Reloading!' Jake rose and took over, maintaining a steady rate of fire that was at least enough to keep the enemy at bay and, with any luck, would eliminate some.

I finished reloading and waited for him to shout the command, at which point I immediately took over to keep up the pressure.

I was now confident that, as long as we kept firing, we would be safe. I just hoped our ammunition would last. I dropped back with a cry of, 'Reloading!' Jake didn't move, he just hunkered down and listened. There was silence. The Commancheros (for that's who I guessed they were) had stopped firing. We didn't know why. They may have gone. Equally, they may have stopped because we were no longer offering a target or they may be waiting in the hope we would come out in the open to present easy targets.

'What do you think?' I asked Jake.

He shrugged and carried on listening.

Nothing.

He put his hat on the end of his rifle and lifted it above the rock.

Nothing.

He waved it about.

Nothing.

'I'm going to make a dash for the next rock. You cover me. When I get there, you follow and I'll cover you.'

I lifted up over the edge of my boulder and watched the woods waiting for a flash for me to aim at. Seeing nothing that warranted a change in plan, I shouted, 'Go!'

Jake shot off like a scalded cat and skidded to a halt behind the next rock. He looked over the rock and told me to, 'Go!'

Closely followed by Lupus, I ran through the gap as fast as I could and threw myself down next to Jake.

We were now growing in confidence, but still decided discretion was the better part of valour and so we repeated the manoeuvre until we rounded the bend and were out of sight of the woods.

Buck and Jacob were waiting a little further on. We ran to them vaulted into our saddles and rode hell for leather away from the danger area, putting our Winchesters in their holsters as we rode so we could draw the more suitable Colts if the need arose.

It didn't. We pulled up after a couple of miles to take stock.

'That fucking bastard sent us into a trap,' cursed Jake.

I nodded in agreement.

'I should have guessed when he gave such detailed instruction for the route, he was making sure we were where they wanted us. When we get back, I'm going to beat the shit out of him.'

'How did you know they were there,' I asked.

'I saw a large flock of birds fly off and I looked carefully to see what had disturbed them. I saw too many bushes on the edge moving for it to be natural and decided not to take any chances.'

'I'm glad you didn't.'

'And I'm glad you had the nouse to follow.'

'I haven't been that scared since I was a kid. I didn't know what to do until you showed me.'

'It's a new form of fighting for you, you'll get used to it. I'm glad you worked out early that we have to shoot separately to keep firing. It could have been the end if we reloaded at the same time.'

'I also copied your slow, aimed fire. I'm sure that made them keep their heads down.'

'We may have knocked a few of them over, which is why they became discouraged and decided to leave.'

'They weren't very good. They were shooting all over the place.'

'That's typical Commanchero. They're good up close, but they sacrifice accuracy for rate of fire at other times.'

We took a different route back to town and were vigilant the whole way. We didn't want to camp and so we pushed on and arrived in town late in the evening.

We bedded down Jacob, Buck and Lupus in the livery

and headed for the saloon.

We had a meal and were standing at the bar when I heard a commotion behind me. I looked in the mirror behind the bar and saw the reflection of five rough looking characters with rifles in the crook of their arms. They spread out line abreast and scanned the room. They were obviously Commancheros and I guessed they were looking for us.

This was much more my sort of fight. I nudged Jake and whispered, 'Five behind us. You take the two on the right, I'll take the three on the left.'

I moved a couple of paces to my right to put more space between Jake and me.

The atmosphere of violence was palpable and I could see in the mirror that the bar was clearing. The Commancheros now had an unobstructed view of us and my movement attracted their attention. As recognition dawned on their faces and they moved to bring their rifles to bear, I made my move.

I pivoted to my right because, although my body had to make a full one hundred and eighty degree turn to face them no matter which way I turned, my Colt was effectively half way there on my right hip. This meant I only had to move the gun through ninety degrees to bring it to bear, whereas it would need to travel two hundred and seventy degrees if I turned to my left.

I swivelled, drawing at the same time and thunder seemed to fill the room as I put a bullet through the heads of each of the three on my left before they had time to raise their rifles. As I took my third shot, I was aware of

Jake shooting and saw the Commanchero on the far right drop. Not taking any chances, I continued to sweep my gun across them and put a bullet in the fourth man's head just before Jake shot him in the chest. They had not had time to fire a shot.

'Christ!' Jake exclaimed, ' I knew you were fast, but you hit three of them in the time it took me to shoot one. You even got the last one to go down before I did.'

I ignored his comment, simply telling him to, 'Keep the door covered. Reloading.'

We had no way of telling if there were any more and I had only one bullet left whereas Jake had three.

I reloaded while he kept a watch. When I'd finished I told him to reload.

I scanned the room and doorway for more signs of trouble while he replaced his empty cartridges. He was obviously still hyped, as he went on, 'This really is your battlefield, isn't it?'

Still ignoring his comments, I moved forward telling Jake to check the bodies while I looked outside. It was all clear and so I went back. Jake said, 'The four with bullets in their heads are dead. The one I hit in the chest is still alive, but not for long. He was spitting venom and I had to take his gun away. He said they were here for vengeance because we killed three of their friends back at the ambush.'

When he arrived, the town sheriff didn't show any interest after he had heard there were two of us, five of them and they were Commancheros. We left him to clear up the mess and went to look for Jake's informant. We didn't find him and concluded that he had either fallen foul of his so-called friends who decided the ambush had gone badly for them because he had warned us, or he had decided to make a career out of keeping as much distance between himself and us. Either way, we were unlikely to find him and so we gave up.

*

Over the next eighteen months, Jake and I formed a bond. Our close understanding helped us in many tight situations as we hunted down Commancheros who were praying on settlers and travellers. We were invariably outnumbered, but a combination of better organisation and discipline, our significant fire power and greater ability with our weapons, and superior horses meant we invariably came out on top. There was no money in hunting Commancheros, but I had my reasons and Jake had his. Nevertheless, our income from the bounty hunting we fitted in alongside and around our vendetta against the Commancheros was more than enough to meet our outgoings and so our bank accounts grew steadily.

We didn't trust informants any more, but we travelled extensively and met a wide range of people and so we were able to collect intelligence from time-to-time that put us on the trail of various lawless bands. We heard of one particularly unpleasant group that had been preying on groups of settlers travelling a specific trail. We cruised up and down this trail for a week or so before we came across them.

We were on higher ground about one thousand yards from the trail. We had tucked ourselves in amongst boulders so we could see without being seen. The immediate descent took us down a gulley from which we could neither see or be seen from the trail. About half a mile along the gully was a wood with trees right up to the edge of the trail.

A wagon came into view. Jake watched it through his telescope and let me know there was a young family comprising father, mother and daughter of twelve or thirteen. As they drew level with the trees, a group of about 12 Commancheros burst from the woods, shooting in the air. The family did not shoot back and so the attackers had soon surrounded the wagon and pulled all the occupants to the ground. From the distance we were, the cries of excitement from the Commancheros and the shouts of despair from the victims were faint. Two men held the father as the mother and daughter were pushed from one man to another to be manhandled before being pushed on to the next. There was a clear leader who was overseeing the proceedings. He looked familiar. I borrowed Jake's telescope and my blood ran cold as I focused on him to see he was the man who had killed my mum and dad.

As I watched him, he took control and ordered his men to tie the father to the wheel of the cart. His obvious intention was to torment the father, as he had the mother and daughter held in front of him with one of the filthy devils holding each of their arms. He went behind the mother and, just as he had with my mum, bent down and slit her dress from hem to neck. He then slit open the arms, allowing the dress to fall to the ground, and cut off her underwear. Putting his knife away, he pushed his hands under her arms, fondled her breasts and then pushed his hand between her legs. She struggled, her husband shrieked his outrage and their daughter sobbed. The leader then made his men turn her around and bend over while he repeatedly slapped her backside.

We had both seen enough, so we mounted up and lost sight of them as we headed down the gulley towards the wood. There was a gap between the end of the gulley and the woods. We slowed and peered around the edge of the gulley to make sure we weren't observed. We needn't have worried as the gang's attention was now entirely on the young girl. The leader had cut off her clothes and was fondling her small buds of breast. As we crossed the gap, he made his men lay her on her back with one holding both her arms and one holding each of her legs so they were splayed apart.

We lost sight of them again when we entered the woods and threaded our way through the trees as fast as we could. We paused at the edge of the woods to get our bearings and plan our attack. The leader had been kneeling next to the prostrate girl facing both the father and mother so that he could taunt them as he fondled and pulled her little breasts and pushed his fingers into her immature vagina.

As we reached the edge of the trees, the leader stood up and stepped across the girl to stand between her legs. He dropped to his knees and lowered his trousers readying himself to lay on top of the girl and rape her.

Taking control as he normally did in this sort of fight, Jake ordered, 'You take the bastards with the girl, I'll go for those by the wagon.'

We drew our Colts, looped our reins around the saddle horn so they would not drop and trip our horses, nudged our heels into our horses sides and set off at a gallop. I set off first with Lupus to my front and right and Jake behind me and to my left.

The sound of our horses' hooves attracted their attention. The leader stood up and turned towards us pulling up his trousers. His three henchmen let go of the girl and stood next to him. The girl jumped to her feet and ran towards her mother.

The leader had just enough time to hitch his trousers up to his waist before Lupus hit him in the chest. He bowled over backwards and screamed in terror as Lupus tried to get at his face and throat.

His shrieks shook his men out of their shock and they reached for their rifles. Too late, as I put a bullet in each of their heads.

The Commancheros were recovering from the surprise attack. The two holding the mother let her go. She ran to her daughter and they held each other close. Their captors bent to pick up their guns from the ground. I dropped them both before they reached them.

Lupus and I had dealt with six and Jake, who was behind me and had further to ride, had shot three, which left three by the wagon. They picked up their guns, raised them and fired as Jake and I shot at them. I felt the bullets fizz by me and heard a grunt off to my left. Two of them went down. I killed the last one and immediately carried out due diligence by checking there were none that represented a threat. They were all dead except their leader. Lupus was still savaging him, but hadn't been able to get to his throat as the Commanchero had crossed his arms over his face, which he held in place even though Lupus had torn them to shreds. As I rode up to them, Lupus stood back. The scar-faced Commanchero looked up at me with pleading eyes, 'Please,' he whined, 'Call him off.'

He had no idea who I was. How could he? He hadn't seen the little boy hiding as he watched this monster torture his parents to death. Even if he had, he wouldn't recognise me now. He had seen the merciless way in which I fought and killed and maybe he hoped that, as a kindred spirit, I would have some sympathy. He was right inasmuch as we were both killers, but the similarity ended there. He was wicked and killed gratuitously. He delighted in the pain of others and took every opportunity to inflict it. Although I also killed, I had retained principles established as a boy when I had killed the weasel threatening the reverend, but they did not make me weak. I looked down on the two of them. My faithful dog and the evil man looked back at me. Lupus in anticipation of the next order and the bloodied Commanchero in the hope I was going to call him off. There may have been hope in the monster's mind, but there was no doubt in mine. A simple and softly spoken command from me was all it need for Lupus to renew his attack. The monster had no time to raise his hands and so he was dead within seconds, the remains of his throat hanging from Lupus's jaws.

I reloaded my Colts and turned to Jake. He was ashen. I couldn't see a wound as I rode over to him. 'What's the matter?' I asked.

He nodded his head towards the other side of Jacob, the side I couldn't see. I looked over and saw his trousers were soaked with blood, which was beginning to pool on the ground.

I dismounted and went round to his wounded side to help him get down. He was almost a deadweight and collapsed to the ground immediately. Lupus had finished with the leader, who was now silent, and came over to lie beside us. I took my knife and cut up Jake's trouser leg to find the wound. It was high on his thigh. The bullet had gone through the meaty part of his hamstring. If he had been lucky, it would have been a significant, but simple wound that would have healed if kept clean. He wasn't lucky. The bullet had severed the artery and blood was pumping out of the both the entry and exit wounds.

The father, who had been released by his wife, came and stood beside me. His wife and daughter were looking for new clothes in their wagon. 'I need dressings,' I shouted.

He ran over to the pieces of dress the leader had cut off his wife and brought them back to me. I packed them into and around each hole as best I could, but the blood continued to pump. 'More!'

He brought his daughter's clothes, which I wrapped

tightly around Jakes upper thigh. pushed the handle of my knife into the loop and twisted, tightening it as much as I could in the hope my improvised tourniquet would stem the flow of blood.

It didn't.

I asked the father to keep up the pressure on the tourniquet and I shuffled up to cradle Jake's head. He opened his eyes and smiled wanly, 'Luck's run out,' he said in a low voice.

'Don't talk like that, I'll pull you round.'

'I know you think you can beat anything, Jimmy, but I reckon this will defeat even you.'

I couldn't think of anything to say.

He closed his eyes and, as though he'd just remembered something, muttered, 'Shirt pocket.'

I fumbled in the top pocket of his shirt and took out a folded envelope. I unfolded it and read my name on the front.

'It's to you. Read it.'

I stuffed it into my top pocket and said, 'Plenty of time for that when your better.'

I looked down and saw the blood was in a large pool around Jakes lower half. The distinct coppery smell of fresh blood pervaded, but the flow had eased. I hoped this suggested the padding and tourniquet were working. I looked at the father. He shook his head sadly.

I turned back to Jake. His eyes were closed and his breath was getting shallow. He breathed in and then out. The in breath didn't come and I thought he had died, but, with a shudder, he gasped in a lung full of air.

This happened twice more and then he started panting, each breath being short and shallow. He reminded me of a young, injured bird I had taken in as a child. I'd tried to nurse it back to health, but it deteriorated. Just before it died, it panted in exactly the same way as Jake was now and so I knew it was near the end.

I put my arms around him and pulled him close. His panting continued for a few seconds and then stopped. He was dead. I buried my head in his shoulder and wept. I wasn't aware of the father standing quietly and respectfully leaving me to my grief cradling Jake's head as he lay in a pool of his own blood with that coppery smell all around.

I didn't want to let him go, but the only thing I could do for him now was to bury him. I also had to deal with the aftermath of the battle. I looked up to see the small family standing by their wagon. The women had found some clothes and the mother was hugging the girl, who was sobbing.

I stood, wiped away my tears with my sleeve and walked over to them. The father came forward nervously moving the rim of his hat through his hands. 'We're so grateful and so sorry,' He started. 'You were both so brave to attack those men when you were so badly outnumbered. You saved our lives, but at a terrible cost. What can we do to help?'

Taking charge and keeping busy would help me deal with the initial stages of grief and so I started giving orders, 'First of all, strip everything that's useful from the dead Commancheros.'

'We don't want anything of theirs.'

'That's not the point. You may not want them, but there are plenty of people of the wrong sort who would want their guns, so we can't leave them here for anyone to pick up. If you don't need them you can sell them.'

The daughter went to the wagon while the mother and father moved from one body to the other collecting guns, ammunition and everything else that may be of use. I went back to Jake's body. Lupus was lying beside Jake protecting him in the way he did when we slept.

I removed his gun belt, laid him flat on his back with his legs out straight and his arms by his sides and dragged him away from the blood. I didn't like the idea of him lying with his blood congealing around him. I then stripped off the blood soaked dresses, made sure his eyes were closed and covered his face with his hat.

Returning to the wagon, I put Jake's things in, making sure they were separate from the Commancheros' possession. 'Can you help me lay out the bad guys?' I asked the father.

He nodded .

We dragged each of the bodies to the side of the trail and laid them in a row. I had no intention of paying them the compliment of treating them with respect. As far as I was concerned, they were carrion, but the trail had to be clear.

Without me asking, the father went to the wagon and came out with a shovel. 'You must let me help you with your father. It's the least I can do.'

Although it was a tragic moment, it struck me as funny that he should think Jake was my dad. I suspect it would have amused Jake, too. 'We're not related,' I corrected him, 'But you're right, he was like a dad to me and so I should bury him. Go back to your family, they need you.' I took the shovel and he went back to his wife and daughter. Lupus growled at him as he went by, warning him away from Jake's body.

I chose a place off the trail, but not so close to the trees that their roots would create a problem and started to dig.

The sun was low in the sky by the time I had a hole the right length and width, but only four feet deep because I'd hit bedrock and couldn't go any further. I walked over to Jake, squatted down and lifted him the way a husband carries a wife over the threshold. Lupus followed as I carried him to his grave.

I had a dilemma. I could easily drop the body into the grave, but I wanted to treat Jake with respect and give him some dignity. Dropping would leave him at the bottom of the pit in a tangle of arms and legs, so it was not an option. I squatted and laid Jake next to the grave. I could have rolled him into the grave, but this was no better than dropping him. The frustration of not seeing a way of burying Jake properly added to my grief. I sank to my knees and sobbed again.

I became aware of a noise behind me. I looked to see the family standing at a respectful distance, not wanting to intrude on my pain and distress. The father was holding a plank that was about two feet wide and just under six feet long. I recognised it as one of the planks that had made part of one side of the wagon. He must have torn it off. The mother was holding a blanket and two lengths of rope while the daughter was holding two short lengths of wood.

I stood and they came over to me. Lupus growled, but stopped when I told him to be quiet. The daughter placed her two pieces of wood across the width of the grave. The father laid the plank on the pieces of wood so it was held above the hole and would fall in directly if the cross pieces were removed.

The mother laid the blanket on the plank. The father and I then lifted Jake, I took his shoulders and the father his legs, and laid him on the blanket on the plank. The blanket was wrapped around Jake, hiding his wounds and making him look comfortable.

The two lengths of rope were passed under the plank. I held the two ends on my side, one in each hand. The father did the same the other side. We walked backwards, tightening the ropes and lifting the plank with Jake on it away from the cross pieces. The mother and daughter removed the cross pieces and the father and I walked forward, lowering Jake gently into his grave. I was relieved I had been able to give Jake a dignified send off and thanked them for coming up with the solution when I was at a loss.

It was now twilight and we needed to finish quickly. I asked them to collect fist sized rocks and stack them next to the hole. As they did so, I filled the grave. I took time with the first few shovels, which covered the blanket with earth, saying my last goodbyes as Jake disappeared. After that it was just piling earth on earth and so I finished as quickly as I could. I patted down the pile and we covered it with the stones. It was unlikely that a predator would dig him up from four feet deep, but I didn't want to take the risk and the stones also acted as a marker in what would otherwise have been an unmarked grave.

For a while, we stood around the grave in silence.

The mother broke the silence, 'We should say some words.' Turning to me, she asked, 'Would you like to say them?'

I shook my head. I had nothing more to say to Jake and my beliefs with regard to the absence of a god were unchanged.

The mother continued, 'We understand. Perhaps we could say a few words for you.'

She assumed I was too distressed to speak. She was wrong, but now was not the time to tell her my reasons. 'What was his name?'

'Jake Cody.'

They all bowed their heads and clasped their hands in front of them as she said quietly, 'Please. God, welcome Jake Cody into your heaven. He may have been a man of violence, but in our short acquaintance, we knew him as a good, brave man who gave his life to save ours.'

In the silence that followed, the tears ran down my cheeks as Lupus whined and licked my hand.

It was now dark, but no one wanted to stay close to the place of death. The moon provided enough light for us to pick our way along the trail. The family climbed up on the wagon while I collected Jacob and what I thought was the Commancheros' leader's horse. I hoped their other horses would follow.

In just over a mile, we came to a spot where a stream came bubbling close to the trail. We agreed this was an ideal spot to camp and it was far enough from our little battle field.

The mother and father started a fire and cooked some food.

I unsaddled Buck.

The daughter didn't speak to me, but followed and did the same to Jacob.

The Commancheros' horses had followed and so we unsaddled all twelve together. Still without exchanging a word, we set the saddles neatly under a tree and went to join her parents around the fire.

The girl sat close to her mother, the father a little away from them. I sat opposite. There was an uncomfortable silence. As they stared at the pot on the fire, I looked them over properly for the first time.

The father was studious-looking, tall and slim with sandy hair. His wife was short and matronly with black hair cut short. The daughter looked what I thought as typical of a girl in her early teens. Her build was more like her father's, but she had long black hair that covered her face when she looked down.

The father turned to me, 'I'm Roger Amiss, this is my wife, Emma, and our daughter, Anna.' Emma looked at me and smiled. Anna looked down and hid behind her hair.

'Jimmy Kidd.' I looked for a reaction as I gave my name, but there was none. It seemed my notoriety had not spread as far as the circles in which they moved.

'We are so grateful to you, Jimmy,' Roger continued, 'And so sorry that your friend, Jake, should have died.'

I thought for a moment. 'He knew the risk, just as I did. Commancheros killed his family, but I don't know the details because he didn't like to speak about it. When I was young, they killed my parents, so we both had good reason to hate them and spent most of our time trying to prevent it happening to others.'

'We were so lucky that you were passing.'

'We weren't exactly passing. We'd heard that there was a band praying on travellers and had been watching that trail for some time.'

'We were still lucky you were there.'

'That's true, you certainly weren't in any position to defend yourselves. Where are your guns?'

'We don't like guns.'

My response was angry, 'I don't <u>like</u> guns. I don't <u>like</u> hammers and saws either. They are just tools that each have their job.'

They all looked a little crestfallen and so I moderated my tone and continued more quietly and less vehemently, 'Out here you have to be able to defend yourselves. There is no guarantee that if you had fought back that they would not have taken you, but at least you had a chance. Without guns, you had no chance at all. If you had knocked a few of them off their horses, they might have decided the price was too high and left you to find an easier target. As it is, you are the easy target.'

Roger looked at Emma. There seemed to be some sort of unspoken agreement.

'We don't have any guns and we don't know how to use them.'

'You've plenty of guns now, kindly donated by our late, unlamented friends.' In spite of everything, I was able to grin at my weak joke before continuing, 'And I can teach you.'

'Thank you,' they said in unison.

We ate and, being exhausted, laid down to sleep. They said they were frightened that more bandits would creep up on us while we slept, but were reassured when I told them that Lupus was always on guard and no one would get anywhere near us without him knowing.

I woke at first light and sat up and stretched. As I did so, I felt the envelope in my pocket. I retrieved it from my pocket, took the note out and read:

'I, Jake Cody, being of sound mind, do hereby appoint Jimmy Kidd as my sole beneficiary.

For the avoidance of doubt, my estate comprises everything in my possession at the time of my death including my horse, Jacob, or any horse that may replace him in the interim, and all the goods on my horse plus the balance in my account in the National Bank in my name and account number 52084163.

The presentation of this note by the said Jimmy Kidd may be taken as proof of my death.'

It was signed by Jake, dated nine months earlier and was witnessed by a bank manager and one of his senior clerks.

I was shocked. It had not occurred to me that Jake had anything worth leaving, although I knew he had a bank account. I certainly would not have guessed he would leave anything to me. His loss struck home again and I sat on ground where I had slept as sobs wracked my body. Lupus came to me and laid his head on my shoulder. It was a great comfort to take him in my arms and bury my head in his neck.

I had put the will back in my pocket and recovered my composure by the time the others awoke. Anna and I saw to the horses while Roger drew water from the stream and Emma cooked breakfast. Anna was shy, but it seemed that this was normal and she was being remarkably resilient following her ordeal. She obviously loved horses and asked me about Buck. This broke the ice and she was soon telling me her plans for when they reached their destination.

After breakfast, I took stock of the weapons. Including Jake's, there were seven pistols, thirteen rifles, twelve belts full of cartridges and twenty boxes of cartridges. Jake's guns were by far the best, being of much better quality and properly maintained. The bandits' guns were a mixed bag with some so much in need of a clean and service, I was surprised they worked. I chose what seemed the best two Winchesters and the best two Colts, stripped them down and cleaned them.

We had decided shooting lessons would start before

we set off and so I took the weapons to family Amiss, who were waiting for me at a spot well away from the horses. I gave Jake's gun belt with his Colt to Roger. He recognised them and tried to give them back, 'I can't take these. They were Jake's and are rightfully yours now.'

'I don't need them,' I explained. 'I have very good guns of my own and I don't want to carry the extra weight. He left everything to me and I want you to have them.'

He understood, but only took them and Jake's Winchester reluctantly.

I gave a Winchester to Emma and another to Anna and started the lesson.

With the slow wagon and herding all the horses, it took us five days to reach the next town. There was no room on the wagon to carry the saddles, so each day we had to saddle all the horses in the morning and unsaddle them in the evening. I started the first day by riding behind our small herd to keep them moving along. Luckily, they were eager to stay together, which made it easy.

Also, Anna wanted to ride rather than travel in the wagon. I said she could ride Jacob, who was the best horse after Buck. She was a good rider and soon had a rapport with Jacob. I was able to leave her for long periods to keep our herd going and scouted around to ensure we weren't surprised. I didn't see another living soul.

Evenings and mornings were spent practicing with the guns. They were soon able to use them safely and became reasonably good shots. They learnt to keep the guns to hand at all times and I was reasonably certain that they would be able to see off most bandit attacks.

When we arrived at the town, I told them they could have all the guns, saddles and horses and that they should sell those they didn't want or need. They insisted they couldn't, but I assured them I had all I needed and couldn't carry any more. All I wanted was to replenish my ammunition.

I picked up Buck's and Jacob's reins. I'm sure they expected me to mount up and ride away with them both, but I walked across to Anna and put Jacob's reins in her hand. 'I know Jake would want him to go to a good home and I can't think of anyone better than you, Anna.'

Her look was of total surprise and then delight. She caught her breath and laughed as tears filled her eyes. Keeping a tight hold on the reins, she threw her arms around my neck as she hugged me and said, 'Thank you, I will love him forever and I will never forget you, Jimmy.'

Her parents were looking on with silly grins on their faces. I extracted myself from Anna, vaulted onto Buck and with a wave to them all, left with Lupus trotting by my side.

As I rode off, I heard a passerby say, 'Look, that's Jimmy Kidd! They say he's the deadliest killer in the territory.' I don't know if the Amiss's heard it and found myself wondering, if they did, would it tarnish their memory of me?

*

On my own again, I felt Jake's absence more keenly and lost my sense of purpose. I had more money in the bank than I knew what to do with and I didn't want his money, so I left it all in the bank. I wandered aimlessly and was angry with the world. In one bar there was a great thug who was throwing his weight around. I deliberately placed myself in his way so that he pushed me. I then beat him senseless. It didn't make me feel any better.

In another town, there was a girl who took an interest in me. She invited me to her room and told me how much it would cost for various services she could offer. I was taken aback because I hadn't paid for sex before, but I agreed to pay for the her 'full service'. The soulless, mechanical, perfunctory, impersonal sex that followed was completely unfulfilling. I walked out before morning, leaving her money on the bed. The experience made me feel more lonely.

As had become my habit, I was wandering aimlessly along yet another anonymous trail when, up ahead, I saw a group of people under a tree. When I was close enough, I saw that it was three men around a member of the indigenous peoples who they had tied to the tree. He had bruises on his face, one of his eyes was closing and blood was running down his chin from a split lip. In spite of this, he seemed unafraid, had a proud and haughty bearing and was looking at the men abusing him with disdain. When he saw me, his eyes opened wide in astonishment.

Two of the men were standing close to their prisoner. I rode up to the one standing slightly apart and looked down at him. 'Welcome, stranger,' he greeted me, but had a wary eye on Lupus.

I dismounted and faced him, 'What's going on here?'

'We found this filthy savage riding along as though he owned the place. We jumped him and have been teaching him a lesson.'

I decided not to comment on the fact that the 'filthy savage' could trace his ancestors back many generations in this land and that there was a good argument that he did 'own the place', but decided the subtlety would be lost on them, so I simply commented, 'Three against one seems extreme and the lesson is a little ambiguous. What are you teaching him?'

'He's sort've got to learn their place.'

One of the others chimed in, 'I know you, you're Jimmy Kidd. I was in a saloon a while back and I saw you and your partner take out eight Commancheros, you shot seven of them.'

As with many such incidents, the story of Jake's and my run in with the Commancheros had 'improved' with the telling. It was not only exaggerated, it was impossible as I carried only one Colt and could only have shot five at the most. However, I didn't correct them, as an enhanced reputation might come in useful.

This seemed to be the case, as the first man became uncertain and decided justification was needed. 'Anyway, we aren't doing him any real harm. We were just having a little fun.'

I grinned and said, 'That's all right then.'

They all relaxed.

I continued, 'What you're saying is that, if you're just having fun and don't do any real harm, it's perfectly okay to take advantage of someone who is in a weaker position than you.'

They all laughed a little nervously and nodded vigorously.

I told Lupus to watch the two by the tree. He took a couple of steps forward and stood watching them closely.

I turned to the other one and, smiling widely, said, 'I'd like to join in.'

Obviously pleased and believing the crisis was over, he stood back and with a sweep of his hand towards their prisoner, said, 'Be my guest.'

Still smiling, I stepped up to the grinning idiot and, keeping my right hand by my side, slapped him in the face with my left.

'What's that for?'

Saying, 'No real harm done, I'm just having some fun,' I slapped him with the back of my left hand on the other side of his face. I caught his lip against his teeth and a very small trickle of blood ran down his chin.

The other two started to protest, Lupus growled, they fell silent, I hit their colleague for the third time. He put his had to his right cheek.

Slapping him on the other side again, I explained, 'You have a choice. You can stand there and bleed while I keep hitting you; you can do something about it; or you can all mount up and ride off.'

They made their decision quickly, ran to their horses, mounted and galloped off as fast as they could.

I went over to their prisoner and cut him free. He was a man of about fifty, but was tall, strong and confident. He made nothing of his injuries. He put his hands on my shoulders, looked deep into my eyes and said, 'Kraspa.'

I had no idea what he meant and obviously looked as confused as I felt.

He poked me in the chest with the forefinger of his right hand and each time his finger touched me he said, 'Kraspa, Kraspa, Kraspa.'

I thought he may have confused me with someone else and so I tapped myself on the chest in the same way and said, 'Jimmy, Jimmy, Jimmy.'

He shook his head and repeated the process, 'Kraspa, Kraspa, Kraspa.'

I gave up.

He took hold of my arm and pulled me away. He said something in his own language and then, sifting through his mind for a word, he said, 'Come.' Turning and mounting his pony, he waived his arm in the way people all over the world do when they want someone to follow them and repeated, 'Come.'

I had nothing better to do. He seemed to have some sort of purpose and so I thought, 'What have I got to lose?' I mounted Buck and followed him.

We travelled together and didn't meet another living soul. He carried a knife, a skin for water and an old Henry rifle, a forerunner of the Winchester that carried the same number of rounds, but had to be loaded by dropping the rounds from the front into a tube mounted under the barrel. It was slow and required great care, especially with the first few rounds because, if they hit one another too hard, the cartridge would ignite and shoot the bullet out of the tube as you were loading. By my standards, he was severely underarmed, especially as he carried few bullets.

He was a master of living off the land. He knew where to find water when we needed it and foraged, including finding ample grazing for the horses. Meat came from game, which I shot. I could well afford the one or two bullets a week required, he could not. He admired my Winchester and nodded his head in approval at my marksmanship, but only once. I was to learn later that, for this taciturn man, nodding was equivalent of glowing praise, but even he was unable to hide his amazement at the range and accuracy of my Martini Henry.

From the first day, he taught me his language. He started by pointing at trees, boulders, clouds, the sky, the sun, the moon, etc. while speaking his words for them. After I had acquired a reasonable vocabulary of nouns, he put them into simple sentences. During the evenings, he would talk at great length. I learnt later that he was relating stories of his people, the Kikatchi clan of the Hoopa tribe. Of course, I understood nothing of what he said, but it helped as I learnt the rhythm, sounds and cadence of the language.

After three months, I could understand a lot of what he said. After four months, I had enough understanding to answer simple questions. Once I reached this point, my ability to speak improved exponentially. By the end of the sixth month, we could hold conversations, even on more abstract subjects.

I learnt that his people were ancient. He said they came from the beginning of time. They had a rich, semi-nomadic culture based on respect for the environment and a deeply routed code of honour.

I asked him, 'Why were you wandering outside your territory and all alone?'

'A chief has many things to consider. As time goes by, thoughts crowd in and so we take time alone to meditate and commune with nature to clear our minds. These times are called 'the wanderings'.'

'But you made yourself vulnerable. Why not stay in your own lands?'

'It is a tradition to travel abroad. Other tribes have the same tradition and if we see one of them on our land, we will respect their privacy and leave them alone. All tribes extend the same courtesy to one another. A loan chief does not represent a threat. Your people do not seem to have the same level of respect.'

Not having any inclination to defend 'my people' I continued, 'Are you normally away for so long? Won't your family be worried?'

'I can be away for a few months, but this has been longer than normal because you have taken so long to learn Hoopas. They will understand.'

Early in the sixth month, we came across an enormous herd of great shaggy beasts. There were thousands of massive, big horned, long coated bovines that ambled before us as we sat and watched. Although I thought the herd was endless, he told me that there were far fewer than there had been, which may have been why I had not seen them before.

These animals were the mainstay of his people's lives. They hunted them only to meet their needs and used every part of each body, without any waste. Since the beginning of time, the Hooplas and the great beasts had lived alongside one another and thrived, but, now the immigrants were hunting them, their numbers had declined. He told me that his father had named him after the leader of the herd, it translated as *Raging Bull*. He had not told me his name before and when I asked him why, he said it was because, like the bull, he was the leader of his people. I had not realised I was in such exalted company.

As we skirted the beasts, Raging Bull turned to me and said, 'You are now ready to meet our people.' By 'ready' I assumed he meant able to communicate, but he would not confirm this and refused to comment on why they were 'our people' rather than 'my people'.

After a week, we crossed a great river into a land that marked the boundary between the relatively barren wilderness in which we had been travelling into a land that had a lush beauty. It was largely green grassland and much of it was flat, but it was punctuated by small woods, streams and hills that turned what would otherwise be plain countryside into one of great interest.

Raging Bull paused and, with a sweep of his hand, explained, 'This is my people's land. We are as numerous as the great beasts and we live here between the Oza river we have just crossed in the east and the Inda river four days ride to the west. Our northern boundary is the White Top Mountains and our southern border is the Great Forest. It would take seven days to ride between them.'

Assuming the land was a rough rectangle and working on the basis of travelling 30 miles a day, I estimated it was one hundred and twenty miles wide and two hundred and ten miles long, just over twenty thousand square miles. This was pretty big, but I didn't think it would support the many thousands of people he implied, but I didn't comment.

An hour or so after fording the river, the rattle of gunfire filled the air. It sounded like a small battle that must have just started because it was not too far away. Without a word, we broke into a controlled gallop that would get us to the fight quickly, but would reduce the chances of our running into trouble.

We topped a rise and looked down on a small village comprising lodges that were triangular tents made of poles widely separated at the base, but meeting at the top. They were covered with skins. I estimated there were about thirty Commancheros attacking the village. Strewn around were a few bodies, mainly Kikatchi youths and women. As we watched, a boy hurled himself at a mounted Commanchero intent upon knocking him off his horse, but he was too small and light and he was swatted aside and then shot as he fell to the ground.

From behind one of the lodges, a muscular Kikatchi warrior appeared with an arrow already strung on his bow. He drew and loosed in one smooth action, knocking the Commanchero off his horse before he ducked back behind the lodge.

We could hear screams from the villagers as they ran for shelter and whoops of delight as the Commancheros cut them down.

I'd seen enough. I drew my Colts and, closely followed by Lupus, pushed Buck down the slope shouting to Raging Bull, 'Let your warriors know I'm on their side.' The idea of being mistaken for a Commanchero and being killed by a Kikatchi warrior did not appeal to me.

There were only fifty yards from the base of the hill to the village. The Commancheros were in groups attacking villagers at random. I galloped along their flanks to keep them to one side of me to avoid meeting any Kikatchi, weaving to present a difficult target and picking off the bastards as targets presented themselves.

In what seemed no time, we were through them having emptied both Colts and eight Commanchero saddles. Lupus had been unable to find a target and so he was still by my side. There was no time to reload and so I holstered my saddle Colts and drew the one from my hip with my right hand and my Winchester with my left.

As I returned to the fray, I saw Raging Bull had downed two of the enemy and had made contact with the muscular warrior. He pointed at me. I hoped he was telling him that I was on their side.

I hit them again, dropping four more before my Colt was empty. Raging Bull and the warrior were working together standing back-to-back, the warrior loosing arrows and Raging Bull firing his Henry. They were doing well, but the Commancheros were rallying and I could see they were about to charge and overrun the two of them through sheer weight of numbers.

I brought my Winchester to my shoulder. I was about thirty yards from the action, a long shot for their poor marksmanship, but well within my scope. Six shots emptied six saddles and destroyed the momentum of their charge.

Raging Bull and his ally took full advantage and poured arrows and bullets into the ever smaller group, emptying three more saddles. This broke their attack completely and the five remaining retreated at a gallop running directly away from Raging Bull and diagonally across me. This gave me another opportunity and I hit two more before they disappeared behind a hill.

I reloaded the Winchester and my saddle holster Colts and then rode slowly to Raging Bull as I reloaded my hip Colt.

As I got there, I looked down at his companion, 'You are a fine and brave warrior.'

He didn't answer, seemingly fixated with Buck. Then his gaze turned to Lupus, who trotted up and sat beside us, and his eyes opened wide with astonishment.

He then looked up at me and the face of the warrior who had just fearlessly faced overwhelming odds went as white as a sheet.

Raging Bull nodded and said, 'Yes, Wind-in-the-Hair, this is our *Kraspa*, Sky-in-the-Eye!'

Book 2 - Sky-in-the-Eye

8

Kraspa

Before Raging Bull could explain further, eighteen warriors galloped into the village.

'Where were you?' raged Wind-in-the-Hair.

'You know we were out hunting,' replied their apparent leader.

'How did they get past you?' Wind-in-the-Hair pointed at the body of a Commanchero.

'We were looking for the great beasts, not them.'

Before Wind-in-the-Hair could reply, we heard the crack of a rifle in the distance. On looking up, we saw three Commancheros who had escaped the battle standing on a ridge about six hundred yards away. They were too far away to hit us with their Winchesters and I assumed they were just taunting us. They had lost most of their comrades, but they were unconcerned and were selfishly revelling in their escape. The shot had been to attract our attention so they could taunt us for the casualties they had inflicted, safe in the knowledge they were out of range.

They were wrong.

I dismounted, pulled the Martini Henry from its holster and laid down. I needed two further bullets, but couldn't lay them in the ground as they would collect dust and grit, which would foul the gun's mechanism, and so I passed them to Raging Bull, who knelt beside me ready to pass them to me.

I pulled down the lever, pushed a bullet into the chamber. Pulling the lever up, I looked up to check the range and saw the three bandits in a line against the horizon. I pulled up the ladder site and set the V at the what I thought was the correct range. As I sighted, the one in the middle turned, pulled his trousers down and bent over in the universal insult of the coward. His companions' shouts of delight were cut short as I shot the one on my right.

I pulled down the lever, ejecting the used cartridge. Raging Bull passed me a live round. I watched the two remaining Commancheros as I went through the instinctive process.

I pushed the bullet into the chamber.

The Commanchero on the left ran away.

I lifted the lever.

The one in the middle tried to run, tripped on his trousers that were still around his ankles and fell.

I took aim.

He stood up.

I shot him.

I looked up to see stunned faces. Wind-in-the-Hair

started chanting, 'Sky-in-the-Eye, Sky-in-the-Eye, Sky-in-the-Eye.' The other warriors turned to me and joined him. 'Sky-in-the-Eye. Sky-in-the-Eye. Sky-in-the-Eye. Sky-in-the-Eye ...' I had no idea what it meant and, as I looked around, decided now was not the moment to ask.

There were bodies strewn around the village, mostly Commancheros, but there were some Kikatchi mothers cradling their young sons and daughters. The youths had fought bravely to save their families, but were no match for the better armed Commancheros. Those who had survived had found cover in and around the lodges. They would have been found and suffered the same fate if Raging Bull and I had not mounted our surprise attack. I noticed a particularly beautiful young woman kneeling by the body of an elderly man and assumed she was grieving for her father.

Raging Bull and Wind-in-the-Hair organised the newly arrived warriors and survivors. The Commancheros' bodies were stripped of anything that was useful, had ropes tied around their legs and were dragged by mounted warriors out of sight.

The Kikatchi bodies were gathered with respect and laid out in a dignified manner at the edge of the village. Wooden platforms of about ten feet high were raised about a mile from the village and the Kikatchi dead were laid reverently, one on each platform.

I asked Wind-in-the-Hair, why they had been laid out in this way.

Apparently surprised by the question, he explained as though talking to a child, 'Nature is a circle. All living things are born, move through life and then die. In death, their goodness is returned firstly to the insects, birds and animals. Finally, we make meal of their bones and spread it on our crops. In this way, the goodness of our ancestors is returned to the land and then to us.'

Being used to burial, this seemed a strange custom. 'And the Commancheros bodies?' I asked.

'They are taken away from the village so as to avoid disease and are left on the plains for the insects, birds and animals. We have no use for them and so they are left.'

I needed to think about this and so I changed the subject. 'How did the Commancheros surprise you? Raging Bull told me the Kikatchi are numerous and so why were there no warriors to defend the village?'

'It is our custom to live in a large number of small communities. It was unfortunate that so many of our warriors were away at the time of the attack. I think the Commancheros had watched them and had waited until they had gone.'

Raging Bull joined us and I took the opportunity to ask him, 'Why do you say I am 'Sky-in-the-Eye' and what do you mean when you say I am the 'Kraspa'?'

'We have a story handed down from one generation to the next. It tells of a great warrior who rides a brown horse, has a wolf for a companion and has eyes the colour of the sky. All our people have brown eyes. You are the first person we have met to have blue eyes.'

I had seen many people with blue eyes and, although it was not uncommon for people to say mine were an unusually bright shade of blue, as far as I was concerned they were not especially rare. As many as half the horses I had seen were bay, Buck was only slightly unusual in that he didn't have any white. Dogs were also common companions. All-in-all, I didn't think there was anything unusual about me, but decided now was not the time to comment and so I changed the subject again, asking them to explain the word 'Kraspa'.

This was far more difficult. At first I thought they meant a saviour or messiah, but soon realised these were too vague and had too many spiritual connotations. 'Kraspa' was far more specific. The closest I could get was *'warrior chief who will lead us to victory'*. I needed time to consider this and said so.

Raging Bull brought the discussion to a close, 'It has been a long day and there is much for you to consider, Sky-in-the-Eye. Go to your lodge and sleep. We will discuss this further in the morning.'

'I don't have a lodge.'

'When a warrior is killed, his wife loses her protector. Lodges are the property of the warrior and, when he has gone, his widow had nowhere to live. This is our custom, which sounds harsh, but works well as widows invariably find a new protector. Broken Lance was killed in the battle. You should take his lodge and his wife, Prairie Flower, so that she has a place to live. She will welcome you.'

Given the recent demise of her husband, I thought this unlikely. However, I needed a place to sleep and would decide on my future in the morning. Raging Bull pointed out the lodge. I made sure Buck was settled in the corral and, together with Lupus, took my saddle and other possessions with me to the lodge. The entrance was covered with a flap. There was nowhere to knock and I didn't want to burst in. As I was deliberating, the flap was pushed aside and the lovely young woman I had seen mourning her father stood before me.

I was dumbstruck. She was not just lovely, she was the most beautiful girl I had ever seen. Standing a head shorter than me, her body was lissome, but well formed. Her complexion was the colour of very milky coffee and was completely flawless. Her brown eyes were deep pools below the longest lashes I had ever seen. Her hair was black and long and shone like spun silk.

She stood aside and gestured for me to enter. In order to do so, I had to brush past her. Her fragrance was intoxicating.

The inside of the lodge was surprisingly large and well ordered. Various items were stacked neatly around the edges. There was a fire in the centre with smoke escaping through the gap at the top where the poles forming the main structure met, but were not covered. The floor was covered in skins and there were blankets piled along one side of the fire. She indicated an empty space at the back where I placed my saddle, saddle bags and guns. As was normal, Lupus settled beside my possessions to guard them.

She gestured towards the pile of blankets, which I took as an invitation to sit. As I did so, she spoke for the first time, 'Your food will be ready very soon, Kraspa.' Her voice will lilting.

She moved with a gentle athleticism and grace. I could not take my eyes off her and followed her every movement around the lodge. Feeling that I should say something, 'I am sorry for your loss.'

'Thank you.'

'You must be very sad to have lost your husband and father on the same day.'

She gave me a puzzled look and then realisation hit her. 'It was just my husband who died today, my father died many years ago.'

Seeing my puzzled expression, she continued, 'A year ago I married a young warrior. He died in a riding accident the day after our wedding. Broken Lance had just lost his wife. I lived in his lodge and cared for him so that I had a home. He was very kind and I was fond of him, but he was never really a husband to me. I am sorry he was killed because he was a good man, but I am not so very sad because I did not love him.'

The food, a stew with meat and vegetables, was excellent. I sat cross legged on the blanket to eat and Prairie Flower sat opposite me. We did not speak, but I could not take my eyes off her. She sat demurely looking at the floor.

When we had finished, she took our dishes out to wash them. I laid down with my back to the entrance. She came in, put the plates away and laid down next to me. I had my back to her and I did not know what to do. She was radiantly beautiful, but I didn't want to take advantage of her in her moment of need. I fell asleep.

When I awoke, Prairie Flower was preparing

breakfast. We ate in silence. When she took the plates to wash, I left the lodge. Exploring a little, I found a stream not too far from the village. I stripped off and plunged in. The cold water was invigorating. Refreshed, I dressed and walked back to the village.

As I entered, I came across a young warrior with one of the Winchesters taken from the Commancheros. I could see he had tried to clean it because the stock and barrel had been wiped down, but I could also see the mechanism was filthy. 'This gun is dangerous,' I told him, 'It must be cleaned to make it safe and work properly.'

'How is it cleaned, Kraspa,' he asked.

'Go and get all the other guns and bring them to my lodge. I will show you.'

Ten minutes later, thirty young men were at my lodge. I sent them to get blankets to sit on so they could keep the guns out of the dirt and sat on my blanket with Lupus by my side and my Winchester on my lap to wait for them.

After they arrived, I explained, 'The first thing to learn is how to handle your guns safely. The idea is to kill your enemies, not your friends.'

Starting with the basic premise of not pointing a gun at anyone, even if it's empty. I them moved on to unloading, stripping down, reassembling and loading. Some of them were very receptive and understood quickly. There was one strapping young lad of about eighteen, who was constantly posing and waiving his gun around pointing at an imaginary enemy. With a 'bang' his gun discharged. Fortunately, the bullet flew harmlessly above the heads of the others, but this was too much for me. I went over to him and held out my hand, 'Give me that rifle, you are not responsible enough to have it.'

He glared at me and spat out, 'A Kikatchi warrior surrenders his weapons to no man.'

I tried to exert my authority, 'I am the Kraspa and I order you to give up that gun.'

This gave him pause for thought, but only for a moment. Dropping the rifle to the ground, he reverted to a more familiar weapon. Pulling his knife from his belt in one fluid motion, he lunged at my chest. I stepped to my left, allowing his knife hand to pass in front of me before I grasped his wrist with my right hand, placed my left forearm under his elbow and pushed down just enough to hurt him and make him drop the knife without damaging his arm.

He screamed at me in rage and tried to kick me. I took my left arm from under his and hit him hard in the face with my elbow. He fell onto his back unconscious.

I looked down to see his nose was broken and pushed to the side, laying almost on his cheek. It was not my intention to maim him and I knew how to mend his nose, but it would hurt and would be better done while he was still unconscious.

Squatting down, I took his nose between my first finger and thumb and pulled it up straight. I then asked one of the others to pass me an arrow from which I removed the fletchings before pushing it into his right nostril. I moved it around to push the cartilage on the inside of his nose into place and make sure his airway was clear. I then moulded the right side of his nose with my finger against the arrow. I repeated the procedure on his left nostril and then cut of two strips of buckskin from his shirt. Using the arrow, I pushed a piece into each of his nostrils to ensure the airways would be clear when his nose had mended and to hold it in place while the cartilage and bone set, leaving a small piece dangling from each to facilitate their removal when no longer needed.

He moaned, started to come around and put his hands to his face. I held them away and told him to leave his nose alone. It would need at least a week to set, after which he could remove the buckskin strips. In the meantime, he would have to breath through his mouth. He started to get up and I told him to sit at the edge of the class until we had finished.

I sent one of the class to get a replacement who could be responsible and gave him the confiscated gun. I've never seen anyone so proud and pleased. I sat him next to the quickest pupil and told him to help the new boy. I then got them to go through the whole process again and then again until I was sure they could do it on their own.

When the class was over, they all left talking excitedly, except the boy with the broken nose. As he walked towards me, I could see his nose was badly swollen and he had the beginnings of two really impressive black eyes.

I thought he was downcast, but he looked at me with

pride and said, 'From this day I will be called Broken Nose to remind me of the lesson I have just learnt. From now on I will work hard to become a warrior worthy of riding with you, Kraspa.'

I nodded.

Without another word, he walked away.

For the remainder of the day, I walked around the village. I was impressed by the way the Kikatchi went about their work in an efficient, but unhurried way. How everything was well organised and the animal husbandry was outstanding. Even so, I did not see my place amongst them and, although I was greeted in a polite and friendly, if slightly reserved, manner, I was still not certain how, or if, I fitted in. I was pondering this as I went back to my lodge.

Prairie Flower was making the evening meal. She took my breath away as I saw her again.

We ate in silence again.

When she came back from washing the dishes, I was standing by the sleeping blankets. I turned as she walked in. She came up and stood close to me with her head bowed and asked, 'Do you not like me?'

I was completely taken aback by this and couldn't think what to say. She looked up and I knew what to say, 'It is more than like, Prairie Flower, you are the most lovely woman I have ever seen.'

'Then do I not please you?' She undid the laces at the shoulders of her dress, which fell to the ground. She looked into my eyes. I was bewitched. She was perfect.

Dropping to her knees, she started to unbuckle my

belt and continued, 'It is my greatest wish to please you.'

All uncertainty left me. I now knew exactly what to do. Taking her hands in mine, I pulled her to her feet. 'Not this way. I do not want to have sex with you, I want us to make love.'

I lifted her and laid her gently on the sleeping blankets, removed my clothes and laid down beside her.

We were not in a hurry. For ages we lay on our sides looking at each other and stroking one another's faces, just revelling in the pleasure of our closeness.

I kissed her and then we made love.

Although it involved the techniques, gestures and acts I had used before, this time they were an expression of our love, a blending of our bodies that was spiritually uplifting instead of simply pleasurable.

All the time I had spent with Josie and others were no more than preparation for that night. I reached higher peaks than I'd previously experienced, but did not sink to the depths of the valleys that I had before. Instead, we came down to a high plateau that was the launching pad for each subsequent journey into the stratosphere.

Prairie Flower eventually fell asleep in my arms.

I couldn't sleep. I was frightened that, if I slept, I would miss the first soft light that precedes dawn when I would be able to see her face again.

When she woke, I was lying with my head on my hand looking at her.

She smiled. Her lips were like pink roses flavoured with honey and her teeth like pearls.

If I hadn't realised before, I knew at that moment I

was in love and there was no question of me leaving the Kikatchi.

I dressed and ran to the stream to bathe.

I ran back and, although I hadn't slept all night, I was invigorated.

After a quick breakfast, I set out to see Raging Bull, but came back immediately - I had not asked the most important question: 'How do we get married?'

I realise now that it should have been, 'Will you marry me?' but, at that moment, the idea of not spending the rest of my life with her was unthinkable.

She laughed, 'If we decide we are married then we are.'

'Have we decided?'

She wrinkled her nose and stuck her tongue out.

I took it as a, 'Yes!'

I went to Raging Bull's lodge. He was sitting outside as though he was expecting me. I went straight to the point, 'I need to understand some things.'

He nodded.

'Do you believe I am Kraspa?'

He nodded.

'Do you want me as your war chief?'

'Of course, the Kraspa is the War Chief, but, when I met you, you did not speak Hoopas. My people would not have believed that the Kraspa does not speak our language and so I had to take you on a great trip to teach you.' This was a long speech for Raging Bull and explained a lot.

'But you are the Great Chief?'

He nodded.

'What is the difference? Who is in charge of what?'

'You are in charge of everything to do with war, I am in charge of everything else.'

'There will never be a conflict between us?'

'No! Anything to do with the warriors and waging war, I will defer to you. In all other matters, you will defer to me.'

I was reasonably happy with that, but had one more question. 'What if I ask for the Kikatchi to change how they live?'

He recognised that there was an overlap in such matters and spent several minutes thinking about it. He decided, 'I will agree to anything that is for the greater good of the Kakatchi.'

'Thank you. You say that the Kikatchi are numerous, but you don't know how many?'

He shook his head.

'In order to organise the warriors, I need to know how many there are. I also need to know the number of women, children and elderly so that I can plan their defence. The way you live at the moment with small groups spread all over the land makes counting them difficult. It also makes it difficult to protect them, as the Commanchero attack a few days ago showed. We should live in two or three large villages so that all warriors can protect everyone and we can assess the numbers.'

This was a radical change and I realised he needed time to think it over. He decided to consult the senior members of the tribe.

My best ally proved to be Wind-in-the-Hair. Many of the others were loath to dispense with their traditional ways and the argument went back and forth, but he won the day by saying, 'Our greatest tradition is the legend of Kraspa, Sky-in-the-Eye. The legends tell us he is a man of great vision who will lead us to many victories. It would be a foolish man who rejects his vision.' The decision was unanimous and word was sent to all groups that they should gather around our village.

As the groups came in, I arranged with Raging Bull for them to gather in large villages of no more than one thousand. We ended up with three villages within a two mile radius, two with a thousand inhabitants and one with seven hundred.

We now knew the total, but I needed to know the breakdown. They did not have a tradition for writing and so I had to go to each village to collect my own data. The figures worked out as follows:

Women of all ages: 1195
Boys below the age of 12: 175
Boys from 13 to 15: 165
Boys from 16 to 17: 145
Men from 18 to 50: 890
Men over 50: 30

I now had the information I needed to start my plans.

9

Legions

Raging Bull said we needed to address the senior warriors. There were about fifty in all and he gathered them on the open ground between the three villages. At his suggestion, we waited until they had gathered and then we and I made a grand entrance. He wanted them to see Buck, Lupus and then me so they could confirm for themselves that I was, indeed the Kraspa.

It seemed to work, as there were gasps as we rode up and dismounted. The warriors gathered round. Raging Bull opened the proceedings. 'My brothers. Times are changing. Outsiders come to our land. They kill us and they kill the great beasts in such numbers that they threaten our very existence. If we do not take radical action, the Kikatchi and all the Hoopas will be nothing more than a memory. Our legends tell us that, when he is most needed, our Kraspa, Sky-in-the-Eye, will come. As you have all seen, he is here with us now.' He made a sweeping gesture and I stepped forward.

The warriors muttered to one another. It was apparent that the most my appearance had achieved was to make them willing to listen. I was going to have to win them over. 'My brothers,' I started, 'I have been with you for only a short time, but I know you are a great people with proud traditions. Your warriors are strong and brave and no war chief could wish for better men to lead.' This seemed to hit the right note, as most of those gathered nodded and murmured their agreement.

I continued, 'The old ways have worked for you for many generations, but the world is changing and we have to change with it if we are to survive. My plan is to take the best of what you have and mould it into a new way of fighting.'

No reaction.

'Many years ago in a land many thousands of miles from here, there lived a people known as Romans. Like you, they were proud and brave, but, like us now, their enemies were numerous. They devised a way of fighting that enabled them to overcome the odds. By combining and working together, they were able to defeat their enemies even when they were seriously outnumbered. They did not rush in to meet their enemy head on, they stayed in formations, each man fighting with and for his companions.' I took an arrow from a warrior close by and held it up. 'This is a finely honed and effective weapon, but on its own it can be broken.' I snapped it. I then took fifteen arrows and held them up. 'These are also finely honed and effective weapons, but together they are far stronger.' I bunched the arrows and showed I could not break them.

A warrior about the same age, height and build as me stepped forward. His face was full of contempt and disdain as he almost spat out his words, 'So this is all our Kraspa has to offer. He wants us to hide behind one another. A Kikachi warrior is not made of wood like an arrow, we are as hard as flint and throw ourselves at our enemy to intimidate and show our superiority. If we fight in the way the 'Kraspa' suggests,' his tone was dripping with contempt, derision and disgust, 'Our ancestors will be ashamed and our enemies will laugh at us and lose all respect.'

The gathered warriors started to talk excitedly amongst themselves. It was apparent that, although some were asking for me to be given a chance to explain further, many agreed with the dissenter.

I turned to Raging Bull and asked the name of the warrior. 'Honey Badger, our most hotheaded and short tempered warrior.'

The gathering turned to me to see if I could say anything to counter his argument. 'Honey Badger is right, Kikatchi warriors are as hard as flint, but even flint will flake if it is hit hard enough. Fighting my way allows you to bring this hardness to battle in the most effective way so as to increase our chances of success.'

Honey Badger had the bit between his teeth and was not about to concede an inch. 'The Kikachi do not need clever tactics to win. For generations we have cowed our enemies with our ferocity. I will not sacrifice this reputation for the sake of adopting tactics invented by another people. They lived many years ago and many miles away, so we have no way of knowing if they had the success claimed for them or if they are relevant today.' Encouraged by the cheers of a section of the listeners, he went on, 'Let us test this according to our traditions. Does Sky-in-the-Eye have the courage to take the Circle of Truth?'

I had no idea what he was talking about and so I turned to Raging Bull for an explanation. 'He is challenging you to fight within a circle drawn on the ground. By tradition, the winner is telling the truth.'

With Asuka's training I had no fear of man-to-man combat and so I agreed.

The crowd parted and one of them pushed his knife into the ground, attached a rope to it and then scribed a circle of about twenty feet diameter. He removed the rope, but left the knife.

I raised an eyebrow at Raging Bull. 'You each stand opposite one another on the circumference. On my signal, you race to the centre. Whoever gets the knife has the advantage. There are three ways to win. The only certain way is to kill your adversary. The second is to throw him clear of the circle. If you do, he can retire without loss of honour, but he may also choose to continue. There is no limit to the number of times this can happen. You can also render your opponent unconscious or otherwise unable to fight, in which case he can retire without loss of honour. However, he can also decide to continue when he regains consciousness. If you break his arm, or nose,' (he gave me a meaningful look), 'The contest will be suspended. He may retire or choose to continue when he is better. The Honey Badger from which he takes his name is notorious for being the bravest, most savage, and fearless animal who will attack no matter how badly injured. This warrior is most aptly named. He will not give up even if you injure him so badly that he takes weeks to recover. This would mean the matter would be unresolved for too long. You will have to kill him.'

That was not what I wanted. I gave my gun belt and knife to Raging Bull, told Lupus to stay with him and took my position on the circumference opposite my opponent.

Raging Bull shouted, 'Go!'.

Honey Badger sprinted for the knife, dived the last few feet, pulled it out of the ground, rolled away and sprang to his feet in one smooth movement. He expected me to be close, having lost the race for the knife, but I hadn't moved. He snarled in contempt, crouched and ran at me with the knife held in front of him expecting the speed of his charge to surprise me. He lunged with the knife without pausing in his charge, but I had thrown myself to his left, away from the knife, and swept my legs forward, tripping him so he fell headlong out of the circle. Some of the crowd laughed. I wished they hadn't. It had not been my intention to humiliate him, which would anger him further and strengthen his resolve.

I backed away to the other side of the circle reflecting on the fact that he was fast and agile and, I suspected, strong and so I could not underestimate him.

He leapt up and charged again.

This time he paused in front of me and lunged at my head with the knife.

I moved my head to my right, allowing the knife to pass over my left shoulder, grabbed his knife arm with both hands, pivoted and hurled him over my shoulder.

He was out of the circle again, but had rolled and recovered his feet very quickly. I moved away from him, but this time stopped about half way between the centre and the circumference.

Honey Badger didn't pause, he just gathered himself and charged again.

I let him get in close, pushed his hands to the sides, took hold of his shoulders and rolled back using his momentum to take him over and above me. I got my feet on his hips and, when he was immediately above me, kicked upwards, making him spin through the air to land on his back.

Once again, he landed outside the circle, but was agile enough to roll as he landed and regained his feet immediately.

I moved to the opposite side of the circle hoping he would retire, but expecting him to charge.

He did without even pausing for thought.

He hadn't slowed, but this time he weaved as he approached, trying to disguise the angle of his attack. He held the knife low and, as soon as he was close enough, brought it up in a sweeping movement designed to disembowel me. I swayed back so the blade passed in front of my face, caught his knife wrist and, again using his momentum, pushed it up high above his head and back so he was off balance. I then swayed to the side and kicked his legs from beneath him, bringing him crashing to the ground again. As he started to rise, I kicked him in the side, sending him out of the circle again.

He took a moment to gather himself.

I hoped he was considering giving up. I took the time to reflect that, if he didn't retire this time, he wasn't going to at any time. Raging Bull had implied it would be counter productive to maim him because our plans would be in limbo until he recovered.

As I resolved to kill him, he attacked again.

As before, he did so in a mad rush. The only variation was that, this time, he changed his grip from having the blade coming out the front of his hand between his forefinger and thumb, to having the blade coming out the back of his hand by the little finger. This meant he had to strike with a downward, rather than upward, stroke.

He raised the knife above his head.

I caught his wrist with my left hand, bent it back to release his grip and took the knife with my right hand.

I pushed hard to make him bend backwards and drove the knife up through his lower jaw.

He grasped my knife hand with both of his and tried to pul it down. I held firm and pushed up hard under his chin.

He opened his mouth to scream, but just gurgled. Before the blood came, I caught a glimpse of the blade going through his tongue into the roof of his mouth.

His eyes glared their hate for a second.

He then looked surprised.

This, in turn, faded as life left his body.

Using all my strength, I straightened my arm to heave

him above my head so that he swung like a puppet. As he was one of the talisman that set me apart and gave me status, I called Lupus to my side before I addressed the stunned crowd, 'This was a brave man. But he was a stupid man and now he is a dead man. Five times he attacked me in the same way. A successful warrior needs more than bravery, he needs the intelligence to see what will work and what will not work. He should have seen that he would not overwhelm me with a mad rush, but didn't change his tactics. I don't want you to die protecting your families. The man who dies can only do so once. We will kill our enemies and live to protect our families again and again.'

As the blood coursed down my arm, fifty fists punched the sky and the the surrounding countryside resounded to, 'KRASPA!'

I washed the blood from my arm and rinsed my shirt before returning to my lodge. As I entered, Prairie Flower ran over and held me as she rested her head against my bare chest. 'You fought Honey Badger.' The story of my fight was already widely known. 'You could have been hurt'

'Honey Badger was a brave warrior,' I explained, 'But I was trained by one of he best fighters in the world from a very young age. I had to fight him to resolve the dispute and I knew I would win, but I hoped he would retire with honour when he knew he could not win. He would not stop and so I had to kill him. If I had not, many warriors would have thought me weak and would not follow me.'

'Out there, you are the Kraspa. In here, you are my husband.'

'Out there, I am Sky-in-the-Eye, in here I am Jimmy.'

'What is Jimmy?'

'It is the name my parents gave me.'

'To me, you are Jimmy.'

*

Honey Badger had paid the ultimate price, but the point had been made and there were no more dissenters. I needed to find leaders and consulted Raging Bull. I was not surprised that he suggested Wind-in-the-Hair as a senior officer together with another warrior by the name of Running Deer. I split the 890 warriors into two 'legions', which we called war parties, with Wind-in-the-Hair and Running Deer the leaders, known as War Chiefs. The war parties were broken down into groups of 100, which included their 'centurion', known as War Leaders. So the ranks were warriors, War Leaders, War Chiefs and Kraspa.

The boys from thirteen to seventeen were grouped into third scouting parties comprising an approximately even number of thirteen to fifteen and sixteen to seventeen with one of the older boys as their leader. This left a group of ten in that age group who were designated as my couriers and messengers. They came with me wherever I went and, when I needed to send a message, they would carry it. All officers knew them by sight and would know that any message they carried was legitimate.

The war parties were trained so they could move together in various formations. This sort of regimentation went against the grain with such free spirited people, but they managed to compromise with fluid formations that retained the essence of the organisation I needed, but allowed room for improvisation. This not only satisfied their natural reluctance to follow orders, but provided a level of flexibility and gave scope to the use of initiative, which was essential as plans fell to pieces in the heat of battle, especially as the absence of drums or bugles made communication so difficult. The overall effect of the training was not so much to mould them into regimented troops in the Roman fashion, but a large group of individuals who were able to co-operate effectively within an established framework.

The scouts were mounted on the swifter ponies and fifteen groups were on patrol at all times. They patrolled for ten days before returning to be replaced by those who had been resting. Ten of them worked within a radius of twenty miles from wherever we were encamped to provide close cover. The others ranged more widely to provide an overall picture. As the three large villages moved two or three times a year, the area covered varied from time-to-time. If we were camped close to one of the rivers, we would patrol the other side to avoid surprise attacks.

The scouts were under strict orders not to engage an enemy. If they encountered anything, two of them were required to bring the information back while the remainder kept a distant watch. If there was a significant change, a further two were dispatched with this information.

During their rest periods, the boys of seventeen were given warrior training so they could take their place in the war parties when they reached eighteen.

*

Life settled into a routine. Each night, Lupus and I would go to the lodge. He would settle in his corner and I would spend my time with Prairie Flower. Buck was happy to spend the night with the main herd, but ran to us each morning as part of the inseparable trio to complete the day's work. On the days that my duties took me away from the village, we rode off. When my duties kept me within the village, Lupus and Buck followed me around in the way they had since we were all young together. This was unusual, but no one gave it a second thought because a bay horse without any white and a wolf-like dog were the emblems of their Kraspa.

During the day, I worked hard to establish the right organisation. My nights with Prairie Flower were spent talking, mainly about our day's activities, but sometimes more profound subjects and I learnt a lot about the Hoopas' philosophy concerning man's place in the world. We also enjoyed companionable silences and, of course, making love.

My objective was to make the war parties self sufficient and, as this came about, I was able to delegate training and the general running of the army to others. I used this time to become familiar with my new land and spent days at a time travelling with my band of couriers. They accepted Buck and Lupus as an integral part of their Kraspa.

One day, I was told a herd of the great beasts was close by. I went with Wind-in-the-Hair and a group of four young warriors, including Broken Nose, to see them. We found them within a couple of hours and, as previously, I marvelled at their number and size. Wind-in-the-Hair said we needed to take five to meet our needs. I drew my Martini Henry, as I would have been able to take them down within a matter of minutes, but he laid his hand on my arm, 'No, brother, we must respect the great beasts and take them in the traditional way.'

The others galloped off. I sat on Buck and, with Lupus by my side, marvelled at their skill and bravery as they road amongst the bolting beasts, shooting at them with their arrows. They downed five and sent a message back home to arrange for a party to skin and butcher them and transport them to the lodges. Nothing was wasted and so it took a long time and many people to achieve this.

As we waited, we heard gunshots in the distance. Leaving one of our number to greet the skinning and butchering party, the remainder, including Lupus, galloped towards the sound.

We came across five buffalo hunters who had used their Sharps rifles to kill thirty beasts in the few minutes it had taken us to find them. These rifles were single shot breech loading like my Martini Henry. Their effective range wasn't so great, but even in unskilled hands, their

.52 calibre bullet could down a beast at 500 yards. Although single shot, they could achieve up to ten shots a minute and, as they didn't chase them, the beasts tended to stand in circles with the bulls on the outside to protect the herd, which made them sitting targets.

When they saw us coming, the hunters mounted their horses and rode out to meet the four members of our party. From their attitude, it seemed they felt their greater number and superior armaments they could adopt an aggressive stance.

Their leader greeted us, 'What the fuck do you fucking savages want?' His associates chuckled.

'I'd like to reason with you,' I replied. He was momentarily taken aback by my perfect English, but recovered his composure.

'What the fuck has reason got to do with anything.'

'Let me explain,' I continued. 'These beasts and the Hoopa people,' I indicated my companions, 'Have lived in harmony for thousands of years. The Hoopas respect the natural world including the great beasts. Like the wolves that my dog resembles (I pointed at Lupus), they kill only what they require to meet their needs and use the whole of the carcass without any waste. In this way, the beasts and the Hoopas live in harmony. You kill indiscriminately and in great numbers. You take only the skins and leave the rest to rot. You have already depleted the beasts significantly and in a few years they will all be gone. The Hoopas will then die and you will have to find another way to make a living.'

'Very touching, but what's your fucking point.'

'My point is that, as you will have to find an alternative living shortly, you could do so now. You would lose nothing and the Hoopas and the beasts would continue to live as they have for thousands of years.'

The leader turned to his companions and they all laughed. The were cretins unable to listen to reason. Their only response was, 'You're breaking my fucking heart. I don't give a shit what happens to you, your filthy savages, or your fucking wolf dog and, while the beasts last, we'll make a fortune. If you don't mind, we'll carry on the way we are,' he finished sarcastically

Being rational was getting me nowhere. Trying to reason with the ignorant is like giving medicine to the dead: a complete waste of time. I narrowed my eyes and changed my tone. 'I'm afraid I do mind.'

My companions hadn't understood a word, but they recognised a change in the atmosphere and stiffened.

'And what the fuck will you do.' In his over confidence, he was playing to the gallery.

'I will give you a choice: drop your guns and leave or die here.'

They were becoming uneasy. Superficially, it was five men with guns against one man with guns and three with bows. They were asking themselves why I was so confident when we were at such a disadvantage. They looked to the horizon to see if we had reinforcements. When they looked back, they were staring down the barrel of my Colt.

Their expressions changed to surprise and fear. They lifted their hands above their heads and let go of their guns, which dropped to the ground. Lupus moved forward and growled at them, which destroyed the last vestiges of their bravado.

'Your ammunition belts and your saddle bags, too.'

They took off their belts and dropped them, together with their saddle bags, to the ground.

'Two days that way,' I pointed with my gun to the east, 'Is the Oza river. There are streams for water and grazing for your horses. You will have to go hungry. When you get home, pass the message that hunting is prohibited on our lands. Anyone caught hunting will be killed. Now go, you will be followed.'

They gathered up their reins and left in a hurry.

I turned to Broken Nose, 'Collect their things,' and then to Wind-in-the-Hair, 'Is there anything we can do with the beasts they killed?'

Wind-in-the-Hair blew his cheeks out, 'I have never known so many beasts killed at the same time. I will arrange for them to be skinned and butchered. If we dry the meat carefully, it may last.'

I was annoyed that the hunters had not been discovered by the scouts. It was my fault because I had given only vague instructions and it turned out that the scouting parties were simply following one another. I gave them search patterns to ensure the land was covered more effectively.

None too soon, because shortly after I received a report of a large number of Commancheros, who had entered our land from the west. I put together a party of one hundred and fifty warriors. Thirty five of them had guns, the others were armed with bows.

We set off towards their last known location, with scouts ranging ahead. They made contact with the scouting group that had first sighted the Commancheros. They, in turn, had carried out their instructions to the letter and had shadowed the Commancheros without being seen. This enabled us to set a trap.

Taking them completely by surprise, we cut them to pieces, killing forty five without suffering any losses ourselves. Five of them escaped. Although annoying at the time, it was probably a good thing because we were not troubled by Commancheros again. I think the message got through that the Hoopas were well organised and best left alone.

*

I was acutely aware that the major flaw in our defences was a lack of firepower. No matter how well organised, we needed guns to effectively oppose a serious invasion. I had not previously worried about how much he had left me, but I now had a use for Jake's money. Added to mine, I could at least increase our arsenal by a few guns and so I started to plan a shopping trip.

I had adopted the dress and style of the Hoopas and so I had to change my appearance if I was going to buy guns - no one would sell them to a 'filthy savage'. Firstly, my hair had not been cut for more than a year. Prairie Flower hacked it short with a sharp knife. It wasn't pretty and she laughed at my appearance, but it was good enough. I put together a set of clothes that approximated to something worn by men in 'civilised society' and set off with Lupus and Buck.

My journey took about a week because I had to find a town large enough to have a bank, a decent-sized gunsmith and a railway. I reckoned the last was needed as I doubted even the largest town gunsmith would carry the number of guns I needed and I didn't want to wait while they were hauled along trails in carts.

My first stop on reaching the town was the bank. I was still covered in trail dust when I presented myself at the counter and the clerk was a little sniffy. I gave him my name and account number and asked him to check my balance. He made a note and said that the information would be available the following day after they had time to telegraph their head office.

I then passed him Jake's will and asked him to let me know the balance on his account, too. He said he would let me have it back the following day. This was the only document that connected me to Jake and his money and I wasn't going to let it out of my possession. 'Just make a note of the name and account number. I'll keep the will.' He agreed reluctantly.

I had a day to kill, but I was no longer comfortable in towns, so I rode five miles out and made camp. I took the opportunity to dust myself down and wash in a convenient river. That night I bedded down in the open with Lupus and Buck, just like the old days.

Mid morning the following day, I went back to the bank. Seeing me walk in, the clerk I had seen before cut short the customer he was dealing with, got up from his desk and walked across the room to greet me. 'Oh, Mr Kidd, so good to see you again. The manager is expecting you and has asked me to take you to his office as soon as you arrive.'

Something had happened that had changed his manner from disinterested and condescending to deferential. His body language was telling me, 'Nothing is too much trouble.'

He led me to the back of the bank, knocked on an office door and took me in without waiting for an answer. He introduced me to the bald, portly man sitting the other side of a large desk, 'Mr Kidd, sir,' and left.

The manager struggled to his feet and waddled around the desk with his hand extended, 'So kind of you to come, Mr Kidd, I'm Phileas Hart, the manager.'

I took his hand and immediately regretted it as it was like holding a week old lettuce leaf. He gestured me to a chair in front of his desk, doddered back to his side and collapsed in his chair. 'We have the information you require, sir,' (respect of this kind was uncommon, but I could get used to it), 'but could I see Mr Cody's will first? Just a formality, you understand.'

I passed the document across the desk. He read it and passed it back, 'Yes, everything seems to be in order. Here are your balances.'

I picked up the first piece of paper offered and saw my account had the amount expected with the addition of a year's interest. It was an amount of money I could not have dreamt I might have when growing up. If Jake had a similar amount, I would be able to buy a good few guns. Jake didn't have anything like the same amount of money as me. He had about ten times more! My face obviously registered my surprise as the obsequious manager felt the need to explain. 'It would seem that Mr Cody deposited a very significant sum many years ago. I believe this was from the sale of a rather substantial property. Since then, there have been deposits without any withdrawals.'

Jake had never told the complete story of the years before I met him, but anyone could make a reasonable guess.

I was aware that the unpleasant little man was still droning on, '…. and substantial sums such as these can provide excellent returns if invested wisely. I am pleased to say that the bank is highly regarded in this sphere and I can assure you we would be proud to assist.'

I found it difficult not to sneer at his obsequious efforts to ingratiate himself, but decided alienating him at this stage would be counterproductive and so I said politely, 'I don't believe that will be necessary as I have earmarked these funds. Can you please confirm that, if I were to make a purchase, I would be able to transfer funds without withdrawing cash.'

'Most certainly, Mr Kidd. I can assure you the bank will assist in any way you wish.'

'Thank you. In the meantime, I would like to make a withdrawal.'

'By all means, Mr Kidd. I won't trouble you to go to the clerk in the bank hall, please complete this form and I will take it for you.'

He pushed a slip of paper across his desk. I completed it to withdraw the amount I guessed I would need. He scuttled out with it and came back a few minutes later with the money. 'Is there anything else, Mr Kidd.'

'Please arrange to transfer the balance from Mr Cody's account to mine.'

With a, 'Yes, sir,' he bustled out again.

He returned several minutes later with some papers. I read them through and, satisfied they made the transfer as required, signed them.

I then stood up, collected the slips with the balance and couldn't resist, 'Goodbye, Phineas, thank you for your help.'

Unfazed, he replied, 'Goodbye, Mr, Kidd,' and escorted me to the front door.

I laughed at the farcical performance as I walked into the gunsmith's and metaphorically picked him up from the floor after I asked him how long it would take to fulfil an order for 700 Winchester repeaters with 100,000 rounds of ammunition plus thee Martini Henry's with 200 rounds. When he asked me what they were for, I told him I had secured a contract to supply a small army across the border. It pleased me that he was satisfied with an honest answer, but no doubt made assumptions that were far from the truth.

We agreed a price, the inclusion of the requisite amount of oil and cleaning materials and he promised they would be with him within five days. He then became slightly embarrassed as he enquired, 'How would you like to pay?'

I showed him the official bank notes with balances in excess of the required amount and asked him, 'Would a bank transfer be okay?'

I used the five days to buy four wagons each with a team of two horses. I enquired at the livery stables where I could hire drivers and it was suggested I should ask for Slim Perkins at the saloon.

Slim was a tall, skinny man with a hawkish face. He recommended three others and called them over.

The first, who went by the name of Bronco, was six feet six inches tall with muscles bulging out all over. The second was a nondescript, stocky man called Brad who had the florid look of a drinker. The last, introduced as Michael, was a boy a year or two younger than me. He was finely built with dark, long lashes that made him look pretty. He looked unsuitable, but Slim assured me he was a fine driver.

I offered them a modest amount. They bridled and argued. I held up my hand for silence and said that was for the outward journey and that they would get the same amount for coming home. Their eyes lit up. I was hoping my generosity would buy some loyalty and ensure they worked well in expectation of a double pay for their three weeks' work. I arranged to meet them at the livery yard on the day of delivery to hitch up the wagons and take them to the rail yard.

The day the train was due with the shipment of rifles, it was pouring with rain. My team of drivers gathered in the livery yard soaked to the skin. They stood around waiting for instructions while Buck and Lupus watched from one of the stalls.

As I walked along the line giving them their initial payment, I said, 'All I expect is a good days work through to the end of the trail. In return, I will treat you with respect and honesty.'

Bronco, the giant, was last in the line. He took the money, turned and walked towards the door, 'All I expect is to take your money and go for a drink and there's fuck all you can do about it.'

It was apparent that he was used to getting his way by throwing his, not inconsiderable, weight about. He knew I could have shot him in the back, but, quite rightly, assumed I would not resort to cold blooded murder.

I didn't have to. I called, 'Lupus,' and pointed towards the retreating figure.

Within three bounds, Lupus was on him.

Big and heavy as he was, Bronco could not withstand the weight and speed of Lupus's attack as he hit him square on the shoulders and sent him sprawling in the mud and puddles. As he stood on his back growling with his fangs only inches from his spine, Bronco screamed, 'Get him off, please call him off …..'

I took my time to walk over to his prostrate figure.

Leaving Lupus on his back, I put my foot on Bronco's wrist and squatted down to remove the cash from his fist. Fortunately, it was clenched tight and so the money was largely dry. Putting my mouth close to Bronco's head I could hear just how ferocious Lupus sounded. 'Big mistake,' I shouted in Bronco's ear.

'I'm sorry, please call him off.' All his bullying

bravado had evaporated and was replaced by a whimpering coward. In all the rain, I couldn't see if he had wet his trousers, but I wouldn't have been surprised if he had.

'Do you want to live?' I asked

He nodded.

'Then listen carefully. When I tell him to get off, you will run as fast as you can as far away as you can get. If I see you again, I'll let him tear your throat out. Do you understand?'

He nodded so vigorously his face splashed in the puddle.

I stood up and called Lupus to me. Bronco jumped to his feet and ran away.

I sent Lupus back to the stall with Buck and looked at the others. They were line abreast, each with a look of horror etched on his face. Brad had pulled a bottle from his pocket and was taking large swigs. I walked along the line and took the bottle as I passed him.

Turning to face them, I said, 'I don't seem to have made myself clear. I have two rules, the first is that you fulfil our agreement and do a good day's work for a good days pay.'

I threw the bottle in the air, drew my Colt and shot it to smithereens as it reached the apex of the arc. Like the bottle, their nerves shattered and they all jumped at the sudden and unexpected noise.

'The second is, no alcohol while you work for me.'

I looked along the line. They nodded. 'Is that understood, Brad?'

239

He nodded.

'Okay,' I continued, 'If that's true, Brad, you can clear up that glass while I make arrangements to replace Bronco.'

I turned to Slim. 'Go, find someone who I can trust.'

I didn't like what seemed to be a gleam in his eye and so I went on, 'But it's a lawless place out there, so I'll hang on to your money until you get back.'

He passed his cash to me and left.

Slim returned about twenty minutes later with someone who looked like a sober version of Brad. He introduced him as Pete. I gave them each their money and told Slim to explain the terms of the contract. He did so to my satisfaction and so we got on with harnessing the horses to the wagons.

The rain had stopped by the time we were ready and had driven down to the rail yard. The train was on time and the crates were unloaded onto the ground. There were twenty Winchesters in each wooden crate, making thirty five crates of Winchesters. The Winchester rounds were in boxes of ten thousand each, making ten boxes. The Martini Henry's were wrapped in oily rags with their 200 rounds in a separate box and the ancillary items were in a box of their own.

We placed the ten Winchester crates onto each of the first three wagons with the remaining five and everything else onto the fourth. We loaded one wagon at a time. I stood on the wagon bed and opened each crate as it was loaded to check the contents before nailing it shut. After two hours, I was satisfied the order was complete and went to the bank, leaving my men to tie down the cargo with tarpaulins under Lupus's watchful gaze.

As soon as I walked into the bank with the gunsmith, the clerk who knew me left the customer he was helping and took us to the manager's office. Phineas stopped what he was doing and waddled around his desk to greet us. I explained that I needed to transfer money to the gunsmith's account and he sent the clerk to prepare the paperwork. He offered us coffee while we waited and made small talk.

The clerk returned and we completed the transaction.

As we left the office, Phineas and his clerk stood either side of the door as a sort of guard of honour and were almost pulling their forelocks.

I'd had enough. Their manner annoyed me more than I could say and so I turned on them, 'You are the most slimy toads I have ever met. When I arrived covered in dirt from the trail, you assumed I was a penniless drifter and treated me in a condescending, patronising and supercilious manner. When you realised I had money, you became sycophantic, greasy and tried to ingratiate yourselves to me. I can have nothing but contempt for someone who behaves in this way and suggest that, if you don't want to create the same impression again, you treat everyone with equal courtesy and respect. You are not better than the man who has just ridden in and the man with money is not impressed by false flattery.'

With that off my chest, I left them with their mouths open.

As we left the bank, the gunsmith said, 'I would

almost have completed our deal without payment just for the opportunity to see those smug bastards taken down like that.'

Everything was tied down when I got back to the wagons, so we set off.

With heavily laden wagons and saturated ground, the first leg of our journey was slow. We made better headway when the ground dried after a few days and established a good work pattern. I had no intention of getting close to the drivers and so I camped thirty to fifty paces away from them.

We drove out into the wilderness. After the first day, we didn't see another living soul. On the tenth day, we were skirting a wood. Up ahead we could see some riderless horses. As we got closer, we could see there were four and they were tethered to a tree.

'Okay, gentlemen,' I said, 'This is the end of your journey.'

They looked confused.

I rode along the wagons paying them the balance of their money.

'That's it, you have fulfilled your contract. Those horses are yours. Take as many provisions as you need from the wagon and go home.'

'But how are you going to cope from here?' enquired Slim. I had a feeling his question was prompted by curiosity rather than concern for me.

'That's no longer your worry, Slim. I'm perfectly happy with the arrangement. Just mount up and ride off.'

It was obvious I was not going to explain and so they

pulled from the wagon all the supplies they could carry, loaded them onto the horses and headed back. They went about fifty yards, stopped, gathered in a group, spoke for a while and then Slim came back. 'Truth is, we don't know where we are or how to get home.'

As a driver, he was embarrassed to admit this.

'Well, Slim, that's really your problem. These heavy wagons must have left quite a trail to follow and where they haven't, heading east won't take you far off course. I'm sure four upstanding fellows like you will manage.'

He wasn't entirely convinced, but joined the others and they set off together.

I watched them until they were out of sight.

A few minutes later, Broken Nose and nine other warriors appeared from the woods, six mounted and four on foot. I pointed in the direction the drivers had left, 'Make sure they haven't doubled back to see what is happening.'

Broken Nose nodded at one of the warriors, who set off after them, riding close to the woods so he could disappear when he caught sight of them.

Broken Nose and his party had been following us. They had been checking that my little column of wagons was not being followed while I led the drivers in an aimless meander around the wilderness so they had no idea where we were headed. He had come into my camp on several nights to update me. I was now certain that no one could possibly know that the guns were bound for the Hoopa nation. If anyone had guessed, they would almost certainly have tried to stop me. Our deception meant that we would be far better armed than anyone would expect.

The warrior returned to report that the drivers were travelling fast in what they hoped was the direction of home and seemed to have lost all interest in the wagons.

The four riderless warriors, who had given up their horses for the drivers, climbed up on the wagons and we headed for home.

My subterfuge would mean it would take at least ten days, which increased the chances of accidental interception, but Broken Nose and his warriors provided us with scouting cover and so we were unlikely to be surprised.

Our journey was without incident and, when we got back, there was a crowd waiting to greet us. The sight of so many guns was a novelty and there were many willing hands to help unload the wagons and store them in a lodge specially set aside for the purpose. There was no need to mount a guard, as the Hoopas did not steal from one another and no one else could gain entry.

Prairie Flower was amongst the crowd. As I saw her, the breeze caught her hair and pushed her dress against her body.

We didn't get around to eating that evening. As we lay in one another's arms, she said, 'When you came into my life, I thought I was as happy as I could be, but in six months I think I am going to be even happier.'

She smiled into my eyes and realisation hit.

10

Invasion

The following month was filled with organising the distribution of the Winchesters to the war parties. There were not quite enough to provide one for each warrior. For complete versatility and because they still had a use, all warriors carried a bow. Those with rifles carried ten arrows and a bandolier of ammunition. The few without rifles had twenty arrows and a spear.

No warrior was issued with a rifle until he was properly trained in its maintenance as well as firing. This was achieved by progressive delegation. The few who already had rifles trained the senior war leaders. They trained the remaining war leaders who, in turn, trained their warriors. As each teacher had ten pupils, the knowledge grew exponentially and so each warrior was a competent shot after a relatively short time. They were taught to fight together. To achieve the maximum field of fire and reduce the number of shots being taken at the same target, they fired from formations. To minimise waste and maximise effectiveness, they learnt to take controlled, aimed shots.

Training was refined by taking the war parties on

patrol and applying different ambush, attack and managed retreat tactics. We were preparing for the expected invasion. When it came, we were ready.

It was a day like many others. The sky was clear with just a few fluffy clouds. It was hot, but not unpleasantly so with a light breeze. It was morning and I was preparing Buck for a day's inspection, when I saw two young scouts galloping in. They had been ordered to take all reports to Wind-in-the-Hair. As they pulled up outside his lodge, he came out and I walked over. They were breathless, but the senior one was keen to do his job properly and to make his report in a complete and professional manner. 'War Chief,' he addressed Wind-in-the-Hair formally, 'I have to report an invasion. As best we could count, five hundred horse soldiers have crossed the Oza at the main ford and are travelling north west in a column. They are not coming in this direction and they have not as yet sent out scouts of their own. Running Otter and the other members of our scouting party are trailing them.'

Wind-in-the-Hair complimented him, 'An excellent report. How fast are they travelling?'

'They are not hurrying. I estimate they will achieve between twelve and fifteen miles a day.'

Wind-in-the-Hair turned to me and raised and eyebrow.

'We will take your war party and leave Running Deer here with his as reserve and as protection for our homes in case there are more following. In addition, my couriers and ten of the resting scout groups will come with us.

The others will remain under Running Deer's command.'

We were underway within two hours.

From the information provided, we headed for a point that would allow us to intercept the invaders. However, we didn't want to run into them unexpectedly, so I put a screen of outriders ahead and to both sides at all times with orders to report at regular intervals.

Three hours after we had set off, all the scouts to our front galloped back. Their leader reported, 'Kraspa, the horse soldiers are two miles ahead. They are still moving north west, which is diagonal to your line of march.'

I called to Wind-in-the-Hair, 'I am going to reconnoitre. Stay back out of sight until you hear from me.'

I galloped off with the scouts. They guided me to a rocky outcrop. From there, I could look down on a vast expanse of open grassland. The grass was quite thick and about waist high. There were no other rock outcrops in sight and there were no trails through the grass and so the soldiers were having to push their way through.

It was a clear day and so I had a perfect view from my hiding place. They were a mounted column, each man armed with a rifle. Six wagons carried their supplies. There was no sign that they had sent out scouts and neither was it apparent why they were headed north west. As I watched, their leader called for them to halt and they started to make camp.

The soldiers busied themselves. Firstly, they used the wagons to create a rectangle about one hundred paces by two hundred paces with two wagons along each of the long sides and one along each of the short sides. It was neat and regimental, but made the wagons more difficult to guard. They then set a wider perimeter of pickets and pitched their tents in the rectangle.

I had seen enough. Leaving four scouts with strict instructions to stay hidden and to report any changes, I rode back to Wind-in-the-Hair and set out my plan.

The night was moonless and dark. I took fifty warriors back to the rocky outcrop.

The scouts reported that there had been little change. The camp had settled down for the night. The pickets did not seem to be taking their duties very seriously. They had not been inspected by an officer, some were gathering to talk and some had laid down to sleep. I told my men to remain there and, together with Lupus, crept down onto the grassland.

At the foot of the outcrop, I crouched enough to see along the top of the grass. This put the nearest guards and wagons in silhouette against the sky. Having established their bearings, I dropped to my front and started crawling.

The pickets were pretty static and I was able to avoid them completely. When we arrived at the nearest wagon, Lupus and I crawled underneath. Depending on Lupus to keep a watch, I took my knife from its sheath and started to shave away the inside of one of the wheel spokes.

I had only just started when Lupus's low growl warned me and I stopped work. I heard the voices of two men as they approached. When they got to the wagon, they stopped and the wagon lurched slightly as they leaned against it. I heard the clink of glass and the smelled alcohol.

'What's the colonel's plan?' one of them asked.

'Don't think he has a plan and don't think he needs one,' replied the other. 'These stinking savages have no guns and only one strategy and that's to shoot some arrows and then to charge us with their spears. All we have to do is wander around until they see us and then shoot them to pieces as the mad bastards throw themselves at us.'

Now I knew why they were so badly led and unprepared. They had made the elementary mistake of underestimating their enemy. Even so, I needed to be careful because it would not go well for me if I was caught.

Suddenly, one sat down and rested his back against the wheel I had been working on. Deciding this was a good idea, the other joined him. Lupus and I were just a couple of feet from their backs. Dark as it was, all they had to do was turn and we would be discovered. I held my knife ready to strike if either of them should turn. It would have to go for their throats to silence them and my strike would be impeded by the wheel spokes. Even if I silenced the first one, the second would probably raise the alarm before I could get to him.

Time passed slowly as they chatted idly and drank. They finished their bottle and tossed it aside. 'Best get back to our posts. It's a waste of time because I don't suppose there's a savage within a hundred miles, but there'll be hell to pay if we're found here.'

They got up, stretched and sidled off. I let out a long, slow breath and got back to my whittling.

It took me about two hours. When I had finished, I had whittled the inside of two spokes down to a fraction of their original thickness. All the wood had been taken from the inside, from the outside they looked like the others.

I spread the shavings out so they were difficult to see before Lupus and I crawled back to the others at the rocky outcrop. I gave fresh orders and, leaving the scouts there, I took the fifty warriors down to the grassland. They spread out in a line about fifty paces from the wagon with the doctored wheel, silently dug themselves shallow scrapes, lowered themselves in, covered themselves with soil and waited. Our low profile, the long grass and the covering of soil meant they would probably tread on us before they saw us.

Camp fires were re-ignited at dawn. The soldiers' camp came to life as they ate their breakfasts, saddled their horses and harnessed the wagons.

The wheel on my doctored wagon broke very shortly after it started to move. Both the shaved spokes broke causing the wheel to collapse as the remaining spokes couldn't take the strain. An officer came over and shouted at the driver as though it was his fault. He told him to replace the wheel and catch up with the column at the next camp, leaving nine others to help.

As the column pulled out, the men left behind started to unload the wagon.

As soon as the column was out of sight, they stopped. Like so many 'workers', they saw the absence of supervision as a chance for a rest and just sat around smoking and talking.

The driver became agitated and so they set to and finished unloading.

As soon as it was empty, the nine men lifted the wagon for the driver to remove the broken wheel and replace it with a new one.

They then reloaded the wagon, the driver climbed on board, the others mounted their horses and we attacked.

The signal to attack was my shot, which killed the driver. It was immediately followed by two volleys. One hundred bullets aimed at nine men at fifty paces equals no survivors.

The warriors ran forwarded. One of them climbed on the wagon and drove it away immediately. The others caught the horses and stripped the dead bodies of their guns and ammunition. Nine of them mounted the horses and rode off.

At that point, another two hundred warriors ran out from behind the rocky outcrop. I had left instructions that they should be collected from Wind-in-the-Hair's party and were to join me after we had taken the wagon.

I positioned the warriors fifty paces back and either side of the track the soldiers had made through the grass as they left the campsite. They dug themselves in as before.

An hour later, two of the scouts who had been following the column galloped in to tell me that, when they heard the shooting, the soldiers had halted the column and held a meeting. They then split the column, sending two hundred soldiers back while the remaining three hundred continued.

This level of stupidity was completely unexpected. Why would an already small number split its force in this way? I had expected they would all return and intended to hit and run before they could retaliate, but we were now equally matched in numbers and we had the distinct advantage of surprise and concealment.

After a wait of another hour, the column of two hundred cantered into view. They came up to the dead bodies of their comrades and stopped, retaining their formation. I commenced firing immediately.

It was not a battle, it was a slaughter.

The first volley of two hundred bullets was aimed at stationery targets in a row and emptied more than one hundred saddles. The others ran backwards and forwards trying to find a way out. I had arranged for both the front and back doors to be closed and so, whichever way they tried to flee, they ran into a hail of bullets. It was all over within two minutes.

Half the warriors formed a screen in case the remaining soldiers returned The rest went amongst the soldiers making sure they were dead and removing their weapons.

We then mounted their horses (they had obligingly brought exactly the right number) and returned to Wind-in-the-Hair's camp.

Our scouts reported that the main party had stopped

when they heard the shooting. They had waited, apparently expecting their victorious colleagues, or at least a significant number of survivors to return. When they didn't, they made camp.

Certain that there were no other hostile forces in the area and that the present one no longer represented a serious threat, I sent word back to the lodges that all the remaining warriors and anyone else able to ride was to assemble at Wind-in-the-Hair's camp. If they didn't have guns or spears, they were to carry staffs that, at least from a distance, would look like weapons.

I assumed the only logical course of action for the soldier's commander was to retrace his steps. This would keep his remaining soldiers in one force, would allow him to discover what had happened to his other party and, if he had to retreat, he would be on his way.

Early the following morning, my scouts reported that the column was returning. I placed my much enhanced force in a large semi circle around the previous day's battle sight, but just too far to be seen. Wind-in-the-Hair, my couriers and I waited at the rocky outcrop.

We didn't have to wait long. The column approached slowly, the front stopping when they saw the bodies of their comrades. I moved to the top of the outcrop where I could be seen by the soldiers and my warriors and fired once into the air. The soldiers milled about in confusion and stopped in horror as they saw what looked like an army of thousands of well armed warriors approaching from their front and sides. My people stopped at a distance so that this illusion could be maintained. It was an imposing and frightening sight. My entourage came from behind of the rocky outcrop and rode under a white flag of truce towards the soldiers. When we got to the front of the column, I took stock of the man at the front, who I assumed was their leader.

About my age, he was wearing a smart, blue uniform with epaulettes, which I assumed indicated a senior rank. He was sweating profusely and was ashen. I addressed him directly, 'I am Sky-in-the-Eye war chief of the Kikatchi Hoopas. You are invaders. I have sent warning that invaders will be destroyed, but you have ignored my warning.'

He was apparently surprised at my fluent English and seemed unable to reply.

I continued, 'As you can see,' I spread my arms in an arc to indicate the 'army' around is, 'We are a very powerful people with many skilled warriors. We have already killed half your number without suffering a single casualty. Can you give me a reason why we should not now kill you all?'

Their officer was scared, but he was intelligent and hadn't entirely lost the ability to think, 'No, sir,' he was ingratiating himself, 'I cannot think of a reason, but I suspect you may have one because you have approached us under a flag of truce. If you intended to kill us you would have done so.'

I smiled and nodded my acknowledgment of his perspicacity. 'I have two reasons: the first is that I want to demonstrate that the Hoopas are not savages and can show mercy. The second is that I have a message for you to take to your leaders. Would you like to hear my terms?'

He nodded.

'You will all dismount and leave all your belongings here. You will walk back to the Oza river. You will be escorted at a distance. You will camp each night near water by which we will leave you food. Provided you stick to these rules, you will not be molested and will be allowed to return to your own lands.'

'How can we trust you? How do we know you will not slaughter us the moment we put down our weapons.'

'Only a man who was raised in your land could ask such a question,' My reply was indignant and haughty. 'The Hoopas are men of honour and my word is my bond and this is my word:

Walk away leaving your belongings here and you will live.

Stay or try to leave with your guns and you will die.

That is my word.'

He took a deep breath and acknowledged, 'I suppose you could kill us anyway and so at least we have a chance by taking your word. I accept.'

With that he gave the order to dismount and remove all their guns, ammunition and other belongings and prepare to leave on foot.

'You will also take this message,' I nodded at Broken Nose. He rode up to the dismounted officer and passed him an envelope. 'Read it out loud,' I commanded.

He opened the letter and read:

'The land of the Hoopas extends from The White Top

Mountains in the north to the Great Forest on the south, from the Oza river in the east to the Inda river in the west.

Travellers may cross our land, but they may only camp overnight. They may not settle. Anyone trying to settle will be moved on.

Traders may enter our land to trade, but they may not settle and may not trade in alcohol. A trader trying to settle will be moved on and may not return. A trader with alcohol will have it confiscated and may not return.

No outsider may hunt on the land. Anyone caught hunting will be executed.

Any further attempts at military incursion will be opposed with the full might of our army and the invaders will be eliminated.'

'Do you understand?' I asked.

He nodded.

'Will you take this message to your leaders and make sure they understand?'

He nodded.

'You may go.'

My party and I moved to the side to let them pass. The 'warriors' in my 'army' saw we were letting them leave and dispersed. To the soldiers, it looked as though they had melted into the countryside.

They trudged home escorted at a distance by two scouting parties at all times. True to our word, we placed food by water sources for each night's camp. A very foot weary, but relieved, group of soldiers eventually forded the Oza.

The mood amongst the Hoopas was jubilant We had

defeated the invaders without suffering a casualty. The captured weapons and ammunition, carried by the soldiers and the wagons, more than doubled our arsenal. We could arm all the warriors with rifles and have some in reserve.

*

Our reputation spread beyond our lands. Young men from the neighbouring Siskate clan wanted to join us as warriors. We were able to integrate them into our existing war parties to begin with, but the trickle turned into a flood. Some brought their families. The senior chiefs were concerned that we might be overwhelmed as our way of life required a lot of land. We needed to find a compromise. We sent word to the chiefs of the Siskate that we could accept a further six hundred men of warrior age, but not their families. The warriors would be given leave to return to their families at regular intervals. In return, we would defend them if they were attacked.

This was accepted.

Most of the new warriors were young and wanted adventure and were not yet concerned about domestic life. We were able to form a third, fully armed and trained war party, bringing our warrior numbers up to fifteen hundred.

11

Loss

I was in my mid twenties, I was the war chief of a powerful clan, my hair had grown and so, apart from my blue eyes, I looked one of the clan. I had a beautiful wife who had just given me a son, who we named Spirit of Asuka. My days were spent at my duties to the clan and the army and my nights with my family. Life was pretty much perfect.

Since my early teens, Lupus had been my constant companion and my life with the Kikatchi had not changed this. As part of my family, he lived with us in our lodge and was always ready to accompany me when I left. One day, he was slow to get up. I called him and he followed. I didn't think any more of it at the time, but, over the next few months, he lost a considerable amount of weight. I tried feeding him more, but this made no difference.

One morning, he wasn't there. He must have wandered off during the night. Extensive searches didn't find him, but he came home a few days later.

I was sitting outside the lodge one morning when he crawled up to me. He had lost even more weight and couldn't stand properly. He whined and laid his head on my lap. I stroked his head I ran my hand across his back and his tummy. I could feel large lumps. He whimpered when I touched them. He had growths that were causing him excruciating pain. I was faced with a terrible dilemma.

Here was my most loyal friend.

He would have died for me and had saved my life several times.

Life without him was unimaginable.

I looked down at his big, beautiful head. His deep brown eyes were fixed on me. He always looked at me like that when he wanted something. He was pleading with me to do something. I was helpless, totally useless. My best friend needed my help and I could not make him better. There was only one way I could take his pain away and I didn't know if I had the courage to do it. I knew I could ask someone else, but that would be letting Lupus down. I couldn't do that at his moment of greatest need.

I laid his head on the ground and stood up.

He turned so he could see me.

I took my pistol from the holster.

I couldn't see him properly because my eyes had misted over. I wiped them with my left hand to clear my sight and squatted down to stroke his head. 'I'm sorry my old friend,' my words were catching in my throat and I could barely speak, 'I don't want to say goodbye.'

He just kept his eyes on me. He seemed to be so wise and was saying, 'It's okay, Jimmy, I have always trusted you and I trust you now. You won't let me down. I know you will do the right thing.'

I stood up, raised the hammer, put my gun close to his head and pulled the trigger.

He died instantly.

I was overcome and fell to my knees.

Prairie Flower came from our lodge and put her arms around my shoulders. A number of people gathered around. I stood and turned to Prairie Flower. She wiped my tears away and said simply, 'I understand.'

I replaced my pistol and picked him up.

I carried him to where Buck was grazing and laid him on the ground as I saddled Buck.

As I did so, Buck nuzzled Lupus saying his own goodbyes.

I lifted Lupus and climbed into the saddle. It was a struggle, but I wanted to do this by myself. I turned Buck and we wandered off into the grasslands.

I found a remote spot with high, rock outcrop. I carried Lupus to the top and laid his body on a large, flat rock. It was his own, special sky burial. I knelt close to him stroking his side and sobbing.

Buck had followed us to the top and stood with his head on my shoulder saying his own goodbyes.

My words spilled out, 'Goodbye, Lupus, I will miss you more than I can say. I know dogs live much shorter lives and that the pain I feel at your loss is the price I pay for the joy you brought and the love I have for you. I may have taken you for granted sometimes, but I think you had a good life and I hope you think so too. I will now leave you to complete the cycle of life. Goodbye, Lupus, and thank you.'

I mounted Buck and rode off into the wilderness.

Days later, I rode into Smalltown. It had changed very little. The livery yard was there. The sheriff's office seemed to be closed. There were a few people going about their business, but no one took any notice of me.

I left Buck by the hitching rail and went into the saloon.

It was mid afternoon and the place was deserted apart from a chubby, dark haired girl behind the bar. I thought Josie may have moved on and she was her replacement, but I thought I might see Carl. She was pleasant and friendly as she asked if she could get me anything. For old time's sake, I ordered steak, beans and coffee.

She suggested I sat at a table and said she would bring the food over when she had cooked it.

I asked for a glass of water and took it to a table at the back of the room immediately opposite the door.

She brought me my food and coffee.

I was half way through the meal when Carl appeared behind the bar. He scanned the room, saw a Hoopa was his only customer and got on with polishing glasses.

I had finished eating and was drinking my coffee when a stocky, angry looking man burst into the room. He strode up, stood opposite my table and launched into the predictable tirade, 'We don't want you fucking filthy savages here. Fuck off out of it or I'll kick your arse from here to kingdom come.'

As I stood and lifted my head to look at him, my hair

fell from my face.

Carl recognised me, 'Jimmy Kidd!'

The stocky man looked less confident. 'Are you sure, Carl.'

'Sure as I am it's you, Grouty.'

'If I draw on him, he'll probably kill me.'

'No, Grouty, if you draw on him, he will definitely kill you.'

Grouty raised his hands with his palms facing me, partly to show he wasn't holding a gun and partly as a gesture of holding me back. 'I'm sorry, Mr. Kidd, my mistake.' He was backtracking fast. 'I can see now, you are no more a filthy savage than I am. I expect you've just had a long journey. You have as much right to be here as me.' Still holding his hands out, he backed up to the door and, as soon as he was outside, scuttled off.

I picked up my coffee, moved two tables to my right and sat down.

A minute later, the door crashed open. Grouty burst in with his gun in his hand and emptied it into the space I had been occupying when he left. As his eyes became accustomed to the gloom, he saw I wasn't there and pulled bullets from his belt to reload.

My chair scraped the floor as I stood up, which attracted his attention.

He turned to his left, saw me walking towards him and became so flustered he dropped his gun and bullets.

Carl was still polishing glasses, 'Thought you'd make a name for yourself as the man who killed Jimmy Kidd. Big mistake, Grouty.'

Grouty started to grovel, 'Yes, that's right, Mr Kidd, my mistake again. You know I'm sorry, don't you? I haven't got a gun. You won't shoot me, will you?'

I stood in front of him and shook my head.

His relief was palpable.

My left arm shot out like a ramrod and the heel of my hand hit him in the nose.

He dropped like a stone and I walked over to the bar.

'It's been a long time, Jimmy,' Carl felt the need to say something, 'Where have you been?'

'Out in the prairies, mostly.'

'What brings you here now?'

'Lupus died and I had a yearning to see the old place.'

'Sorry to hear that, he was a great dog. Have you seen it?'

'I went out to the homestead, but it's sad and derelict. It was a mistake to go.'

'Old Mr Schmidt's brother couldn't make a go of it. He sold the stock a few months after you left and went back to where he came from.'

Relaxing and feeling a little emboldened, he went on, 'You've changed, Jimmy. A bit older, but with your hair and clothes, you can almost understand old Grouty's mistake. If it wasn't for those sky blue ....' His voice trailed off as realisation dawned. 'You're that Sky-in-the-Eye. Been on the plains. You led the filth ....'

'Filthy savages,' I finished his sentence. 'I've lived with the Kikatchi Hoopas for years and so I know we are cleaner than most people around here. We are savage only when attacked and have to protect our homes and families. At other times, we are loving caring, honest, honourable and noble.'

I knew I was in the wrong place and turned to leave.

As I walked by the prostrate form of Grouty, Carl tried to redeem himself, 'Grouty got what he deserved. You must have hit him pretty hard, he hasn't moved.'

I looked down at the body, but didn't tell Carl he was dead. I'd pushed the cartilage and bone from his nose into his brain. He had died instantly. He was the sort of man who would hide in an upstairs window, in a dark alley or behind a rock to put a bullet in my back. I'd given him one chance, I couldn't give him another. I was completely justified, but I didn't tell Carl because I didn't want to waste time explaining myself. I just raised a hand in a wave goodbye.

I went outside, mounted Buck and rode out of Smalltown for the last time. We were going home.

When I got home, I went to my lodge immediately after I had unsaddled Buck. Prairie Flower was outside feeding Spirit of Asuka. She looked so beautiful and serene as she got up to greet me. I took them in my arms. I wanted to explain that they were more important to me than anything, that my need to be alone during the first few days of mourning Lupus did not change the way I felt about them and that I would never leave them. As I opened my mouth, she put her finger to her lips and smiled, 'I understand.'

Nine months later our second son, Spirit of Tor, was born.

Although the pain faded, I did not ever entirely come

to terms with the loss of Lupus. I would instinctively look for him as I left the lodge, make sure I didn't catch him with my foot as I mounted Buck, depend on him to guard when I camped, and a myriad other things that had become habitual to the boy who had grown up with his friend the wolf.

*

For nearly two years there was peace. We had the occasional brave souls who travelled across our land without incident and some industrious merchants willing to trade, but there was no suggestion of aggression from outside. I believed the lesson we had taught the horse soldiers had been well learnt and that maintaining the cutting edge of our training and vigilance would be sufficient to deter further incursions.

I was wrong!

As before, the warning was delivered by two scouts who galloped up to Wind-in-the-Hair's lodge. I had an uncomfortable feeling as I walked over to listen to their report - they were from a local scouting party. First warning should have come from an outer scouting party.

'Two thousand soldiers marching directly for us and about two days march away. They have Fahka scouts.'

The Fahkas were sworn enemies of the Hoopas. They had not caused trouble since I had been with the Hoopas, but they had obviously seen this invasion as a chance to gain a victory.

Being two days from us meant they had been on our land for at least two days before they were sighted. The major questions were, 'How had they managed to approach so close without us seeing them and how did they know where we were?' These would have to wait; we had to respond to the immediate threat. I called a meeting of the chiefs and, while they assembled, I considered our options.

When they had gathered, I advised them of our predicament and went on, 'It would seem that the Fahkas have been able to bypass our outer scouts and have discovered our encampments. They are now leading two thousand soldiers directly towards us. Our first priority is to safeguard our people. We will then have to find a way of neutralising the Fahkas before we can deal with the soldiers. We must break camp now and go south. Raging Bull will oversee the movement of our people, I will take the resting scouts and two hundred warriors under Broken Nose, Wind-in-the-Hair will take charge of the army in my absence to protect the people.'

Within two hours, the lodges had been dismantled and loaded for travel. Nearly three thousand people were heading south.

I used that time to brief my party.

'We must expect the Fahkas to be watching us and to inform the soldiers that our people are on the move. They will change direction to cut us off. At present, they are travelling west. We are going south and so they will head west-south-west to intercept us. The Fahka scouts will be trailing us to report any change in direction. When night falls, we will head out to find them and neutralise them. As we leave, our people will turn around and march north during the night. If we kill the Fahka scouts, the soldiers will not know of this change in direction.'

We travelled the remainder of the day and stopped at dusk. The night was clear with the moon in its first quarter, making it possible to travel, but nothing like as bright as a full moon.

As soon as it was dark, the main group about faced and headed north. The two hundred warriors and fifty scouts in my party remained concealed. We waited about thirty minutes before heading east. We expected the Fahkas to be following the main group and hoped to outflank them. We had to ride at a speed that was fast enough to catch them, but not so fast that we would run into them and scare them off. I sent out three scouting parties of ten each, one obliquely to our left, one obliquely to our right and one directly ahead. I also sent a party of fifty warriors east-north-east to intercept any scouts who might have been sent to report our change of direction to the army.

We were in grassland that comprised the majority of our land. The grass was long and it was dotted with occasional rocky outcrops and small woods. Visibility was good enough for us to ride without risk of tripping or stepping into holes, but we could not see far.

After about an hour, the front scouting group returned. 'There is a group of thirty Fahkas about half a mile ahead, Kraspa,' their leader reported. 'They are following our main group, as expected.'

I needed to get them all and so I would have to encircle them.

I sent Broken Nose with fifty warriors off in an arc to the left to get around the Fahkas so they could approach them from the front. He would have to risk a fast gallop in poor light, but there was no alternative.

I sent another fifty to the right, but ordered them to stay abreast of my party; their responsibility was to mop up any Fahkas who managed to escape the main attack.

I arranged the remaining fifty warriors line abreast with the scouts behind.

We proceeded at a pace that would allow Broken Nose to get into place, but would enable us to catch the Fahkas.

They were nearly half a mile ahead when we spotted them. We all dropped our reins, I drew my Colts and the warriors raised their Winchesters. At that moment, the rearmost Fahka must have heard us because he turned, saw us and shouted to his comrades.

They broke into a gallop in an effort to escape us.

We increased our pace to catch up.

We had only been chasing them for a minute when Broken Nose's party appeared in front of them and slightly to their left. They wheeled to their right and galloped away from Broken Nose. They were travelling diagonally across us and ran slap into the fifty warriors I had placed on my right whose first volley decimated them.

Not wishing to run head on into such fire power, they pulled up, which made them sitting ducks.

I replaced my Colts, drew my Winchester and joined my warriors in shooting them down.

They were brave and did not try to surrender.

There was no roar of repeated volleys, there was just the regular crack of aimed shots as our horses stood and we picked off the Fahkas.

Some of them charged us, but they were not prepared for battle and we shot them down.

It was all over within a couple of minutes.

I sent half the scouts to find the soldiers with orders to link up with the scouts already trailing them. They were to let me know if the soldiers changed direction or if they continued as though we were still heading south.

We loaded the Fahka bodies onto their horses and thirty of my warriors led them back south. They placed them where they would have been if they had been trailing us south. The rest of us went to catch up with our people.

Our main group walked throughout the night and the following day.

Two Fahka scouts had been intercepted, which suggested they had not been able to report our change of direction. This was confirmed when we learned that the soldiers had maintained their line of march. Our subterfuge had worked. We had bought some time, but we were still in real danger.

Over the next few days, I was able to form a picture of what had happened.

Our scouts found our outer scouting parties. They had been ambushed and killed without exception. Our only consolation was that the main objective was to prevent any of them escaping to warn us and so they had been killed immediately rather than captured and tortured. The Fahkas must have been observing from the other side of the river and had ambushed them shortly after they had started their shift. We assumed this because it would give them the maximum amount of time before they were to be relieved and so the report of their arrival would be delayed. This suggested very careful planning and organisation.

It was estimated that there were a further twenty Fahka scouts. They represented our greatest threat because they were the army's eyes that could enable them to focus their attention on our weakest points.

I had been in danger before and I had been scared before, but I had never been as angry as I was at that moment. My anger was largely centred on the fact that these people threatened my wife and children. I was also annoyed that they should be a threat to the people of the clan I cared for and respected. We did not represent a threat to them, we just asked that they leave us to follow our way of life. I had travelled extensively and knew there were vast open spaces that were more than enough for others and could not understand why they should go to such lengths to prevent us from leading our lives peaceably on what was, in the overall scheme, a small piece of land.

I also realised I had made a mistake. I had thought that by letting the survivors of the previous invasion return safely, the authorities would understand that we did not want to kill for its own sake. I had hoped my message would prove that we had no aspirations outside our land, that we were accepting of other peoples' culture and asked for nothing more than the same in return. I was naive because they had seen it as a sign of weakness and had not taken my message as intended, but had used the information the survivors had provided as intelligence on which they could base their plan for a further invasion. This meant they presented a much more intractable problem.

They had three key strengths:

1. The Fahkas were able to provide them with information. If they found us, they could direct the soldiers to our settlements. Furthermore, their scouting parties would make it difficult for us to lay ambushes.

2. They seemed to be well led.

3. They outnumbered us.

Against that, our strengths were:

1. We had more scouts who had a far more intimate knowledge of the land.

2. We were well prepared and were fighting for our survival.

Using advantage 1, our scouts become adept at keeping the soldiers under observation while avoiding the Fahkas. We made every effort to maintain the illusion that our new site was south of our original position while we consolidated our homes in a secluded pocket in the far north.

We started to harry them with guerrilla tactics. To begin with, we were able to isolate some of their night guards and leave them with their throats slit. We hoped to undermine their morale, but they responded by reducing the spacing between pickets and having four men at each guard point and so we had to discontinue this.

We mounted a couple of lightning raids on the rear of their column and were able to kill a several soldiers for far fewer casualties of our own, but they strengthened their rear guard, which brought this to a halt, too.

The problem we had was that time was on their side. They had plenty of supplies, which they could supplement by foraging and it was only a matter of time before they located our settlement. We might be able to move again, but we couldn't depend on that. If they attacked our settlements, we would have to defend them, which would result in the sort of conventional battle that we had to avoid as this would be fighting to their strengths and we simply could not withstand the casualties that such a battle would inevitably entail.

By killing more than a half of their scouts, we had reduced their effectiveness, as they could not afford to venture too far from the main body of soldiers. However, they were still a threat as they were difficult to pin down and could provide vital information. We had to isolate them and then eliminate them without attracting the attention of the army and pulling down its full force before we had time to escape. For their security, the twenty survivors tended to remain within hailing distance of one another and mainly acted as a forward scouting party. Although they would take occasional forays on the flanks, their normal position was in an arc about a mile ahead of the main force. They could then warn the army of any traps or ambushes.

One day, my scouts reported that, unless they changed direction, the soldiers' line of march was going to take them through two rocky outcrops. Being only about a quarter of a mile long and of sufficient width to allow a column to pass through without breaking formation. They did not represent a good location to ambush the army but they had a bend to the right, that meant it was impossible to see along the whole length from the entrance. So, if we could lure the Fahkas in ahead of the main column, we might be able to reduce their numbers.

I took fifty warriors. We approached the outcrop from an angle that hid us from the army and took up position. We could see the army approaching with the Fahkas providing their normal frontal screen. Half a dozen broke formation and galloped up and stopped at the entrance. They cautiously walked around the bend, looked at the exit and made a quick retreat. They galloped back to the column to make their report. An officer waved in the direction of the outcrop and all thirty of the Fahkas galloped in a group back towards us. They formed up line astern as they entered the gap and proceeded with some caution between the two outcrops.

As soon as the last one had passed the bend, we attacked. We used bows because the soldiers were now less than half a mile away, but there were fifty warriors loosing arrows at the rate of ten a minute against only twenty. Two hundred and fifty arrows in the thirty seconds before we sprinted for our horses. The bodies the soldiers found looked like a group of porcupine.

The monster was now short sighted, but far from blind and still extremely dangerous. Time to cut off its head.

We observed them for days on end trying to find a weakness. They were extremely well organised, if a little too regimented. They habitually travelled in four columns of five hundred men in each column. The second was behind and about fifty paces to the right of the first, the third was behind the second and fifty paces to its left, the fourth behind and fifty paces to the right of the third. After the loss of the Fahkas, they had nominated fifty of their own number to act as a screen travelling a quarter of a mile ahead and fanning out a quarter of a mile to each side of the marching columns. This formation and their sheer number made it impossible for us to lay ambushes in the grassland in the way we had for the previous invaders.

We watched and bided our time.

By keeping clear of the wooded areas, they made ambushing them very difficult. We discontinued our harassing attacks because the casualties we were able to inflict did not justify the casualties we incurred. We also hoped they might lower their guard a little.

One day, our scouts reported that their line of march was taking them towards one of the largest rock outcrops in our land. It looked as though they were heading for it days before they arrived and we laid our plans on the basis they would not change direction. We had done this before, but our planned ambush had to be aborted when they changed from the anticipated direction.

I left one war party of five hundred warriors to guard our encampment in case something went wrong and took the other two, comprising one thousand warriors.

In addition to me, we had three snipers each practised in using the Martini Henry. The four of us were on the top of the large outcrop as the soldiers approached in their usual formation. We allowed their scout screen to get within a quarter of a mile, which put the front of the main body half a mile from us. At this point, we commenced firing.

Our aim was to kill their senior officers in the first instance, effectively removing the monster's head. They were leading the first column. At half a mile range, we each aimed at our designated targets and shot.

Four officers went down.

Little happened in the first few seconds as we reloaded and shot again, taking down the next four.

The first response was for the flanking scouts to turn and gallop back to the main body. As they did so, we took down four of their number.

The leaderless soldiers lost their cohesion and started to mill around in their columns. It became apparent that there was one individual who was not panicking as he rallied the first column, got them to draw swords and then to charge straight for us. I think he was assuming that, as we had only fired four guns, we were few in number and he would be able to rout us.

They came up very fast, the earth shaking as they thundered towards us. As they closed the gap, we four snipers brought down a few, but we made little impression on the five hundred. When they were three hundred paces from the outcrop, the two hundred warriors who had been lying in the grass immediately in front of the outcrop, rose to their knees and the thunder of the charging horses hooves was drowned out as they opened up with their Winchesters.

Although they were outnumbered, the warriors were in line abreast and so they could all fire upon the charging soldiers. The soldiers were in a column only five wide, at the very best, only five could return fire. Their plight was even more precarious, as they had drawn swords in preparation for running us down and so they had to scabbard their swords and pull out their rifles before they could fire. This slowed them, making the remorseless fire from two hundred Winchesters even more effective.

My warriors' training meant their shooting was controlled with only aimed shots, but, even so, they were firing at the rate of twelve rounds a minute, which meant that the soldiers had been hit by one thousand two hundred bullets within thirty seconds. This more than halved their number. The survivors paused for a moment to fire one ragged volley before turning to gallop back to the main body.

As they did so, four hundred mounted warriors led by Broken Nose charged from behind the right side of the outcrop in line astern, they overhauled the retreating soldiers and rode alongside them pouring fire into them like the broadside from a ship. They continued down the length of the main body emptying their guns before peeling off to the right to reload, go around in semicircle and then repeat the manoeuvre.

As the four hundred led by Broken Nose broke cover to the right, a further four hundred warriors led by Running Deer charged from the left of the outcrop. They did not mirror the attack made by their comrades on the right for fear of shooting one another. Instead, they rode in a wide arc taking them past the soldiers. As they reached a point in line with the back of the rear column, they wheeled right and then right again to ride along the flank of what had been four perfectly formed columns, but was now a rabble. As they reached the front, they peeled off to their right to repeat the procedure.

From my vantage point on the rocky outcrop, I could see my warriors taking it in turns to ride along each flank of the milling soldiers. I could see the smoke puffs from rifle barrels and the delayed sound of cracks carried to me as they kept their formation line astern and poured fire into the soldiers.

The soldiers had one exceptional leader. He convinced about one hundred of his colleagues immediately around him to dismount and return fire. They now presented smaller targets and were able to take careful aim as my warriors rode by them. I saw several warriors fall as this tactic paid dividends.

My strategy depended on us taking out their officers so that they were leaderless when attacked. I had not allowed for a resourceful, courageous individual from the ranks. In the chaos of battle, he had recognised that

277

the threat was coming alternately from one side and then the other and that he could, therefore, direct their fire on one side and then turn to concentrate it on the other, confident in the knowledge their backs were safe. He had his men kneeling in a single line to fire one way. He would then get them to about face to deal with the next wave of warriors from the other flank. When he was sure the men he had rallied in the first instance understood what was required of them, he ran towards the main body of soldiers who were still milling around in a rabble. If he was allowed to rally the thousand or more in the same way as he had the first hundred, my plan would be in tatters and he could snatch victory from the jaws of defeat. Full of admiration as I was, I could not allow this. I raised my Martini Henry and took careful aim as he was running away from me. As I shot, he tripped, fell flat on his face and I missed.

The situation was now desperate. He was up in a flash. If he got amongst the main body before I could reload and bring him down, he would be difficult to pick out and may be able to rally them with impunity. This was a moment for calmness. I controlled my breathing as I drew back the bolt, pushed another bullet into the breach, pushed the bolt forward and raised the gun to my shoulder. I sighted on his running figure and, just before he ran into the main body of men, pulled the trigger.

He fell to the ground.

Although their hero had gone, the men in his original one hundred continued to fight effectively and continued to inflict casualties on my warriors.

I became aware that a group of warriors on the right flank of the soldiers who should have been riding away from me as they fired at the enemy, were galloping towards me. I recognised Broken Nose leading about fifty warriors. When they came alongside the line of organised soldiers, they were facing away from the warriors because the next attack was due from the other side. Broken Nose halted his warriors in line with the soldiers and took careful aimed shots at their backs as they aimed at Running Deer's men approaching from the other side.

Within thirty seconds, they were cut to pieces and demoralised, at which point their cohesion disintegrated. Without the guidance of their now dead charismatic leader, they lost direction. Broken Nose had shown them that we, too, had a combat leader of great vision and the ability to think clearly in the most stressful environment allowing him to improvise a plan that would resolve the problem. He had saved the day for us.

When the decimated remnants of the charging column turned and fled, the two hundred warriors who had halted their charge rose and walked towards the milling mass, shooting as they went.

The confusion created by the alternating attacks on their flanks and the approach from their front coupled with the loss of their officers and the one resourceful colleague, meant the soldiers were unable to mount an effective defence. There were small pockets of brave individuals who dismounted and returned fire, but for the majority, their main concern was to escape.

The natural line of retreat from the first flanking attack was to their right, but they ran straight into the attack from that side. Some survivors repeated the error by running to their left only to run into the return of the attackers on their left. Some tried to run forward, but were cut down by our party advancing on foot.

As it transpired, it was the members of the rear column who were lucky, or at least thought they were. They chose to about face and run back the way they came and so a significant number escaped. By this time, I had mounted Buck and was with the group on our right. The resistance from the three front columns was petering out and so I ordered the warriors in that party to go after the retreating column to harry it.

After our experience from the first invasion and in accordance with the promise I had given concerning destroying any future invaders, we did not show any mercy. We just stood off the remnants of their army and shot them to pieces.

We counted about sixteen hundred enemy dead. We had fifty or so warriors killed or seriously wounded. Although this was a resounding victory, we had suffered the greatest number of casualties of any engagement, which saddened me greatly.

We harried the survivors all the way to the Oza. There were just under one hundred very frightened, damaged, tired and hungry soldiers who made it across. We had killed more than three hundred in the running battle for the loss of a further thirteen casualties.

They had abandoned twenty wagons of supplies.

This, together with the arms and ammunition we recovered from the dead soldiers, was a very considerable boost to our stores, especially our arsenal.

After the main battle, we took our dead to a place between all the villages. Raging Bull, Wind-in-the-Hair, Running Deer, Broken Nose and I watched as the burial platforms were raised and the dead warriors placed on them. I was sad and felt an overwhelming sense of responsibility. 'This is my fault. If my plan had not gone wrong, there would not be so many dead.'

'That's not true, Sky-in-the-Eye,' Wind-in-the-Hair contradicted me, 'If it were not for you, we would not have been able to beat them and we would have far more dead.'

'It wasn't me, it was Broken Nose who prevented more dead. If he hadn't read the situation after my tactics had gone wrong and come up with a plan, we could have lost.'

'Without your tactics, Kraspa, we would not have had a chance,' interjected Broken Nose, 'And without your training and example, I would not have known what to do.'

I was too exhausted to argue.

Word of our victory spread far and wide and with it our enhanced reputation. We were inundated with young men volunteering to join our army. We replaced our losses and created a reserve, but did not increase the size of the army as this would have put too great a strain on our natural resources - an army marches on its stomach.

About three months after we had ejected the invaders,

two scouts brought me a written message. They were scouting the banks of the Oza when they were approached by a small group of soldiers under a white flag of truce. Neither spoke the others language and so they could not communicate, but they were given a short letter in an envelope with the words, 'Sky-in-the-Eye.'

Opening it, I read:

'Governor Jordon and General Lopez send their kindest regards to Sky-in-the-Eye and respectfully request that he meets them for a discussion on the future relations between our peoples. We suggest this meeting is under a flag of truce between the parties and no more than five other members of each entourage and that it should take place on the banks of the Oza river at a date and time to be arranged.'

My first reaction was that they were being insolent. They had been the aggressor on two occasions and we had beaten them resoundingly each time, so their negotiating position was weak. After some reflection, I decided that, provided it gave us what we needed, it would be better to have a formal, enforceable agreement than a series of wars. Deceasing to play my cards close to my chest, I added my cryptic reply to the bottom of their note:

'Agreed.'

I sent my reply with my scouts and received a response four days later:

'Governor Jordon and General Lopez thank Sky-in-the-Eye for his reply to their request for a meeting and confirm the basis of any agreement will be as stated in

his letter.'

Given their acceptance of my terms, a meeting was arranged at the appointed place at a time mutually convenient to both parties.

I arrived on our side of the banks of the Oza with Raging Bull, Wind-in-the-Hair, Running Deer, Broken Nose and another chief and elder by the name of Restless One. Fifteen minutes after our arrival, a group appeared on the other bank comprising an army officer of high rank, a well dressed civilian and four other lower ranking army officers. They were accompanied by a single Fahkas warrior. I waved to indicate they should cross to our side. They duly forded the river and stopped about ten paces from us.

The senior officer opened the proceedings, 'May I introduce Governor Jordon,' he indicated the civilian, who nodded his head in greeting. 'I am General Lopez and we are honoured to meet Sky-in-the-Eye and his comrades.'

Before I could reply, the Fahka spoke. It was immediately apparent that my cursory written response had been taken as a sign I had only rudimentary English and that a translator was required. The Fahka was very perfunctory, 'This is Governor Jordon and this is General Lopez. They have stooped to speak to you stinking Hoopas.'

My companions bridled at this insult, but I held out a hand to restrain them. It was apparent the Fahka was intent on undermining the negotiations by giving an inaccurate translation.

To provide him with more rope, I replied in Hoopa, 'The Hoopas are pleased that such high ranking members of the army and the civil government should honour us in this way.'

The Fahka translated, 'The Hoopas say you are snivelling cowards who fight like women and that they will not lower themselves to sign an agreement with you.'

The General looked confused and his soldiers stirred uneasily. I held up my hand and said in English, 'Your translator has misrepresented both what you said to us and what we said in reply. He would seem to be intent on sabotaging our meeting.'

Realising he had been found out, the Fahka turned his horse and started galloping back across the river. I nodded at Broken Nose, who lifted his rifle and shot the Fahka.

I looked at the two senior figures opposite me. The General seemed unimpressed, but the Governor looked horrified.

'The Hoopas are an unequivocal people. The harsh justice meted out to our traitors and enemies is matched by our honour and loyalty for our friends and allies.'

The General's and the Governor's expressions remained unchanged.

I continued, 'I think we can agree we are better off without his help.'

They looked astonished for a moment and then the General burst out laughing, quickly followed by the other members of his entourage.

My party had not understood a word, but they recognised there had been a change in mood. Laughter is universally contagious and so they grinned, all except Raging Bull, who just nodded.

The ice had been broken and we were able to speak freely.

We dismounted and gathered in a circle. The Governor opened proceedings, 'Not a very auspicious start, but I think we can agree that there is mutual respect and we can open proceedings. Would you please let us know what you want from an agreement.'

'We want nothing more than we have now. We do not have any ambitions to extend our territory or to take anything from you. We may not agree with them, but we respect that you have different priorities and traditions. We merely ask you to respect us in the same way. We need concrete terms that will respect our territorial integrity and that there will be no further attempts to invade our land. We occupy a very small part of the total land available and are happy to let you have everything that lies outside our territory.'

The Governor turned to the General and whispered something to him.

The General nodded and the Governor held out his hand.

I took it and we shook on the agreement.

Although formal documents and decrees were drawn up and signed by the most senior people on both side, the basic negotiations were as simple as that.

The agreement was based upon the terms I sent with

the survivors of the first invasion and could be summarised as:

1. Our land extended from The White Top Mountains in the north to the Great Forest on the south, from the Oza river in the east to the Inda river in the west.

2. Travellers could cross our land, but they may only camp overnight. They may not settle. Anyone trying to settle would be moved on.

3. Traders could enter our land to trade, but they could not settle and could not trade in alcohol. A trader trying to settle would be moved on and may not return. A trader with alcohol would have it confiscated and may not return.

4. No outsider may hunt on the land. Anyone caught hunting would be executed.

5. The Hoopas have full authority to enforce these regulations.

So started a time of peace. The following fifteen years were probably the most contented of my life. On a personal level, I was able to spend my time with my beloved Prairie Flower and my sons. They grew into fine young warriors with my build, but their mother's complexion and deep brown eyes. I taught them karate and how to use guns. They were both very good,. Interestingly, Spirit of Tor was left handed.

My sons were not pure Hoopas, but this was not important and they were accepted without question. Far more difficult for them was to live up to the reputation of being my sons. From the time they were young, they were challenged, but these were no more than scuffles, initially, and the matter was unresolved until a confrontation when Spirit of Asuka was ten and Spirit of Tor was eight.

I was walking through the village when I saw them being confronted by four boys of about twelve years of age. I stood back and watched the action unfold. The leader of the small gang got up close to Asuka, who stood his ground even though he was a half a head shorter. At half a head shorter than Asuka, Tor was by far the smallest. The boy who had got into Asuka's face said something. Asuka's reply seemed to amuse the boy because he turned to his friends and grinned. As he turned back to Asuka, he pulled his head back with the intention of hitting him in the nose with his forehead. Asuka's training made him ready for this move and, as he was already smaller than his attacker, it was a simple matter for him to drop his head further so the boy hit his own nose on Asuka's forehead. He staggered back in pain, Asuka grabbed the boy's shoulders and kneed him in the groin making him drop to the ground semi-conscious. Asuka turned his attention to the boy immediately to his left and started exchanging punches with him. They were well matched and neither was able to land a telling blow.

As the one-on-one continued, the two other twelve-year-olds gathered around to attack Asuka from the side and behind. Tor didn't allow this to happen. Using speed to make up for his lack of bulk, he ran at the boy nearest to him and launched himself feet first into the boy's side, knocking him to the ground. Jumping to his feet first, he kicked the boy left footed in the temple as he was kneeling to rise. He dropped to the ground senseless.

Seeing this, the boy who was planning to attack Asuka decided he could not leave Tor behind them. He turned and side swiped Tor in the head, knocking him to the ground. Tor rolled and kicked the boys legs from beneath him, bringing him to the ground next to him. Tor jumped up and delivered the same coup-de-grace he had to his previous adversary.

While this was happening, Asuka had continued to trade blows with his second opponent. Although bigger and stronger, the other boy seemed to be tiring. Asuka had more stamina and was faster, which enabled him to land a telling left fist to the other boy's ribs. This made him drop his right hand, leaving Asuka an opening to hit him in the jaw with his left. The boy dropped to his knees, looked up and Asuka laid him out with a right to the jaw.

As I watched, my sons checked one another and, seeing they had no more than superficial bruising, turned their attention to their downed enemies. They laid them out on their sides and checked each of their mouths in case any of them had swallowed their tongues. The boy Asuka had kneed in the groin was sick. Asuka pulled him clear of his vomit, laid him out again and stood over them with Tor as they recovered.

They soon came around and sat up with crossed legs. The boy who had vomited was an interesting shade of green and sat cradling his head in his hands. After a few minutes, he looked up. Looking less sickly, he said something to Asuka, who replied and helped him to his feet. The others stood, exchanged a few words and went their separate ways. I melted into the background, so no one knew I had witnessed the fight.

When they came home, Spirit of Tor had a black eye where he had been side-swiped and Spirit of Asuka had a bruised cheek and a cut lip. Unable to hide the fact they had been in a fight, they told their mother and me what had happened, which was exactly what I had seen. When asked what had been said before the fight, they told us that the first boy had said that, as they were the sons of such a mighty warrior, they must be good fighters and should prove it. Asuka had said they had been trained to fight and, if they had to defend themselves, they would inflict more damage than they received. My boys had also shown maturity by not revelling in their victory, but took the time and trouble to make sure their vanquished foes did not suffer unnecessarily. Recognising this, the boys' leader had agreed the brothers had inflicted the most damage and that they were, indeed, not only mighty warriors in their own right, but also wise and humble in victory. In future they would fight with them and not against them. Asuka and Tor did not have to prove themselves again.

As they grew into manhood, I often reflected that they were like a mirror image of one another, each perfectly complementing the other, Spirit of Tor carrying his Colt on his left hip while Spirit of Asuka carried his on his right. I also taught them English, as I thought it may prove useful one day.

They shot most days. When they reached their late teens, their accuracy equalled mine, but they lacked my lightning reactions. Each week we practised shooting five identical stones from a rock. Prairie Flower would fire into the air, we would draw and shoot the stones off as fast as we could. They improved, but for a number of years plateaued at the point were they were just shooting their fourth stone when I was shooting my fifth. When they were both in their twenties, something happened that a father dreads and looks forward to with eager anticipation in equal measure: they both beat me.

It was close, but obvious that each of their fifth stones was knocked off the rock before mine. They looked at one another incredulously while I reloaded. I holstered my gun, put my left hand on Tor's shoulder and my right hand on Asuka's. Looking at them both directly, I said, 'This is a moment that always comes in a father's life. It is one of his proudest, but we must now look forward realistically.' Making sure they were both listening, I continued, 'You are in your prime and you can beat me, but must remember that you are still not as fast as I was when I was in my prime. Be aware that his means there may be someone out there who is faster than you and so you must be prepared to use your other qualities to gain the advantage. Furthermore, you have not yet been in a gunfight, whereas at your age I had experienced many. I don't doubt you have the courage to perform at your best no matter what the danger, but we must now devise strategies to ensure you don't suffer by learning the hard way.

'During my life I had Jake to back me up for a short time and Lupus for many years. You have one another, but must learn how to maximise this. Firstly, whenever possible, face your enemies with Asuka on the right and Tor on the left. This will reduce the chances of fouling one another's draw and will maximise your field of fire. Secondly, create as much distance as possible between you so as to increase the time your opponents have to aim at you separately.

'Finally, we have to devise a system to ensure you do not waste time and bullets by both aiming at the same target.'

I asked Prairie Flower to get some red paint. I picked up ten of the stones and painted a large red dot on one. I placed them in a row on the rock with the one with the red dot in the middle and explained, 'The one with the red dot is the opponent who draws first. You, Asuka will shoot at him and then pan to the right to take out the others. Tor, you will take the one to the left of the first to draw and pan to the left.'

I fired in the air and they did exactly as required.

Tor then made an intelligent observation, 'What if the man who draws first is not in the centre? Using this system will mean one of us has to shoot more than the other and this could be more that five, se we won't have enough bullets.'

'In that case,' I replied, ' We have to come up with alternative tactics.'

This was complicated, but we hit on a plan that Asuka would always go for the one who draws first. If he is 2 from the left, having shot him Asuka would jump 3 opponents and shoot the next four on the right. Tor would start with the fourth from the right and pan to the left shooting the remaining four. Tactics like this were worked out for having the first to draw in any position and with fewer that ten opponents (which was most likely). They practised this regularly for months until it became intuitive for them to deal with any number up to ten with the first to draw in any position. I was confident they could cope with any situation, but hoped they would never have to!

But the skills I taught them were just tricks when compared to the profound teachings of the Hoopas.

They learnt to hunt the traditional ways, which went beyond the simple process of killing to eat. It taught them respectful, empathetic hunting. They fitted into the overall scheme of things like other carnivores. They understood that life was not man centric. They understood that man was not above and separate from the natural world, but an integral part of a number of concentric circles. One of these circles was that life was regenerative; nothing lived forever, each generation produced fresh, new life and then moved on.

Another was that the grazing beasts needed the plants on which to feed, that the plants needed insects to pollinate them and the droppings of the beasts to feed them. The carnivores needed the beasts to feed them and they, in turn, kept the grazing beasts at the right number to crop the plants, but not to eat them all and, thereby, create starvation. Each part of nature was in balance and that balance had to be respected.

They understood that the land needed to rest and so we could not use it all of the time. We would grow our simple crops for a few months and then move to a new location leaving the ground fallow and allowing it to regenerate.

Most importantly, they learnt humility for they knew that if the humble bee were to go extinct, the world as we know it would end, but if we were to go extinct, our absence would have no impact and the natural world would continue perfectly well without us.

To begin with, there were very few visitors from outside. I think this was because we had established a reputation of being warlike and so only the very hardy, brave souls came in the first instance.

As the years passed, word spread that we could be accommodating, if not actually friendly. So, more people took the shortcut across our land to green pastures beyond the Inda river. We prospered from them because they were not allowed to hunt and, therefore, had to obtain rations from us, which they did by barter.

Traders also saw the benefit and the initial trickle grew into a steady stream from which we all benefitted.

Our army was kept in training as a deterrent, but its main function became more of a police force inspecting traders and travellers to ensure they were complying with the terms of the agreement and dealing with those that weren't.

So, although I was still busy with my duties and I worked to retain my fitness and fighting skills, my later twenties, thirties and early forties passed pleasantly and peacefully.

By this time, Buck was in his late twenties. He was still a magnificent steed, but I noticed his joints were stiff and he took longer to get going in the morning. He also lost some of his speed and stamina, but this was not so important now that I was not chasing Commancheros or fighting invaders. I suppose I felt we could grow old gracefully together, revelling in the companionship we had had since my early teens. I no longer needed to carry the Martini Henry or the two Colts in the saddle holsters. I gave the Colts to Spirit of Tor and the Martini Henry to Spirit of Asuka because he was the best shot. This lightened the load for Buck.

Buck became even less active and I only rode him occasionally and then mainly for old times sake and to give him some exercise because we didn't travel far.

A dun mare became my main riding horse. She was a fine horse by any standards with a good turn of speed, plenty of stamina and courage, but she was not Buck. We worked perfectly well together and she did everything I asked of her, but the deep understanding was not there.

One day, Spirit of Tor came running to me, 'Father,' he said breathlessly, 'Buck has moved away from the herd and is lying beneath a tree. We can't get him to stand.'

We ran together to find Buck lying on his side with his head on the ground.

Spirit of Asuka was kneeling over him and I could see he had tears in his eyes as he looked up at me and sobbed,

'He can't stand. He can barely raise his head.'

As he finished speaking, Buck lifted his head, looked at me, gave a short snort of recognition and dropped his head.

I sat down, lifted his head and shuffled across so my back was against the tree and his head was on my lap.

My boys were joined by Prairie Flower. They all dropped to their knees and stroked him. Prairie Flower then stood and took each of the boys' arms and in a faltering voice said, 'Come, let your father say his goodbyes.'

She blew me a kiss and they left.

I sat so we could see one another, I looked into his intelligent, brown eyes and he looked back. I was sure he was trying to tell me that he loved me and that Lupus and I had been his dearest and closest companions. I stoked his head and down his body. I could feel his heart was racing, thundering against his chest as he took short, quick breaths.

I told him the story of an orphaned, bottle-fed foal who had grown into a leggy, athletic colt and then became the finest, strongest, fastest, most tireless horse, with the biggest of hearts. I reminded him of how he had carried me into battles, how he had courageously carried me towards our enemies and how he had outrun them when the odds were too high. Of the thousands of miles I had been able to travel because of him. How he, together with a wolf-like dog, had been the greatest companions a young boy who would have been lost without them and how they had been my only friends through my most difficult times..

As I went on to remind him of our adventures together, I felt him relax and his breathing became easier. I stroked his head. His eyes were on mine the whole time and he occasionally snorted. I was sure he was saying that he remembered, too.

His heart continued to thunder, but his breathing became slower. Several times he exhaled and I thought it was over, but he would catch his breath and go on for a little longer.

After one particularly long exhalation, he didn't breath in again and I saw his eyes become misty and unfocused.

As he went, I called after him, 'Goodbye, Buck, thank you for everything.'

His heart had stopped.

We lay there together for a minute or so.

He suddenly shuddered along his whole body and took in a great breath.

It shocked and frightened me, but he then relaxed completely and was a dead weight across my legs.

I knew he didn't want to leave me and, as he had such a big heart, he had fought to stay with me, even after death.

If it were possible, this deepened my sadness even further.

I threw my head back and let out all my emotions in one primal scream.

My head dropped to my chest and I was sobbing uncontrollably as Prairie Flower ran up to me with our sons. I put my arms up like a child and Prairie Flower knelt next to me and fell into them. She put her head on my shoulder and I placed mine on her hair as we cried out our sorrow together.

Spirit of Asuka knelt next to me and put his had on my shoulder.

Spirit of Tor knelt next to his mother and put his hand on hers.

We stayed like that for many minutes. Although this was the irrevocable loss of the second of my two closest companions, I understood it was part of the circle of life and took great consolation in the presence and love of my family.

I could not see Buck's lifeless body being manhandled. The loss of dignity that this would involve for such a magnificent creature was more than I could bear. I did not want his last moments to be my abiding memory, I wanted to remember him in his majestic prime. My wife and sons understood.

Prairie Flower took me by the hand, 'Come with me, Jimmy, let our sons have the honour of laying him out.'

I said my last goodbye, put my arm around Prairie Flower's shoulders and we walked together back to our lodge without a backward glance.

Spirit of Asuka and Spirit of Tor took Buck's body out into the grasslands for him to complete his circle of life.

12

Eternity

In the years that followed, the outsiders became more bold. Our warriors had to work hard to ensure they adhered to the terms of our agreement, but there were only occasional infringements mostly in the form of camps that were becoming permanent and the occupiers had to be moved on. There were occasional efforts to sell alcohol and to hunt the great beasts, but these were dealt with in a salutary fashion.

Our people also became more confident and mixed with the traders in greater numbers in order to barter goods to our mutual benefit. As those travelling across from the Oza to the Inda were not allowed to hunt, some of the more enterprising Hoopas had quite a thriving business in meat.

The plague crept up on us. To begin with, it was just the elderly who became sick and died. Raging Bull was one of the first. He called me and Wind-in-the-Hair to his lodge and said that one of us should become the Chief. I said that I would prefer to continue as War Chief and that Wind-in-the-Hair would make a much better chief. Raging Bull died after a very short illness and was succeeded by Wind-in-the-Hair.

This was the pattern for a few months. The oldest, most vulnerable members of the tribe became ill and then died shortly after. The plague was slow, but relentless. It took many months to get into its stride, but unstoppable. After most of the elderly had died, it started to attack all ages. When the young became ill, the disease ravaged their bodies far more. I suppose their strength enabled them to withstand the first onslaught that had killed the elderly, but this allowed the illness to really take hold. Constant vomiting, bleeding from the mouth, nose and ears were universal. Bodies would become skeletal and hair would become thin before death claimed its victims.

Very few Hoopas did not become ill, but Spirit of Asuka, Spirit of Tor and I were three of the lucky few. This was possibly because I had been born and had grown up with the people who had brought the plague. As my sons, they could have inherited my immunity. Their mother was not so lucky.

Prairie Flower was one of the last to become ill. We had started to hope that we would all escape. When she became ill, we convinced ourselves that she was going to be one of the lucky ones who survived. We were wrong.

Her illness followed the established pattern. I thought I had been sad at the loss of Lupus and Buck, but I plumbed new depths of misery watching the person I most loved in the world lose her beauty and descend into the depths of the illness with all the pain, delirium and indignity this involved. We nursed her day and night believing right up to the end that we could save her with the ferocity of our love and the intensity of our care. She was lucid until the end. I knelt one side of her and the boys knelt the other. I held one hand and they both held the other. She was painfully thin and her once lustrous hair was dry and patchy. Blood oozed from her nose and ears. She looked at me, 'I am old and ugly, you will find a new, beautiful wife.'

'You are still the most beautiful person I have met. I would give the world for you to recover and it doesn't matter what you look like.'

'Liar!' She managed to smile through her suffering.

Spirit of Asuka could not restrain himself, 'We love you, mother, we want you with us and don't care how you look.'

Spirit of Tor was too choked to speak, he just nodded his agreement vigourously.

She fell asleep and so we sat with her quietly. She slept throughout the night. We stayed next to her the whole time. She seemed to be sleeping peacefully and we dared to hope that she was past the crisis and would recover. Others had got better, so why not her?

When the morning came, our hopes were dashed. She opened her eyes. They were more sunken than ever and we were constantly wiping the blood from her face.

She writhed and spoke with misted eyes, 'It hurts so much.'

'What can I do for you, my love?'

Her eyes focused on mine. 'I'm so tired. It is so hard to fight, but I don't want to leave you all.' Her gaze drifted over the three of us.

I realised she was asking for our permission, 'It's okay my love. We understand, you can go if you need to.' I looked at the boys. They understood and nodded. The last thing they wanted was to lose their mother, but they understood this was a selfish wish and they could not ask her to suffer any longer. I was never more proud of them than at that moment.

I looked down at Prairie Flower and could see the pride in her eyes. She turned towards the boys and said, 'I love you,' to each one.

She laid back, took my hands in hers and kissed them. I could not take my eyes from her face. She looked up at me and, as her eyes glazed over and her grip on my hands weakened, she mouthed, 'Goodby my love. I will always love you.'

As she closed her eyes, I repeated her words, 'Goodbye my love. I will always love you.'

She was gone. I didn't know if she heard me, but it didn't really matter because I knew that she knew.

We sat together in silence, each one holding her hands and plummeting the depths of our sadness and waiting for it to pass sufficiently for us to deal with the aftermath. I could see the misery in their faces. I said to them what I had said to Lupus, 'The price we pay for love is the pain we feel at loss.' I continued, 'All we feel now is the emptiness of bereavement. We will fill that void with the joy, pleasure and great fortune we had in having your mother in our lives.'

My words were true and I think they helped my sons come to terms with the loss of their mother. This was important because they had their whole lives ahead of them. I didn't ever tell them, but I felt that the light had gone out in my life. There was an essence that was now missing. I could never be the person I used to be.

Before the plague, the Hoopas had four large villages each with about one thousand inhabitants. Almost everyone caught the illness and most of them died, including Wind-in-the-Hair, Broken Nose and all the senior members of the army. There were so many dead and so few survivors that we couldn't build platforms for sky burials. Instead, we took the bodies into the prairie and laid them out with as much dignity as we could muster, By the time the plague had burnt itself out, there were no more than five hundred living in one village

We could no longer field an army and it didn't take long for the outsiders to take advantage. To begin with, they formed what could best be described as permanent camps. They then brought families and built homesteads. I appealed to General Lopez and the new Governor asking them to enforce the terms of our agreement. The General was sympathetic, but the Governor was a politician. He said that now the Hoopas were only a few, circumstances had changed and the agreement was no longer relevant. What he meant was that, while we had an army, we could punish any infringement. Now that we couldn't they could do what they liked. We didn't have a vote, but the people he allowed in did, so he was bound to support them and there was nothing we could do about it.

I was disillusioned and so were my sons. We talked

about moving to new lands west of the Inda. As they saw our way of life being eroded and, especially, the way the great beasts were being hunted, they became more keen to leave. They had married. Spirit of Asuka's wife was Harvest Moon the daughter of Broken Nose. Spirit of Tor wife was Wind-in-the-Hair's daughter Running Deer. Broken Nose's son, Broken Arrow, had also survived and had married a girl by the name of Flying Falcon. They had become close friends and decided their future was elsewhere. They gathered their belongings on six pack horses. As they prepared to go, I went to see them off.

'Won't you come?' Spirit of Asuka asked.

'I would like to, but this is my home. I know it has changed, but I don't have the drive to start a new life. Maybe I'm getting old.'

'Never!' they all chorused bringing a rare smile to my face.

Broken Arrow expanded, 'My father told me of the wisest, bravest warrior, the best shot and the fastest gun. You are still that man, Kraspa.'

I had not been called that for a long time and it was no longer relevant. 'I thank you for the thought,' Broken Arrow, 'But even if any of that were true, it is in the past. My time has gone. It is now your time. The greatest gift a parent can give his children is self sufficiency. I am proud to say that each of your parents,' I looked from one to the other, 'Has given this to you. I also believe my sons possess this quality. Although I am sad to see you leave, I shall watch you go with pride, safe in the knowledge that you will all prove your worth and make your way in whatever land you choose to settle.'

I embraced each one as they mounted. They wheeled their horses and led away their pack horses. All except Spirit of Asuka, who just sat on his horse with tears running down his face. I nodded reassurance. He nodded his acceptance and set off after the others at a fast trot.

I lived in a lodge in the village, but I lived all alone. My greatest friends had died, but I knew everyone and we got along perfectly well. Each day, I would take the dun mare and ride the prairies trying to find the ever decreasing areas that were unsettled and unsullied because that is where I was most at peace.

One day, I heard shots in the distance and rode to investigate. Four hunters had killed at least fifty great beasts. As I rode up to them, they mounted and, with their rifles across their pommels, rode to meet me. They were grinning as they approached. I suspected they planned to have some fun with this old savage.

I took the wind out of their sales by speaking to them in English, 'You know what you are doing is foolish.' It was a rhetorical question.

'What do you mean, old man?'

I ignored the slight and continued, 'The beasts cannot breed fast enough to replace the numbers you are killing. In a few months, you will have killed them all and you will no longer have a business. That strikes me as foolish.'

'What the fuck do we care what you think and if anything strikes you, it will be the back of my hand.' He turned to his companions, who obliged him with raucous laughs.

'It's not foolish if you have another career lined up for when the beasts are all dead, but how will you earn a living if you haven't?'

They stopped laughing. Their spokesman continued, 'I'm getting sick of your bellyaching, old man. So just fuck off.'

My anger was rising, but my tone was even, 'Sorry, it was my mistake.'

They thought they had the advantage and tried to capitalise, 'Fucking right you made a mistake. Now fuck off old man before we make you pay for it.'

'My mistake was to think you are intelligent enough to listen to reason. It's now apparent you are not and so I have to tell you that hunting the beasts is illegal and the penalty is death.' This was true as the agreement had not been officially rescinded, it had just been ignored.

They found this funny, 'And who the fuck is going to carry out this execution? All I can see is a sad old man.' He turned to his comrades for their approbation. They obliged by laughing.

As they laughed, they died. I had drawn and shot them all before they could react. My concession to the passing years was that I shot them in the chest. In my mind's eye, I could see Sheriff Brand laughing and nodding in approval.

Two of them died instantly. The third died in seconds. The fourth lay on the ground choking his life away. I walked the dun mare over to them as I reloaded my Colt and looked down at the dying man.

'How?' he asked.

'What you see is a shell of a man worn down by hardship and the loss of loved ones. Inside remains the spark of a once mighty warrior and gunfighter. Your stupidity and derision fanned that spark and made it flare into something like the raging fire that once burned within.'

As his life ebbed away, so the fire inside me wained. I was swamped by the feeling of loneliness and impotence. I had killed four hunters, but I could not kill them all. Very shortly, our land would be overwhelmed and become unrecognisable.

They were building towns all over our land. I rode into one and tied the dun mare to the hitching rail. A little way down the street, a man started whipping a horse. The horse was jumping around trying to escape, but he was tied fast and the man kept whipping him.

I walked up behind him and, when he raised the whip to strike again, pulled the whip from his grasp and started thrashing him. He screamed and writhed and fell to the ground. I hit him a few more times and then threw the whip at him just as a well built man in his mid twenties walked up. I turned to see he was wearing a sheriff's badge.

The horse whipper shouted, 'Arrest this filthy savage, sheriff, he's just horse whipped me.'

'You had it coming, Billy.' The sheriff was talking to the whipper, but looking at me, 'How many times have I told you not to whip your horse?'

He held out his right hand and had a friendly smile on his face as he introduced himself, 'Johnny Crowser, I'm the sheriff here.'

I was completely taken in. I offered my hand, which he took it and gave me a hard pull, making me stagger forward. As I did so, he took my Colt from my holster with his left hand. His tone was just as friendly as he apologised, 'Sorry, friend, but I can't take any chances. You can have your Colt back when you leave town.'

Only a few years before, he wouldn't have been able to do that. Even if I had been taken in by his charm, he would not have got the better of me; I would have moved with his tug and then used the momentum to gain the advantage. My brain still retained the information, but my age had taken the edge off my reactions and strength; the inner fire was dimmed. I obviously posed no further threat, but Billy the whipper wanted his pound of flesh. 'I reckon we should teach this filthy savage a lesson, Johnny.'

I looked at the clear, blue sky above their heads and everything suddenly became clear to me. I spoke in Hoopas. What I had to say was best expressed in that language, using any 'civilised' language would have sounded hollow and I doubted if they would understand my meaning even if they understood the words:

'*I am Sky-in-the-Eye.*

I am the Kraspa of the Kikatchi Hoopas.

You did not see the nobility of living in harmony with nature

And we became savage when you forced us to defend

ourselves.
But we did not understand the real threat.
We thought the plague was the illness you brought to us.
But the illness was just a symptom of the underlying disease.
I now know you are the plague.
But there is nothing more I can do,
You are locusts who take without allowing the earth to regenerate.
One day there will be nothing left for you to take and you, too, will die.'

This simple synopsis of the future as I saw it filled me with sadness. I closed my eyes as tears rolled down my cheeks. I felt something soft on my face and opened my eyes. Standing just in front of me was a pleasant looking, small woman somewhat younger than me. She dabbed my cheeks dry with her handkerchief and then put it in her sleeve. She pushed my hair back and held my face between her hands, 'You are the bravest most selfless person I have ever met.' She held me there for a long time, looking deep into my eyes. She looked familiar.

Letting go of my face, she turned to the onlookers. 'He is older, his hair is longer and his clothes are different, but his sky-blue eyes are the same and I would recognise him anywhere. This man and his friend saved my family from the Commancheros. His friend died in the rescue.' Looking directly at the sheriff, she said, 'Without this man, you would not be here, Johnny. He is Jimmy Kidd and must be treated with respect.'

As she took my Colt from her son and replaced it in my holster, I recognised Anna Amiss, the shy young girl Jake and I had rescued together with her parents so many years before.

'I'm sorry, Mr. Kidd, I've heard the story many times. It's a pleasure to meet you.' Johnny was holding his hand out for me again. I was not inclined to take it. My head was starting to hurt and my vision was a little blurry. I turned and walked to the dun mare, mounted clumsily and road slowly out of town.

My headache worsened and my vision deteriorated. I was now in the open grasslands. I felt at home, but very alone. There was a tree ahead. I pulled up close to it. As I dismounted, I found it difficult to hold the saddle horn with my right hand and my right leg gave way as it took my weight, causing me to stumble. The left side of my head was a mass of pain. I had to sit down. I staggered into the shade of the tree and collapsed, just managing to turn so my back was resting against its trunk.

I tried to put my right hand onto my lap, but it wouldn't move. The pain in my head was excruciating, my vision was almost completely blurred and I was drooling from the right side of my mouth. I used my left hand to wipe it away. I reassured myself, 'I just need to sleep and I will be fine.' The final thought before I drifted away was, 'Prairie Flower, I need you now.'

I was on my feet with my Colt in my hand scanning for danger before it registered that it was Lupus's growl that had woken me.

Just off to my right I could see the Kikatchi clan of

the Hoopas moving to fresh grounds, but there was something wrong. With them were mum, dad, Granny and Gramps. They came over to me all smiles. Mum and Granny hugged me while dad and Gramps slapped me on the bank. Dad said, 'We have been thanking Mr and Mrs Schmidt for bringing you up after we had to leave you, Jimmy.'

Gramps waived the thanks away, 'Ve are all so proud of you, Yimmy.'

Asuka and Tor were there, too, grinning with pleasure and waving to me.

'Yer, you done good, kid.' I looked up and saw Jake. With a wink, he said, 'See you later.'

As he rode off, I saw Prairie Flower behind him. Radiant in her natural beauty, she was perfection. We ran to one another and I held her close, her head on my chest, my arms around her shoulders and hers around my waist. My wish had come true. We didn't need to speak, being together was enough.

Wind-in-the-Hair and Raging Bull galloped up. Buck was close behind. Raging Bull nodded and Wind-in-the-Hair pointed to the war party marching by, 'The army needs you, Kraspa.'

Prairie Flower smiled up at me, 'You still have your duties during the day. We will have our nights together, Jimmy.' She walked off arm in arm with mum, dad, Granny and Gramps.

Buck walked over to me and rested his nose on my chest the way he had since he was a colt. Lupus put his front legs next to Buck's head and I put my arms around

310

them both. We were reunited, together forever.

After a moment, I vaulted onto Buck's back and, with Raging Bull and Wind-in-the-Hair by my side, rode over to the ranks of warriors.

A thousand heads turned in my direction, a thousand fists punched the air and the plains resounded with a thousand voices:

'KRASPA.'

'SKY-IN-THE-EYE'

THE END

The author

Tony Eaton was born in London. His family moved to Harlow when he was five where he was one of the last to benefit from a grammar school education.

After GCE A-levels, he qualified as an accountant followed by a career in industry and finance until his retirement in 2003. This gave him time for serious trekking, e.g. The Inca Trail, The Great Wall of China and Kilimanjaro. He has also undertaken several building and renovation projects and has had time to indulge in his hobby of restoring guitars as well as singing and playing guitar in the rock 'n' roll band, *Jurassic Rock*.

Tony now lives in rural Suffolk with his wife, Sue, an artist. Their four children live with their families in towns and villages close by.

The story of *Sky-in-the-Eye* came to Tony in a dream in early 2023, which enabled him to produce the first draft within ten days. The following year or so was spent in putting flesh on the bones of the bare story, having it critiqued and edited to bring it up to the standard required for publishing.

Tony hopes you enjoy reading the story as much as he has enjoyed writing it.